Fire Between Two Skies

A Novel

Dual-time Odyssey Book 3

R. F. Whong

ISBN: 979-8-88904-014-9

Published by Vidasym Publishing
A Division of Vidasym, Inc.
5013 S. Louis Ave., #532
Sioux Falls, SD 57108

Dedication

I dedicate this book, first and foremost, to my Savior, the Lord Jesus Christ, and furthermore, to my brothers and sisters in Christ who have supported us in our ministry over the years.

I wish to honor the numerous Christians in China and Hong Kong who remain steadfast under tremendous pressure and suffering even today.

Why I Wrote This Book

Since I was young, I've often explored the Cheung Po-Tsai Cave on Cheung Chau Island in Hong Kong. Of course, I didn't stumble upon any pirate treasure. Yet the tale of the pirate king Cheung Po-Tsai and his wife has captivated my imagination and inspired me to write this Dual-time Odyssey series. This is Book 3.

The period of Chinese history in Book 3 is complex and challenging to portray. At times, I wondered if I'd taken on more than I could handle. I tried not to focus on the details of the rise and fall of the Taiping Heavenly Kingdom. Instead, I explored the common human trait of seeking purpose and justice, regardless of our era or circumstances.

I wrote the book using two distinct voices. This is my third attempt at such an endeavor. Readers will notice different writing styles for the past and present timelines.

Note:

The writing in the chapters about the 1800s sounds European and not Asian. My challenge lies in the fact that, despite having studied numerous ancient Chinese texts, I've not encountered any books from nineteenth-century China penned in English. I have, however, become well acquainted with nineteenth-century English literature, particularly through the works of Jane Austen, my favorite author.

Discussion Questions for Book Clubs

1. What parallels between the two eras stood out to you most?

2. How does temptation shape both men's destinies?

3. What does the novel suggest about rebellion—political, spiritual, or personal?

4. How does the Taiping movement echo modern ideological conflicts?

5. Where do you see grace or redemption in the ending?

Glossary

Please feel free to skip the glossary section if you're familiar with Chinese culture.

Attire in the Qing Dynasty:
Hairstyle (pigtail or queue) for men: a long braid and shaved front and sides of the head. The queue was a sign of submission to the Manchu rule and was deeply resented by many Han Chinese. Men in the Taiping Heavenly Kingdom wore their hair long as a symbol of their rebellion against the ruling Qing dynasty. Because of their long hair, the Taiping rebels were derisively nicknamed changmao (長毛), or "long-hairs," by their Qing opponents.

Changshan and Qipao: For men, the changshan (long shirt) and magua (a type of jacket) were common. Women wore the qipao, a figure-fitting dress that later evolved into the modern cheongsam. The early qipaos were loose-fitting, featuring wide sleeves and often elaborate embroidery.

Everyday wear vs. formal attire: Everyday clothing was simpler, often made from cotton or plain silk, while formal attire was elaborate, demonstrating wealth and status. Clothing regulations were part of the sumptuary laws that dictated the color, decoration, and style permissible for each class.

Kung Fu Suits: A variation for training or actual combat might include a two-piece outfit consisting of a jacket and trousers. The jacket often had buttons or toggles, sometimes known as a "tangzhuang," and the trousers were typically loose-fitting.

Bubble tea: A Taiwanese recipe made by blending tea with milk, fruit, and fruit juices, then adding tasty tapioca pearls and shaking vigorously.

Chinese junk and its parts: A junk is a type of Chinese sailing ship characterized by a central rudder, an overhanging flat transom, watertight bulkheads, and a flat-bottomed design. Even today, you can book a tour of Hong Kong's Victoria Harbour aboard a Chinese junk.

Kedge (kedge anchor, to kedge): A small, light anchor used for maneuvering.

Plank: A plank on a Chinese junk refers to the wooden strakes that form the hull of the vessel.

Skiff (tender; in China often a sampan): The small boat carried by or towed behind the junk, used to ferry crew/cargo ashore, to sound depths, and to set a kedge anchor. On many Chinese vessels, this would be a simple sampan, easy to row or scull by one or two people.

Stern: The aft end of the vessel. A Chinese junk's stern is typically high and broad with a flat transom and a raised poop deck containing living quarters and the steering position. The large, deep rudder is hung from the stern and can be hoisted or lowered by tackles to suit depth.

Sweep: A very long oar used for moving or maneuvering the junk when there's no wind or in tight quarters. Crews might pull on side sweeps to warp the vessel or use them to help turn the bow.

City walls: In the late Qing period (including the 1850s), virtually all administrative seats, prefectures (fu), departments/subprefectures (zhou), and counties (xian), were walled cities with gates, gate towers, and often a moat. Quanzhou (全州) in northeast Guangxi was a county seat and therefore had such fortifications, originally built in the Ming and repaired multiple times through the Qing.

First Opium War: The First Opium War, fought between 1839 and 1842, was a pivotal conflict primarily between the British Empire and the Qing Dynasty of China. Stemming from tensions over trade imbalances, Chinese sovereignty, and the proliferation of opium, the war began after China attempted to suppress the opium trade by confiscating and destroying large quantities of the drug stored by British merchants in Guangdong. The British, driven by economic interests and the principles of free trade, retaliated with military force, asserting naval superiority and leading to several key engagements. The war ended with the Treaty of Nanking, which imposed numerous concessions on China, including the cession of Hong Kong to Britain, the opening of several ports to foreign trade, and the establishment of an indemnity to cover British losses. This conflict marked the beginning of the "century of humiliation" for China and highlighted the rising influence of Western powers in Asia.

Hong Kong and China: The United Kingdom governed Hong Kong for a century before handing it back to China in 1997. Upon its return, China established Hong Kong as a Special Administrative Region, pledging to maintain its existing systems and freedoms for fifty years under the "one country, two systems" framework. However, since President Xi Jinping assumed power, democratic freedoms in Hong Kong have progressively diminished. Nevertheless, Hong Kong continues to experience relatively more freedom than mainland China (e.g., religion, education, etc.).

Ji Tong: A spirit medium—a person believed to serve as a living vessel or channel for deities, gods, or spirits during religious rituals. When in trance, the ji tong allows the spirit to communicate with worshippers, deliver messages, provide healing, or perform rituals. The word "乩童, pronounced ji-tong" literally means "divination child" (tong 童 means "child," not necessarily in age, but connoting purity or suitability).

Martial arts/Martial artists: In the 1800s China, martial artists were commonly referred to as "wushi" (武士), which translates to "warriors" or "martial warriors." Another term used is "wusheng" (武生), which translates to "martial artists." Additionally, the term "wulín" (武林), meaning "the world of martial arts," was used to refer to the community or society of martial artists. These practitioners were often associated with various martial arts schools or clans, each with its unique style and techniques.

Mai Po Marshes in Hong Kong: The site is part of several international conservation frameworks. For example, it is recognized as a Wetland of International Importance under the Ramsar Convention. This designation means that the site benefits from international attention and collaboration for its conservation and sustainable use. Additionally, the site is part of the East Asian-Australasian Flyway, a migratory route that brings global conservation bodies together to protect important habitats across countries. It's primarily managed and monitored by the World Wide Fund for Nature Hong Kong (WWF-Hong Kong). WWF-Hong Kong has been responsible for the management of the Mai Po Nature

Reserve since 1983 and works closely with the Hong Kong government and local universities to ensure the conservation of this vital wetland.

Names and ways to address each other: Chinese names comprise a family name followed by a given name. For example, Zhang is the family name of the protagonist in this book, and Xin is his given name.

After the Opium Wars, Hong Kong, Kowloon, and the New Territories were ceded to Britain. Chinese residents in the colony adopted English names, consisting of a Western first name followed by their Chinese last name, to be more memorable to the surrounding British population.

In different regions in the 1800s, people addressed each other differently. Folks in the regions of this book would likely say: Baba for father, Mama for mother, Ye-Ye for grandpa, and Maa-Maa for grandma. Baba or Mama attached to a last name is also a way to address an older person. Another way to address an older person was to use "Old" before their surname, as in "Old Li."

Chinese names of key figures mentioned in the book:

Miao Lan.

Wang Jun.

Wang Hui, Wang Jun's son.

Ying Si-Fen, Wang Jun's wife.

Zhang Xin (Xin pronounced "sheen," like "Xi" in "Xi Jinping").

Zhang Hao, Zhang Xin's older brother.

Real historical figures mentioned in the book:

Cheung Po-Tsai: A nineteenth-century Chinese pirate who later became a decorated naval officer for the Qing dynasty government. He is prominently featured in legends, with tales of buried treasure in the Cheung Po-Tsai Cave on Cheung Chau Island in Hong Kong.

Hong Xiuquan, Feng Yunshan, Yang Xiuqing, Xiao Chaogui, Wei Changhui, and Shi Dakai are all real historical figures associated with the Taiping movement. Hong anointed them kings: Feng as the South King, Yang as the East King, Xiao as the West King, Wei as the North King, and Shi as the Wing King, even though they didn't actually rule over any territories.

Liang Fa, Ying Si-Fen's uncle, a real historical figure. The first Protestant pastor in China. After converting to Christianity through the influence of Robert Morrison, the first Protestant missionary to China, Liang Fa was baptized in 1816 and later ordained as a pastor. He helped Morrison translate the Bible into Chinese and was instrumental in spreading Christian teachings. He was particularly known for his work in printing and distributing Christian literature, which had a profound impact on the spread of Protestantism in China.

Issachar Jacox Roberts (1802–1871), an American Southern Baptist missionary best known for his work in southern China and his association with the Taiping Rebellion. A former shoemaker turned preacher, he reached China in the late 1830s and founded an independent Baptist mission in Canton (Guangzhou), often called the "Roberts" or "Sinim" Mission. In 1847, he briefly taught Hong Xiuquan, the future Taiping leader. Roberts declined to baptize him, though their contact later drew wide attention.

Pearl River Delta: The region's long history goes back more than two thousand years, and the various coasts of the Pearl River Delta can be confusing because the estuary's shape changes over the centuries. Simply put, the Pearl River Delta Metropolitan Region covers the area surrounding the Pearl River estuary where the river flows into the South China Sea.

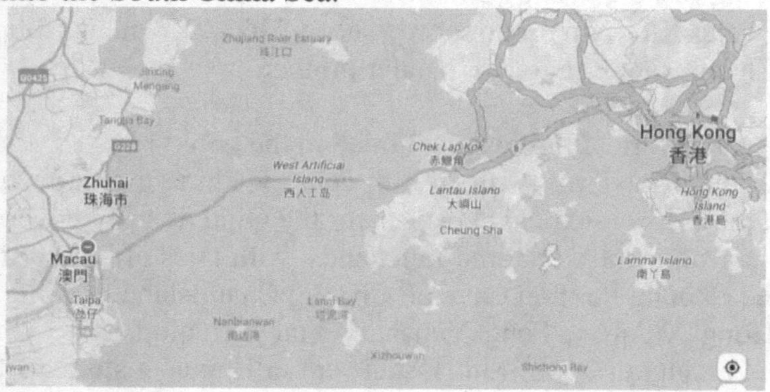

Pirates in the 1850s: By 1850, piracy was still present in the waters around Macau, though it was not at the same overwhelming scale as in the early nineteenth century when fleets commanded by Cheung Po-Tsai and his wife terrorized the South China Sea.

Sedan: In history, this term means an enclosed chair for conveying one person, carried between horizontal poles by two porters.

Tai chi: Tai chi adopts the Taoist idea of softness against hardness. When two forces of yin (softness) and yang (hardness) push each other with equal force, neither side moves. Thus, a key principle in tai chi is to avoid direct conflicts. While it is often practiced today for its health and meditative benefits, its origins are rooted in self-defense and combat techniques.

Taiping: The Taiping Movement was a millenarian Chinese civil war (1850–1864) led by the mystic Hong Xiuquan, who established the rival Taiping Heavenly Kingdom against the ruling Qing dynasty. With estimates of twenty to thirty million deaths, the conflict, which had a significant religious and social dimension, was the deadliest civil war in Chinese history.

Triad (Hongmen): The Hongmen, also known as the Tiandihui (Heaven and Earth Society), emerged in southern China (Fujian/Guangdong) as oath-bound brotherhoods. They mixed mutual aid, secret-ritual culture, and anti-Qing (pro–Ming loyalist) sentiment. Founding legends often invoke the Shaolin rescue myth; historians see them as grassroots societies formed amid social unrest. British officials popularized the term "triad" (linked to the Heaven–Earth–Man trinity in society symbolism) for Chinese secret societies. Over time, some Hongmen-derived groups evolved toward organized crime, especially in treaty ports and colonial cities, while other branches emphasized cultural, charitable, or political identities.

Weapons: Over the whole Taiping Rebellion (1851–1864), edged weapons (swords, spears, shields) were more common in sheer numbers, especially during the early-to-mid war period. Both Taiping and Qing fielded spear- and sword-armed troops, with a smaller proportion of matchlock/percussion musketeers and jingal (wall-gun) crews. Assaults often used shield-and-spear vanguards, with musketeers firing from behind. In the late war (1860–64), Qing "regional armies" (Xiang/Huai) and the foreign-drilled Ever Victorious Army had widespread percussion and rifled muskets (and more artillery). The Taiping never fully matched this shift and retained many cold-weapon troops.

Xiaolongbaos: Soup-filled steamed buns, also known as "soup dumplings." To eat them, you first bite a small opening to sip the soup.

Chapter One

Hong Kong, China
Autumn 2022

Even in October, humidity seeped in. In the sea of pedestrians with face masks, Jason Guan trudged ahead. The city hadn't been the same since the pandemic. Being a Realtor after he lost his job as an assistant supervisor for the Mai Po wetland conservation turned out to be tougher than he'd anticipated. The property market had become a temple. Some arrived to worship, others to offer sacrifices, while most lingered at the margins. The value of stability spiraled into abstraction.

He ducked into Le Jardin, a French café everyone Instagrammed. It had just reopened. Inside, the scent of baked croissants swirled around.

In the corner window, a woman sat, poised as if she were a sculpture poured into a tailored charcoal suit, all clean angles and an odd, quiet gravity. The hairs along Jason's arms lifted. Instincts prickled. His mind skidded from face to memory to name while the rest of him stood there like an idiot. He stared too long. Time kinked. "Vivian Jiang?" The name scraped out before he knew it.

She looked up from her phone. Her jaw dropped. "Jason Guan?"

How many years had it been? Ten? Longer? He stepped forward.

Vivian stood, graceful and confident, but a tautness coiled behind that poise, as if she were ready to spring. He touched his chin. An old image from his high school days at the Methodist Academy flashed in his mind. Didn't she always hide at the back of the class?

Now, her presence soaked into the café like spilled wine—dark, intoxicating.

"Vivian." He rediscovered his smile. "It's been forever."

"I recognized you despite your face mask. Your eyes gave you away. You were voted the guy with the most gorgeous eyes, for obvious reasons." She gestured to the seat across from her. "Sit. You're not in a hurry to go somewhere, are you?"

He lowered his face mask and settled opposite her. "I'm a Realtor. In real estate, it's hustle or starve. Aren't you working in China now? You in Hong Kong for business?"

"Yeah, business." Her immaculate red nails tapped against her coffee cup. "I almost didn't believe it when I saw you, the top student in our class. Life has been good to you?"

"Good, yes." A server swung by, and Jason ordered a cappuccino. "Married, working hard. The city's not easy."

She leaned forward, a single eyebrow arched. "Married already? To anyone I know?"

"Debra Gong." Warmth crept into his chest. "She's a PhD student at Chinese U, studying biochemistry."

Vivian chuckled, a self-assured sound. "Leave it to the class prince. I often thought you'd marry a princess." She sipped her espresso. "Do you have pictures to show me?"

He woke his phone and turned the screen toward her. "Our wedding picture."

She studied the photo. "Did you have a double wedding during the pandemic using Zoom?" She squinted. "I have to say, your wife is more beautiful than a princess. Large, luminous eyes. Full lips. Men will remember a face like hers, stunning, dangerous. I hope you can keep up."

He ignored her remarks and flicked through more images before stopping. "Here is our wedding invitation. 'Maggie Cheung marries Brian Guan and Debra Gong marries Jason Guan.' Maggie Cheung is my mother-in-law. She married my uncle, Brian Guan."

"Must have been a splendid event." She glanced at it again, then raised her coffee for a slow sip. "You still in touch with classmates?"

The gesture showed off the impeccable embroidery on her sleeve and the expensive watch with its understated black leather band. Was it a Patek Philippe? He tucked his phone away. "A reunion once a year, when we're not all running around. Hong Kong feels smaller nowadays."

"Doesn't it?" Her Cantonese sounded slightly accented, as if she'd lived somewhere else long enough to borrow vowels. "I expect to stay for a while if I find the right place."

His Realtor instincts perked up. "Are you moving to Hong Kong?"

"Not quite. I run a biotech company on the mainland. But I need a refuge. Something discreet and spacious. Overlooking Victoria Harbour. Cash, of course."

She placed a slim silver business card on the table, embossed with a government emblem in gold.

He checked the title—Sinogene Pharmatech Holdings. General Manager. Vivian Jiang. "You're running a state-owned enterprise?"

A twitch in her jaw returned her lips to a line that no laughter could smooth. "Yeah. A SOE."

Was this the same nervous girl with oversized glasses asking him for chemistry notes? What kind of metamorphosis had she undergone, and at what price?

His mind flitted over giant towers in Mid-Levels with unobstructed harbor views and penthouses that could swallow up the entire complex where his apartment belonged. "You want to buy? No mortgage, straight cash?"

She stared into his eyes. "No mortgage. Money isn't an issue."

The word, a kind of invitation and declaration code in this city, hung in the air. He steadied his voice. "There are a few options. Do you have a budget you'd like to stick to?"

"My only budget is time. I trust your judgment." She flashed a wry smile. "Do you miss the past?"

"Sometimes." He shivered at the memories. The tragic car accident that claimed his parents' lives when he turned ten, the way Grandpa stepped in to raise him, how he studied hard to make Grandpa proud… "Those years were complicated."

She nudged her cup aside. "Complications are inevitable. But never mind. Is it possible for you to show me a few places this week?"

His phone rang. Debra was checking in from home. He texted her a brief reply. *All's well. Running into a classmate. Will tell you tonight.*

Vivian leaned closer. "From your wife? I envy scientists who strive for a better life for all of us."

"Aren't you running a biotech company?" He stowed his phone away.

She shrugged. "I'm running a company. Period."

"What an answer!" He tipped his head back. "You don't sound excited."

She straightened and smoothed her tailored suit. "Passion is for researchers. Vision is for survivors." Her gaze lingered on him. "I've learned what it takes to win and where the bodies are buried."

"You still need to know the science, right?" He raked his hair with a hand.

Her confident smile wavered. The shy girl from their past peeked through.

"Just enough not to blow myself up." She lowered her voice. "So, are you going to help me?"

His heart thumped. The four-bedroom, three-bath penthouse on Garden Road, priced at over a hundred million HK dollars, he'd seen this morning might suit her. "Of course. It's an honor to help an old friend."

"You're a good man, Jason." She gave his arm a gentle squeeze. "Not many are left."

Her phone vibrated. "Excuse me." Her voice shifted into command, her Mandarin crisp. "Okay. I'll be out in one minute." She turned to Jason. "My driver's waiting. Can you text me your listings?"

"I will." He handed over his phone for her to type in her number. "Let me know if you need anything else."

She put on her facemask. "Thanks a lot."

When she swept out of the café, even the staff glanced at her. He drummed a finger on the tabletop, the rhythm keeping time with the strange unease tempering his nostalgia. Something odd hid behind her confidence. What was that?

His phone buzzed again, a reminder of an appointment he couldn't afford to miss. He downed what was left of his coffee and stepped back into the city's noisy current.

❉ ✧ ❉

Jason entered his apartment. The dusk flooded the living room with a row of honeyed rectangles. Debra curled up on the couch, her tablet and a cup of tea on the coffee table.

"Hey." She straightened up. "Rough day?"

"Long day." He dropped the keys and loosened his tie. "Guess who I ran into at Le Jardin?"

She cocked an eyebrow over the half-smile on her lips. "Who? Our mutual friend?"

"Vivian Jiang. Have I ever mentioned her to you? We were in the same class in high school. She was shy, but bright." He collapsed beside her. "Now she runs a biotech giant in China and asked me to find a luxury flat for her. Cash. No questions asked."

"A request like that out of nowhere?" Debra touched her chin. "That's not normal, is it? Money like that, so fast."

Jason shook his head, anxiety creeping up. "Not normal at her age, anyway. She acted as if privacy were a matter of life or death. I can't figure out if she's hiding from something or someone."

Tiny creases formed on her forehead. "You don't have to get involved if something feels off."

"For old times' sake, I want to help her." He rested his head on top of hers. "I also did a calculation before I came home. If I sell her the flat on Garden Road priced at a hundred and eight million HK dollars, with one percent of the transaction price from both seller and buyer, I'd pocket two point sixteen million. Not bad at all."

Debra released a low whistle. "Two point sixteen million? That's nearly three hundred grand in US dollars."

Jason brushed his fingers along her cheek. "After living in Hong Kong for two years, you still automatically convert every amount into dollars."

She chuckled, her breath warm on his skin. "It reminds me who I am." She leaned back and drew her knees up to her chest. "Promise me if anything about this isn't right, you'll walk away. No hesitation."

His shoulders stiffened. "I promise."

She grasped his hand. "Let's pray for God's wisdom."

They bowed their heads, and she started in a steady tone. "Dear Lord, grant us Your wisdom and guide our decisions. If we stray from Your path, please protect and redirect us. Help us use whatever comes our way for good, for the sake of Your glory. And"—she squeezed his hand even tighter—"and for Vivian too. We pray she'll have the opportunity to know You."

Jason echoed her words. "Lord, I pray for clarity, for integrity. And no matter what happens, I'll have the courage to do the right thing."

When they finished, his mood shifted to something lighter. He cradled her face. "I don't know why," he murmured. "I missed you the second I left home. You've been on my mind all day."

She giggled. "Dear Mr. Guan, we aren't newlyweds anymore."

Her laughter softened the sharp edges of the world outside. The glow from the lamp in the corner bathed her in gold. He nibbled her earlobe. "Well, Mrs. Guan, if you're not a newlywed anymore, what are you?"

"Still yours." She curved into him.

His lips found hers, gentle at first, then deeper. Debra's arms slipped around his neck. He sketched the line of her spine, pulling her closer until there was no space between them.

Time dissolved. The rush in their lives—ambitions, negotiations, worries—vanished into obscurity, leaving only the thrum of hearts in sync.

She sighed, a sound muffled against his mouth. He drew away just far enough to look at her. "Shall we move to the bedroom?"

"Let's stay here for a change," she whispered.

He held her tight. The city lights danced through the thin curtains, yet none reached into their tenderness.

In the hush that followed, they lay on the sofa, her head on his chest. He shifted, propping himself up on one elbow, and nodded toward the tablet on the coffee table. "What are you reading? A scientific paper?"

"You wouldn't believe it." She rolled onto her side to face him. "Even though Dad has been gone for a while, we discover something new every time we sort through his belongings. Uncle Brian and Mom went to the beach house on Cheung Chau Island yesterday and found another unpublished manuscript by Dad. This one is about the Taiping movement, the Heavenly Kingdom of Great

Peace. Mom gave me a USB stick this morning, and I've copied it to my tablet."

She grabbed the device and tapped it awake. Chinese characters appeared on the screen.

Jason's eyes flickered, then widened. "Unbelievable." His breath caught. He touched the bridge of his nose. "Must be a disturbing tale. The Taiping was the deadliest period in Chinese history. I learned about it in high school. Rebellion and danger at every turn. Many people died."

"Yeah. I've read only a few chapters. The story drew me in already." She held up the tablet. "Do you think faith alone can start a revolution?"

He stared at the ceiling. "I've forgotten most of the details about the Taiping. Still, the sense of dread is hard to forget. The pressure, the fear. Every whisper could be reported. I'm afraid our city is falling into that situation."

Her mouth flattened into a thin line. "Strange how something from the 1850s China doesn't seem so distant. People pressed from all directions. Leaders hunted by the strongest power." A muscle ticked in her cheek. "Why don't we read it together? Then we can discuss it."

"I'd love to. Dad's stories never disappoint."

He took the tablet from her and swiped to the first chapter. The words stared back at him: *Guangzhou, Guangdong, China. Summer 1845.*

The chill of danger never quite faded, no matter the century.

Chapter Two

Guangzhou, Guangdong, China
Summer 1844

The savor of boiled pork drew Zhang Xin onward along Thirteen Factories Street. He lingered near a teahouse, his parched lips longing for a warm cup.

A broad-shouldered fellow emerged from the kitchen and laid a generous heap of steamed buns upon a wooden tray. Meat baozi they were, each one plump, soft, their coarse pork filling shiny with fat.

Xin, a skinny stripling of fifteen, edged nearer. Hunger had thinned him to the bone, yet he maintained his jaw in a sturdy, square set. "How much for a baozi?" he inquired in the Canton tongue.

The man grunted. "Three cash."

Such a sum might as well have been the emperor's ransom.

"I have only…" Xin fumbled in his pouch. Ugh, naught but a bent button.

The vendor's gaze swept over him, then slid elsewhere.

Beyond a bamboo screen, foreign merchants' loud voices rang out, their speech a muddle of unknown words.

"Devils." Baba had named the pale-skinned men, their complexions scoured clean, as though water could grant such purity.

A giant among them, with a beard bristling like new millet, sauntered out and pointed at the buns. "Hot and fresh?" He asked with a thick accent.

Xin stole a glimpse of him. He wore a white dress shirt, its sleeves rolled up to reveal pale, freckled forearms. A bowler hat perched atop his head.

The vendor bowed low. "Aye. Very fresh."

The foreigner laughed. Coins jingled. A world barred to someone like Xin. Hunger twisted in his belly. Nausea rose in his throat. He cast a glance at the tray. A cracked baozi teetered close to the rim, then tumbled to the grimy stones below. The bun steamed in the gutter, fat oozing forth in a mournful trickle.

Xin darted forward, seized the fallen morsel, and crammed half of it between his lips. He barely chewed. Hunger flared into a burning ache. Shame seared hot behind his ears.

A shout shattered the marketplace's din. "Ho there! Thief!"

The word struck hard. Xin turned to flee. Yet rough hands seized his collar and wrenched him backward.

Panicked, he writhed, kicked, clawed at air and sleeve, a hooked fish on a line. His eyes watered. Bright dots winked at the edges of his vision.

"Cease!" The new voice, also with a thick accent, thundered. "Do the child no harm. He seeks only to quiet his hunger."

"Thief!" Fury laced the vendor's response. "An example must be made!"

The vendor's steel grip on his neck tightened. Xin kicked, desperation making him wild. He chewed the inside of his cheek, his mouth coppery with blood.

"Calm down." The foreign devil's blue-eyed gaze fastened on Xin.

The onlookers, a rabble of laborers, boatmen, and rickshaw pullers, closed in, drawn by the promise of commotion and justice.

"Cursed stealer," someone muttered amidst the crush.

The stranger stepped forward. "Boy, what compels you to theft?" Camphor, perspiration, and some sharper essence hung about him.

The vendor wrestled Xin upright and scowled. "This is no concern of yours, Reverend."

Reverend? The term reserved for foreign priests?

Xin looked up. Before him stood a tall, gaunt fellow, his hair and beard untamed, his garb consisting not of the stiff attire of Westerners, but of a mended Chinese robe. The pallor of his complexion bespoke long years spent far from home and comfort. A peculiar air, a gravity fashioned of privation and purpose, clung to him.

Xin swallowed hard. "My father used to say, 'Never beg.' We—" The rest choked off.

His baba was gone, and Mama too. The memory hurt worse than the hunger.

The vendor loosened his hold. "Your sort is always full of stories. Who pays for that bun now, eh?"

"Is it right to beat children?" The stranger lifted a finger toward the heavens. "Release him. I shall pay."

"For thieves?" Someone in the crowd hooted. "You devils pay for everything. Silver flows like rain from your pockets, but your morals wallow like swine."

The stranger drew a handful of coins from his pocket. At the sight, the vendor hesitated.

"You feed rats, Reverend Roberts."

Roberts? Was that his name?

The white man dropped the coins into the tray. "My God feeds sparrows. Should we offer less?"

A coarse laugh rippled through the gathering. "Your god is a curious one. Fond of beggars and thieves, is He?"

"He would love us all, were we willing." Roberts turned his gaze to Xin. "And what is your name, child?"

Xin blinked at him. Not once since his parents' death had anyone inquired after his name. "Zhang Xin."

"Zhang Xin?" Mr. Roberts repeated. "Why, child, you appear to have fallen into some difficulty. My name is Issachar Jacox Roberts. I hail from America. You may call me Teacher."

The vendor shrugged. "Keep your eyes on the boy. There are plenty more like him about."

Offered no further entertainment, the crowd dispersed.

Roberts stretched out his hand, deliberate as a careful father. "Come, child."

The foreigner's grip was gentle. Xin twitched to flee. Prudence constrained his limbs, for to take flight would doubtless rouse all wary glances and furnish the foreigner with reason to call upon the constable.

✳ ✧ ✳

Walking alongside Roberts, Xin kept his head down, fists clenched at his sides. The pallid man neither hurried him nor paraded him as a trophy. They passed the high walls enclosing the town toward the Pearl River. Soon the city noise melted into the tranquil whisper of camphor trees.

Beyond the main gate, a square white house stood against the blue sky, windows open to let in the breeze. Xin slowed his steps, gaze roaming the neat rows of a well-ordered vegetable patch and a black dog sprawled in the golden sunlight.

Within, the house's shade held a welcome coolness. They passed a wall mirror. In it, Xin's almond-shaped eyes beneath thick, well-defined brows stared back at him.

Fatigue washed away the last of his anger. As they entered the room, his legs weakened, and he collapsed onto the matted floor.

Roberts kneeled beside him. "Child, are you injured?"

Xin trembled. One of his knees was bleeding, and a dull ache radiated from his jaw. Still, his pride would brook no admission of distress. "I am not a child."

"Forgive me. You are quite right." Roberts flashed a gentle smile. Producing a blue handkerchief from his pocket, he dabbed at the blood on Xin's knee. "May I ask your age?"

"Fifteen."

"Are you quite certain?" Roberts arched an eyebrow. "Most lads of fifteen whom I encounter are rather taller and have a bit more muscle on them."

Xin's hand drifted to the patched garment draped over his shoulders. "Aye, sir. I was born in the year 1830."

"So then, nearly a man." Roberts surveyed him from head to foot. "You have dirt on your face."

Xin's cheeks flushed. He ignored the comment and peered around. Upon the walls hung vast cloths embroidered with foreign characters, mountains, and sheep. A battered wooden chest, lid half-askew, spilled forth books and ragged papers. He returned his focus to Roberts. "Pray, sir, what will you do with me?"

"Feed you first." The white devil sat down beside him. "And give you a bed."

Xin's shoulders remained tense. "Will you deliver me to the magistrate for theft?"

Roberts's eyes sparkled. "You have answered the necessity of hunger, my boy. I shan't send you to the yamen."

"Why?"

"My God commands mercy. He fed the hungry." He winked at Xin. "Were I to do otherwise, what sort of missionary would I be?"

Xin braced for his next request. The foreigners seldom bestowed gifts. They demanded something in return—translation work, menial chores, or worse.

Yet Roberts simply called out, "San-san, bring some food."

A Chinese maid soon appeared with a plate of unfamiliar bread and slices of meat.

"Eat." Roberts motioned for Xin to sit at the table.

Xin settled into a chair and enjoyed the fare, pausing only to break off morsels for the black dog at his ankles.

Roberts sipped tea and waited.

The fog of hunger receded from Xin's mind. The sudden fullness alarmed him, as if he had swallowed more kindness than his body could contain. "Thank you," he muttered.

Roberts lifted his gaze toward the ceiling. "You need not thank me. Give your thanks to the Lord above."

Xin's fingers tightened into fists. He stared at the dusty ground.

The silence stretched until Roberts spoke once more. "Have you family?"

Xin shook his head. "No one remains. My baba and mama…" His voice frayed. "They are gone."

"Gone to the Lord?"

"Gone to the worms." The words dropped heavily. He cleared his throat, but it didn't clear anything. "Baba was a teacher. When the rebels came, they put his books to the flame. The soldiers forced my brother to join them and took what little money we had. Baba became ill soon after. Mama—she also caught cholera and died."

A painful heat rose in Xin's heart. Nay. He would not, could not, shed tears before this foreign devil. Instead, he busied his fingers with the crumbs on his empty plate.

"Grief, I have found, possesses the power to shutter a man's soul." Roberts touched the rim of his teacup. "Yet at times, it may also unbolt doors that once seemed closed."

Xin cast him a sidelong glance. "There's nothing left for a door to hang on."

Roberts didn't respond. Maybe he only partly comprehended him?

"Come." The missionary rose and limped toward the battered chest, a stiffness in his gait.

He rummaged among the books and retrieved a well-worn one. "This marks a beginning." Roberts pressed the slim volume into Xin's palm. "'Tis the Chinese translation of the Gospel according to John. Should you so desire, I would be pleased to instruct you in the English tongue, that you might peruse the entire Bible for yourself in the near future."

Xin frowned. "What virtue is concealed in the Bible? My father often said that foreigners thrust their faith upon us after our nation's defeat and the treaty at Nanjing."

"The Bible proclaims all men as brethren." Roberts didn't raise his voice. "All of us ache for love. Within it lies comfort for sorrow and nourishment for the spirit."

Perhaps seeing Xin's scorn, Roberts returned to the books and withdrew another stitched volume battered at the corners. "You will find greater favor in this. 'Twas penned by one of your own compatriots, Liang Fa."

The title, *Good Words to Admonish the Age*, piqued Xin's interest. He flipped through it, surprised by the tiny, disciplined characters marching down the page in vertical columns. "Liang Fa…" He repeated the name, as though weighing it with his tongue. "I have heard about him from my baba. He argued with the scholars and quoted mysterious sayings about heaven."

Roberts narrowed his eyes. "Liang Fa stands as the first ordained preacher among the Chinese and endeavors to shape the teachings of Jesus for your countrymen. He believes change is possible here, without recourse to violence, without the necessity of war."

Xin's gaze lingered on a single sentence. "Let men recognize their own darkness, that the light may enter."

Memory wandered to the years of hunger, to riots, to foreign ships lying in silent menace. "We know darkness. 'Tis no simple thing to trust that light shall come."

Roberts inclined his head. "Nor is it an easy task to teach. Liang Fa attempts it. And, in my humble way, so do I."

Xin held the book in a tight grip. For the first time since Mama's passing, a sense of transient safety enveloped him. Still, the house was too silent, the wooden chair too tall, and the stranger... At least Roberts was not like the British sailors who, with rough elbows, shoved the porters in the alleys.

As dusk descended and the light of the lantern spread irregular shadows on the floor, Xin slumped beneath the window, the heavy volume on his knees.

Roberts busied himself with the teapot and hummed a solemn tune unfamiliar to Xin's ears. "Shall I tell you a story?"

Xin's gaze traced the scars on his hands, then flicked to the door. Would anyone enter and hurt him again? "Do tell."

The foreigner began, "There was once a prodigal son..."

Xin listened, sleep pressing at his eyelids until they hung low.

Outside, the river carried away the day's dust. Within the missionary's shelter, a space of peace opened. For now.

Chapter Three

Hong Kong, China
Autumn 2022

The city, a forest of concrete and heat, clung to its mugginess even in autumn. Inside the black Mercedes S-Class, humidity slipped away, repelled by the car's relentless air-conditioning. Jason sank into the leather seat and tried to focus. Vivian Jiang sat beside him, her expensive perfume enveloping him.

"I'll introduce you to my friends tonight." She glanced at him. "You may gain more clients."

"Your friends," he echoed, the word caught in his dry throat. "I'm full of hope."

Her mouth quirked. "Relax. You'll do just fine."

He rubbed his palm against his leg. The paper edges of his folder rasped against his fingertips.

As they made small talk, the driver, clad in a black suit, navigated through the cramped tunnel and up to the entrance of a mansion on Victoria Peak. They exited the car, and the guards in crisp uniforms clicked their heels in unison. She smoothed a hand over her pale blue silk dress. He clutched his folder of listings as if it might anchor him before the prospect of having clients at her level swept him away.

Inside the marble-floored foyer, she paused under golden chandeliers. "Don't be nervous. My friends aren't sharks. They won't bite."

His grip on the folder tightened. "I'm not used to this kind of event."

She laughed, a practiced sound. "You'll get used to it soon."

Servers in starched collars glided by, trays packed with abalone canapés and flutes of Dom Pérignon. She called out names—Mandarin, Cantonese, English all blurring together. He shook hands with art dealers, venture capitalists, and men with younger women hanging off their arms. A property tycoon and a tech CEO asked for his card. Through it all, Vivian stood by him.

On a terrace overlooking Victoria Harbour, she introduced him to Esther Fok. "My lawyer and also my problem solver."

Esther's handshake was cool, her jade pendant catching the light with each movement. "So, you're the Realtor Vivian recommended?" she asked in Mandarin.

His heart thudded. He mustered a polite smile to cover his nervousness and shifted his feet. "I'm trying to live up to her expectations."

Esther leaned in. "You're Christian, yes? Vivian says you're honest."

Pressure tightened his throat. Debra's warning about staying away from any wrongs rang in his ears. He swallowed. Honesty— he could live up to that, couldn't he? "That's what I strive for."

Her lips curved up. "Be careful. Honest men don't last."

Before he replied, Vivian nudged him away to another group of guests.

A glass of wine, and the rest of the evening became a blur of faces. As they left at midnight, she tucked her arm into his. "I need your help with something else. Lunch tomorrow. Tai Pan, noon."

Tai Pan, an old-money haunt filled with silver-haired bankers? Jason narrowed his eyes and said yes.

The black Mercedes dropped him off. He entered his flat, slippers lined up by the door with military precision. For a heartbeat, his mind drifted to that peak mansion, where everything shimmered and nothing made sense.

Debra was still up. Her Bible lay open in her lap. She sat up and tucked her feet under her on the sofa. "How did it go?"

"A different world." He dropped beside her, his shirt still smelling of someone else's cologne. "The driveway curled around a fountain bigger than our building. Valets in black gloves, cars lined up like a parade of sharks. Inside, the marble was so polished I kept worrying I'd slide across it. A string quartet played in a corner.

Servers carried trays of tiny food, each with a tag to inform us what it was."

Her gaze locked with his. "And Vivian?"

"Standing by me all the time." He chuckled. "She kept saying, 'You have to meet so-and-so,' and then I was shaking hands with people whose watches could buy our apartment."

She tilted her head. "And you? How did it feel to be there?"

"Like I'd swallowed fireworks, and they were burning down." He tapped the armrest. "The napkins were thicker than our towels. I don't know if I want it or if it wants me."

Debra closed her Bible. "Jason, watch out for temptation."

His breath hitched, and he straightened his shoulders. "Temptation?"

"Yeah. Money, power, losing your way." She grasped his arm. "I trust you. But you must watch out."

His gaze darted to the floor. "Vivian wants to talk at lunch tomorrow. I'll tell you what she says."

"Promise me you'll pray first." Debra placed her palm on his chest, over his heart. "Should we pray together now?"

They bowed their heads and prayed for wisdom and protection from evil. As their voices faded, hope and anxiety wrestled in his mind.

The next day, when he arrived at Tai Pan, Vivian, immaculate in a crimson dress, already sat at the table.

"You're late," she chided with a smile.

"Traffic." He took the seat across from her and scanned the room, all antique furniture and porcelain.

The server swung by, and they placed their orders. Vivian chose the crispy Peking duck with hoisin sauce, while he opted for the steamed grouper and jasmine rice.

She sipped tea. "I need your advice. There are"—she hesitated—"assets I have to move. Large sums. Clean. No questions. Hong Kong is an ideal place for that."

He raked a hand through his hair, a chill icing his spine. "Vivian, I'm only a property guy."

She leaned forward. "You went to Chinese University and know people. If you introduce me to a friend of yours who specializes in those deals, I'll double your normal commission. In cash."

A knot twisted in his stomach. A part of him recoiled. He fought the urge to pull back.

A manicured finger traced lazy circles around her cup. "In my world, some of us don't get to decide the terms of our survival. I had to climb over men who thought they owned me." She gave a sharp laugh that didn't reach her eyes. "I want to protect myself."

Protect herself from whom? From what? The questions rattled in his head. He rubbed his forehead, trying to order his thoughts as something prickled beneath his skin. "Those deals are dangerous. Even in Hong Kong."

One wrong step was all it took to change a life forever.

She smiled, a shard behind it. "Are you scared?"

"No." He pinched the bridge of his nose. "I worry about you."

The server brought two plates. They picked at their food in silence. Vivian broke the quiet. "You're not like the others, Jason. That's why I trust you." She dipped a piece of meat into the sauce. "I'll be careful. Please help me."

"I'll try."

After lunch, he strolled through Mong Kok alone, letting the city's chaos steady him. Hawkers yelled over battered radios. Teenagers clustered around bubble tea shops. Pedestrians hurried by.

His phone buzzed, a text message from Debra. "I'm making your favorite ground-pork stuffed buns for dinner. Mom, Uncle Brian, and little Mateo will join us too. See you soon. Love."

Time to go home.

Debra greeted him in the kitchen, her apron dusted with flour. She looked up from a heap of steamed buns. "How was the meeting with Vivian?"

He braced against the counter. "She needs to move money out of the mainland and asked if I'd find someone who could handle it for her."

Debra's hands stilled, the chopsticks suspended in midair. "Are you…?"

The front door swung open, interrupting their conversation. Debra's mom, elegant in a tailored blazer despite the humid evening, swept in with nine-month-old Mateo in her arms, his fingers clutching a toy dinosaur. Right behind her, Uncle Brian entered and stepped beside Jason. "What's new, partner? Have you heard anything about your Canadian immigration application?"

The question was weighted with significance born of both business and family ties.

"Not yet." Jason took Mateo from his mother-in-law and bounced him on his hip. "Hey, Dino Master!"

The baby giggled, ignorant of the adult world's perils.

Debra cleared her throat. "We were just talking about a complicated request." She set the chopsticks down beside the meat buns and urged everyone to sit at the dining table. "Mom, with years of risk management experience at Hang Seng Bank, you might be able to help."

"Complicated? How?" Mom lifted an eyebrow. "I'm more used to dealing with loan risks. Still, I can spot potential pitfalls."

Jason's pulse quickened. He returned Mateo to Uncle Brian before taking his seat. "A high school classmate plans to move money out of China into Hong Kong."

"That's why you're uneasy." His mother-in-law sat and placed a baozi on her plate. "Lots of folks in China do that. Plenty think they're smarter than the system. Most get caught. Did you warn your friend?"

Debra opened the portable playpen for Mateo. "Jason has always stood up for others. But this sounds like too much."

After placing Mateo in the playpen and giving him a sippy cup of milk, Uncle Brian sat opposite Jason. The steam from buns curled between them as the neon glow from outside flickered on the floor tiles.

"Vivian wants me to introduce her to people who will facilitate the process." Jason exhaled. "I suppose I'll ask around for her."

Uncle Brian intertwined his fingers. "Shall we say grace together? I'll also pray God gives you the guidance you need."

After the prayer, Jason picked up a pork bun. Vivian's request loomed. To distract himself, he changed the subject. "Grandpa likes baozi. We ought to bring him some."

Mom pulled her bun apart, releasing the scent of ginger and scallions. "He'd be delighted. Brian, Mateo, and I just visited him this morning. He looked well."

"Yes, he's fully recovered from COVID. Still, I worry when he coughs." Jason's shoulders eased as he inhaled the steamy scents. "Maybe Debra and I will go see him tomorrow?"

"Sure." Debra pointed at the buns. "We'll save some for him."

He chuckled, warmed by their shared love of his grandpa. The weight of decisions and changes floated aside, and all that mattered was his family. He glanced over at Mateo. "Ha. The baby fell asleep already."

"Good. He didn't take a long nap in the afternoon." Mom spread a blanket over Mateo. "Deb, Jason told me he's joined you in reading your dad's manuscript about the Heavenly Kingdom of Great Peace. How do you like it so far?"

Debra swirled her tea. "Quite interesting. It's an unfamiliar part of Chinese history to me. The chapter about the interaction between Zhang Xin and Issachar Jacox Roberts provides a backdrop for Xin's eventual departure from Christianity." She sipped her tea. "You and Uncle Brian are also reading it, right?"

Uncle Brian raised a hand. "Ah, yes. Another masterpiece, very much your dad's style. I'm curious how he will handle the religious aspect." He reached for the teapot. "Xin tried to fit in. Under Roberts, he learned English and helped prepare tracts in the printing room. Yet a question bothered him. Why does a loving God allow so much hardship in the world?"

Jason swallowed his mouthful of food. "The hard question since human history began, isn't it?"

"Yeah." Debra set her tea down. "He asked why suffering happened, and Roberts just said to trust. That answer confused Xin even more. Dad did such an excellent job. Reading their dialogue, I could almost see Xin's frustration."

Mom brushed a crumb from her lap. "That was the answer I used to receive when I was a seeker." She touched her cup, eyes distant. "Easy to say until you're the one facing heartache."

"For someone as curious and determined as Zhang Xin, I don't think he'd be satisfied with blind faith." Uncle Brian squinted. "Each time he voiced his doubts, Roberts recoiled a little, as if suggesting Xin could only find resolution through his own search."

Drumming the table, Jason exhaled. "That stood out to me as well. Xin was searching for more thoughtful answers. Instead, he ended up testing Roberts's patience."

Debra smiled and lifted her chin. "Dad's writing is powerful. The story says a lot about the era, but even more about human nature."

"We reach for truth, yet the search may lead to more uncertainty." Mom inclined her head. "I often wonder how many changes begin with something left unresolved."

Uncle Brian looked out the window. "Xin ended up leaving Roberts to join Hong Xiuquan in the Taiping Rebellion, stepping into a bloody nightmare. His faith would be tested amid the devastation of civil war."

"Uncle, you're ahead of me in your reading. Please don't spoil it for me." Debra wagged a finger at him. "I want to experience the story myself."

The conversation hung in delicate tension. Jason sighed again. Xin's spiritual confusion seemed to mirror his uncertainty about Vivian.

Chapter Four

Guangzhou, Guangdong, China
Summer 1847

Zhang Xin made his way under the shelter of a battered parasol, its ribs casting shadows across the cobblestones. His hands remained folded within his sleeves.

Three years had slipped by since the foreigner, Reverend Roberts, plucked him from the street. Through his guardian's kindness, he had been granted the rare privilege of learning—numbers, English script, and the peculiar laws of the Western Deity. In requital, he had taken on himself the larger share of the domestic offices in Mr. Roberts's household and schoolroom.

He walked through the doorway and stopped in front of a mirror. The gaunt, ratlike boy of fifteen had vanished. In his stead stood a youth with broad shoulders. His strong stature rose above that of many others. Even so, his tall frame had not outgrown a subtle stoop, nor had he shed the cautious step that spoke of long familiarity with cold stone beneath a beggar's feet.

Inside the parlor, Roberts sat cross-legged and read aloud. "'Blessed are the poor in spirit'…"

Xin stepped closer and cut in, the words burning out of him before he could swallow them. "Teacher, you always say your God loves all." He thrust a finger toward the alleys outside the window. "Why do hungry children with hollow faces still line the jetties, and why does the plague continue to stalk those crowded courtyards?"

Roberts looked up. Creases formed on his brow. "God hears every cry, every pain. Suffering does not mean He has forgotten us.

Rather, it speaks to the fallen state of our world and serves as a trial of our faith."

The same reply, similar to what Liang Fa wrote in his book. Xin contained a bitter laugh. "What good is faith to a famished child or to a mother perishing without medicine? Is it mercy to bid them wait for some world beyond this one?"

Roberts closed his Bible. "Faith is not always accompanied by comfort. At times, it stands as a promise about a life beyond our present misery."

Xin's hands balled into fists at his sides, a useless heat tightening his chest. "Why must we wait for the hereafter? Why must we suffer so much now?"

A ponderous silence descended. Without receiving a reply from Roberts, Xin pressed his lips together.

Maybe he'll give me a satisfactory answer on the morrow.

Xin stood up, took up his broom, and swept the dusty floor in silence. Afterward, he returned the broom to the corner and closed the door behind him.

The following day dawned with leaden clouds. In the far distance, thunder rumbled. Whilst Xin picked pebbles from the rice in the kitchen, Roberts appeared at the doorway. "Xin, I wish for you to meet a newcomer in our community." His smile bore a peculiar reserve common to foreigners, with more hope than familiarity. "Pray, come with me."

They passed into a spare chamber. Half a dozen Chinese men sat around a rough-hewn table, all with dark southern features except for one—a man with high cheekbones, his tall profile impossible to ignore. He wore a plain blue scholar's robe, and his eyes burned with a feverish sparkle.

Roberts gestured. "Zhang Xin, permit me to introduce Mr. Hong Xiuquan. He has declared to us an encounter with God Himself, in a dream."

Hong Xiuquan rose, his intense gaze fixed upon Xin. "Peace to you, brother Zhang," he intoned in a deep bass.

Startled by the singular forcefulness of the man's presence, Xin bowed. "Peace to you, Mister Hong."

Roberts grinned as though he had set some momentous event in motion. "Xin, remain a little. I am needed elsewhere. An errand claims my attention."

After Roberts left, Hong motioned for Xin to sit. Off to the side, a short man introduced himself as Tian Dong, a scholar, and then scribbled in a notebook. "Mister Hong, you were about to share your dream with us."

"Indeed." Hong settled into his seat. "Three years ago, when I lay afflicted with illness, the gates of heaven opened before me. Angels came forth. And God Himself, the heavenly Father, revealed to me my kinship with Christ as the younger brother of Jesus. He commands me to sweep away demons and purify this land."

The men around the table inclined their heads.

Xin furrowed his brow. "Many proclaim dreams and visions of a like nature. The Buddhist monks oft assert such things as well. How do we discern the true from the false?"

"They see only shadows and fumes." Hong's hand sliced the air. "The certainty of my vision lies in this. The heavenly King sorrows alongside His children. Our God turns not away from hunger, poverty, or injustice. He weeps for the lost and has enjoined me to deliver them, not only by prayer but, if necessary, by the sword." His sleeve snapped akin to a banner. "The Heavenly Kingdom, *Taiping Tianguo*, will soon dawn, and the most humble beggar shall stand above the corrupt regime."

Xin's breath caught in his throat. The word *sword* rang in him. Outside, rain lashed the shutters until they rattled in their frames. A draft slid under the door and lifted the hair on his arms.

"Why do we suffer?" His voice rough, he had to swallow to steady it. "How do you remedy evil?"

Tien Dong's brush paused midstroke.

Hong's eyes blazed with zeal. "I have lain on a sickbed, ravaged by fever, cast aside by the bureaucrats who swore to serve the people. As I drifted between life and death, I asked this question. Why such suffering? Why such evil?" He leaned in, the wooden chair creaking beneath him. "The heavenly Father revealed it to me. Evil abounds among us only because we submitted to idols, opium, and wicked officials."

He raised a clenched fist. "The second son of God will break such chains. Not with empty words but through holy rebellion. The Almighty calls me to act."

Xin searched Hong's face for any flicker of doubt. "Would you unsheathe the sword against His Imperial Majesty?"

"I resist all who place themselves betwixt the people and the heavenly mandate." A muscle twitched in Hong's jaw. "Did not even Jesus wield the scourge to purge the temple? How else can I rout out demons, if they clutch at power with iron claws?"

As Dong's brush scratched over the page, Xin studied the men around the table. A chill pressed at him. "And shall all be well in this new kingdom you promise?"

Hong intertwined his fingers. "No more children shiver in alleys. No more landlords despoil fields. In the Heavenly Kingdom, brotherhood rules, and every bowl is filled. Such is the assurance of God and my own solemn pledge."

Thunder rolled beyond the walls. Xin looked down upon his hands, then up at Hong, who glowed with the certainty of prophecy.

"I long to believe, Mister Hong," Xin breathed out. "Yet fear takes root in me."

Hong reached across the table and clasped Xin's forearm. "Fear, my friend, is the instrument of Satan. Together, let us cast it aside."

Their gazes locked. Doubt and destiny converged while the chamber trembled with the distant fury of the storm.

By the next morning, the tempest had passed, leaving a sky mottled with bruised clouds. Xin stepped out to purchase pork. Upon his return, he tarried beneath a teahouse's narrow eaves. Three faded red banners swayed in the wind, their characters blurred by last night's rain.

The shopkeeper approached. "You are Reverend Roberts's pupil, Zhang Xin, are you not?"

Xin stiffened. "Indeed. And you, sir—?"

"Call me Moy. I mind the teas and books here." He pointed at a teapot. "Last night's storm left a chill in its wake. Come, warm yourself, and meet some new friends."

The aroma of jasmine hung in the air. Xin followed Moy inside. Two figures, an aged scholar and a boatman with a graying beard, sat already.

With deft hands, Moy set out teacups and poured chrysanthemum tea. "A friend told me Reverend Roberts has taken on a new student—Hong Xiuquan. Is it true?"

Xin put down the straw bag containing the pork, accepted his tea, and sipped, letting the heat steady the tremor in him. "You know Hong Xiuquan?"

"We all know of him." The boatman spat onto the earthen floor. "He hails from Hua in Guangdong. Raised in poverty, much as we ourselves. He attempted to pass the imperial examinations repeatedly. Failed like most, shut out by the Manchu highborn."

The old scholar cradled his cup. "I know his parents. They spoke of a fever that seized Hong after another failed exam. He drifted in delirium for weeks. When he awoke, he claimed he met angels with golden beards and God called him to battle devils. He has changed, never quite the same."

Xin's fingers curled until the nails bit through cloth. He gripped his thigh. "People speak of family madness in such cases."

"Or a summons from heaven." Moy darted his gaze around as if recalling the well-worn disputes of years past. "He destroyed idols in his village. Smashed ancestral tablets. Spoke against the Buddha, Confucius, and all that has long defined our customs. A large group has already rallied to his cause."

The boatman traced the rim of his teacup. "He did a great kindness to my cousin's son. The landlords would have sent the boy to the yamen for his debts. Hong intervened, negotiated with those landlords, and made good the payment himself."

The scholar snorted. "If you would cast your lot with such a man, be prepared for your life to change. He tolerates neither strong drink nor gambling and strictly forbids opium."

"Does he command his followers to fight against corruption?" The word came out harsher than Xin intended, edged with the bitterness of bribes paid and doors closed. A muscle twitched in his cheek. A dangerous dream flared, and he fought it down.

"Aye." A strange light flickered in Moy's eyes. He slammed a fist on the table, rattling the cups. "What hope have we under the Qing? Hong may be possessed, yet at his assemblies, poor and rich alike dine together, and women are treated as equals in that company."

Silence ensued, broken only by the muted ring of porcelain as the scholar placed his cup on the table.

Xin leaned back. He frowned at the doorway, as if he expected Hong to enter. "If he is already so well-followed, why then did he seek Roberts, the foreign missionary?" He arched an eyebrow. "What does he want from outsiders that he cannot take from his own?"

The scholar's voice dropped to a hush. "That is the crux. After his vision, Hong took up the writings of Liang Fa. Not content with that alone, he sought those from across the seas."

Moy squared his shoulders. "I have heard of Liang Fa's book, *Good Words to Admonish the Age*. A most weighty tome. Nine whole sections, brimming with Scripture, parable, and admonition, all in our common tongue. Five hundred pages, if not more."

Xin's jaw slackened. Was this not the very volume Roberts had bestowed upon him when they first met? How extraordinary!

The boatman's tongue darted out to wet his lips. "Did Hong read the whole of it?"

"He studied it with zeal," the scholar replied. "His parents confided in me. He carried it with him everywhere and inscribed passages in the margins. He recited a whole page to them. 'Heaven and earth tremble at the wickedness of idols,' that sort of thing."

Xin rubbed a thumb along his chin. "Then 'twas no mere dream. Did Liang's writings kindle this fervor within him?"

"Liang Fa is the first among the Chinese to preach in the manner of foreign missionaries." Moy glanced down at his feet. "He wandered from village to village and contended with monks and mandarins alike. His book not only speaks of the foreign God but unveils the corruption at the empire's very core. When Hong read it, he became a man possessed of a sacred duty."

The boatman stroked his beard. "My cousin told me Hong speaks with a fierce conviction of demons and false gods. He claims the appointed hour draws near. All purehearted men shall rally to the Heavenly King, who is none other than his Father in heaven."

The scholar gave a slow headshake. "Hong would upend tradition." His tone dipped to a somber murmur. "It may well be perilous, when virtuous words ignite like wildfire in the mind of a desperate soul."

No one spoke. The hush pressed against Xin's ribs. Heat gathered in his chest, a trembling hunger he feared to name. His palms prickled. He wanted to reach for the faint scent of a brighter future. Outside, sunlight broke through the clouds as if the heavens themselves were awakening.

Fire Between Two Skies

What chaos might erupt when a single righteous flame set the world ablaze?

Chapter Five

In the chamber with windows dimmed by the river's mist, Zhang Xin sat upright upon a plain wooden stool, his restless hands folded in his lap.

"Teacher, Hong Xiuquan has declared a singular revelation. He styles himself as God's second son—nay, the younger brother of Jesus." The words sounded dangerous and blasphemous, a spark Xin could neither swallow nor spit out. He furrowed his eyebrows. A flush crept up his neck at the enormity of the claim. "Do you know this declaration?"

The question slipped out in a hoarse whisper. He looked toward the nearby wooden chest, cluttered with books and ragged papers, as if it might yield answers.

Since meeting Hong three months ago, Xin could not shake the echo of the man's voice. The seed of that certainty had taken root in him. Days once gentle with Bible lessons, errands, and meals turned taut. Prayer no longer soothed. He wanted, with a child's desperation, for his beloved guardian to believe Hong.

Across from him, Roberts's gaze sharpened. His fingers drummed an impatient cadence against the table. "Indeed. I knew of Hong's claim and hoped to persuade him to recant. If he persists, duty compels me to act. Jesus is God's only begotten Son. Tell me, what has he further spoken?"

Xin pinched the coarse string of his tunic until it bit his skin. "He says the heavenly Father appeared to him in a dream and chose him, God's second son, to deliver our people from the demons." His tone dipped low, half awe, half fear.

"Christianity teaches the Trinity. Father, Son, and Holy Spirit, three persons, one God. There is and can be no second son." Roberts pressed his knuckles to his brow. "Jesus—born in Bethlehem, crucified at Calvary, risen the third day—redeems us." He reached for the English Bible on the table and flipped it open. "Read John's third chapter here."

The ink shimmered. Xin bent over the book. His tongue felt thick, but he forced the syllables out. "'For God so loved the world, that he gave his only begotten Son, that whosoever believeth in him should not perish, but have everlasting life.'"

His pulse hammered in his ears. The verse rang clear. Yet Hong's promise rose unbidden in his mind. He clung to the page, while emotions twisted tight in his chest. How could both be true? And if they could not, which one should he follow?

Roberts closed the book, a muscle twitching in his jaw. "People may claim whatever. No truth is fashioned anew by a man's dream."

Xin sucked in a sharp breath. He needed certainty—one solid ground he could trust not to shift beneath him. "If there is only one God, why the three?"

"A mystery to us. We are dust before a God beyond space and time." Roberts rose and sat down again. "The Trinity blazes like the sun. To gaze full upon it will blind us. Hold to truth and beware the pride that remakes heaven to fit our imagination."

Xin rubbed the back of his neck. The fervor in Hong's words would not let go of him. "People follow Hong because they suffer. He gives them hope and talks about God, food, and justice."

Roberts narrowed his eyes. "Hope is a precious thing. It must not be built on falsehood, lest it collapse and crush those who trust in it." He leaned forward. "The Church brings hope without violence or visions that contradict the gospel."

A gust of wind rattled the windowpanes. Xin flinched and looked up, visually tracing the jagged cracks in the plaster above him. "Is it wrong to desire a better world now?" He hesitated, as though his question unveiled forbidden secrets. "The peasants say Hong teaches not only about God, but about peace on earth and equality between men and women." His voice grew firmer, a flicker of defiance burning out the fear.

"Many have clothed their ambitions in holy garments." Roberts put his hands together. "Beware the fire that destroys as it cleanses. Test every spirit, the Scripture says."

Outside, the river mist pressed closer, blurring the line between sky and land.

✳ ✧ ✳

Winter arrived after the last days of autumn. In the dim glow of a low fire, shadows danced along the main chamber's walls, where portraits of stern English ministers gazed down. Rain beat against the windows, weaving a soft percussion through the hush. Upon a wooden chair, Hong Xiuquan perched, his bright eyes undimmed even by the plainness of his hempen robe. Xin lingered behind him, gaze averted from his aging benefactor.

Roberts stood guard before the hearth, the oil lamp's steady light outlining the sharp hollows of his countenance. "Mister Hong, permit me to speak with candor. By what authority do you proclaim yourself the son of the Almighty, aye, the very brother of our Lord Jesus Christ?"

Hong rose, his hands flung heavenward as if summoning a verdict from the unseen. "God gave me a dream. He called me to defeat demons and free people from their suffering. I must not refuse His will."

Roberts's lips thinned. "Dreams are not doctrine, Mister Hong. Scripture admits no new kin to Christ. In tampering with such doctrines, you risk blasphemy, and your message confuses the flock."

Xin's breath snagged. His mentor's usually gentle manner seemed cloaked in cold judgment. The room tilted. Lantern smoke drifted over the two men who had shaped his soul. Now they glared at each other, pulling him taut between them. Was it a betrayal to crave Hong's teachings? Was it cowardice to cling to Roberts's shore if he refused to follow Hong on the path to God?

Hong adjusted his robe and traced a slow orbit along the walls. "What appears as peril to you is promise to me. To the meek, the burdened, and the destitute, I proclaim hope and bring the keys to the Heavenly Kingdom."

Roberts took a step toward Xin. "You lead many astray with fables, and it grieves me Zhang Xin is among them."

At the mention of his name, Xin's shoulder twitched. He rubbed his thumb over the thin scar on his wrist to steady the tremor. His presence, obscure until now, was thrust into the center of this strife. "Teacher, I wish not to offend. You rescued me from the streets—" His throat constricted, the words swallowed by dread.

Roberts's gaze, once full of paternal affection, fell on him in a sorrowful stare. "Xin, remember what I've taught you. The Triune God accomplishes His plan of salvation through Jesus Christ alone. Do not be led into heresy."

A shiver ran up Xin's spine. "I want to believe. Yet my soul is restless." He laced his fingers over the back of the chair where Hong once sat. "I see helpless men and women before cruel landlords. Did not the Lord Jesus lift the lowly into His arms? Is there not a kingdom here for those in need?"

"God indeed called us to serve the least." Roberts inclined his head. "Mistake not fervor for divine command, nor visions for the Biblical teachings."

Hong stopped his pacing. "You fear the old order is ending. But God has chosen me as a new leader. I'm gathering an army under the banner of the Great Peace. The broken and suffering will be the ones to join."

Roberts's voice rose with a rare thunder. "Enough! Your false teaching brings harm. Mark me, Mister Hong. The Christ I follow seeks neither earthly power nor bloodshed. This house shan't harbor such a doctrine, nor shall I permit my flock to be led into rebellion. I insist, sir, that you depart immediately."

Silence ensued. Xin's chest burned as the two men, one his savior who pulled him from the gutter, the other his beacon of future hope, stood irreconcilable. He broke the stillness. "Teacher, I owe you all. My soul aches with gratitude, but it burns with longing for justice. If I err, let God judge me. I must go and seek the kingdom, even if the path is perilous."

Hong stepped closer and placed a hand on Xin's shoulder. "Come, brother. The journey is arduous, but you must trust the calling within you."

Xin hesitated, torn between loyalty and conviction. In his yearning for heaven, had he bidden farewell to earth? Hong urged him to move. At the door, Xin turned for a final look at his guardian.

Roberts stood stoop-shouldered in the wan glow of the hearth fire. "My son, do not leave—" His voice fractured. Then, in English, the words tumbled out in a gasp. "My God, what have I done?"

Outside, the rain stopped. The cobblestones bathed in a silvery sheen. Hong tugged at his sleeve. Xin tore his gaze away from Roberts and hurried out into the open. His heart thundered. Grief mingled with hope. The old life closed behind. The world unfurled in terrifying newness.

Night descended. A damp north wind threaded the fog between moored junks. Lanterns quivered along the wharves. The sweet scent of roasted chestnuts drifted by. Despite his fatigue, Xin's alertness heightened as Hong led him through dark alleys. After the better part of an hour, they slipped into an inn. A mixed crowd, laborers, scholars, and merchants from the market, was already present.

Hong secured a corner table and ordered rice gruel and pickled radish for them both. Steam curled up, sharp with sour brine. "You have left the past and become my kin. The poor will rise because of us."

Xin studied the grooves on Hong's face, so unlike Roberts's open candor. "Do you ever experience fear?"

Hong's eyes flickered. "When heaven calls, fear is useless. Doubt is for those in the darkness. 'Tis not for us."

"I—" Xin's fingers tightened around the warm bowl. Sourness flooded his mouth over other winters carrying the ache of an empty stomach.

Across the room, a fight broke out. Men cursed in Cantonese and overturned stools. A man's knuckles split. Another clung to his sleeve as though it were the last thing he owned.

Why did people suffer? Because their bowls were shallow and their pride was all they had left? If the poor would rise, who must fall for them to stand?

Hong seemed unperturbed and beckoned to Xin. "Remember, we are not of this world's rule. Though others see only want and disorder, the Heavenly Kingdom takes root in brave hearts. On the morrow, we set out for Guangxi. I shall present you to our brethren."

The innkeeper intervened to restore peace. The room smelled of rice wine and old grief. Xin turned back to Hong. "I…" He couldn't finish.

I have burned my bridges.

The inn descended into silence. The lanterns burned low. Xin tossed on his bed, sleepless. At first light, he gathered the few effects from his former lodgings—clothes, rice cakes wrapped in paper, and a notebook with verses he copied from Liang Fa's tract. He and Hong skirted the southern gate and passed beneath the stone archways. None of the guards gave more than a cursory glance.

They journeyed north. Along the river roads, Hong took Xin to visit a few families. Soon, the group swelled to include two scholars, five peasants, and their wives and children. The newcomers brought recent rumors. "Bandits clashed with soldiers because the Qing's grip had grown loose, and the misery of opium fans out like a shadow…"

As if he were moving through a dream, uncertainty accompanied Xin's footsteps. The world he knew faded, and the future was unclear. Yet Hong's compassion, the camaraderie of their little band, and the dream of conquering injustice solaced him.

At night, they stayed at remote inns and sang gospel songs. Beneath a full moon burnished red by smoke, Hong summoned all to prayer. Xin kneeled with the others on mats. Hong's voice, equal parts thunder and sweet balm, echoed in the glade. "We have suffered under the dragon for too long. The time is now, brothers and sisters. Heaven's wrath burns against the Manchu tyranny, and its grace beckons to us."

The air throbbed with a conviction Xin never heard in Roberts's sermons. In Hong's presence, the pulse of destiny coursed through Xin's veins.

Revelation or warning?

Chapter Six

Kowloon, Hong Kong, China
Autumn 2022

Faint golden sunlight from the kitchen window spilled onto the coffee mugs. Jason, clad in a faded blue T-shirt, swirled the spoon in his oatmeal.

Debra sat across from him and sliced a green apple. "In Dad's manuscript about the Taiping Rebellion, Xin asked Roberts why he believed in Jesus but rejected others who claimed to be sent by God. That resonated with me. I mean, the poor guy never got a straight answer, did he?"

Admiring his wife's lovely oval face, he relaxed his fingers, and the spoon slipped from his grasp. "Roberts didn't have an appropriate answer. Or maybe he thought just saying 'believe in the Bible' was enough."

"I have a better answer for Xin." Debra put down the apple. "As a scientist, I have to keep an open mind. If anyone can show me ancient texts predicting someone's coming, and that person actually fulfills those prophecies, I'd study it seriously."

His elbow thudded onto the table, his knuckles whitening. "You know what Xin would probably say? He'd look at all those verses about Jesus in the Old Testament, and"—his jaw tensed, the words twisting in his mouth—"he'd say they were written afterward. Jesus' followers made them up so people would believe."

"Yeah." She pressed her lips into a thin line. "I could imagine Xin wrestled with the questions alone in his room. Finding no satisfactory answers, he strayed into Hong's claims."

He exhaled and let his thumb trace the rim of his mug. "Xin didn't know about the Dead Sea Scrolls." He glanced up with a small laugh. "Even archaeology is in God's control. The discovery of the Dead Sea Scrolls in our era, right when atheism is all the rage and faith has become a punch line, means a lot to me."

"So true." Debra nodded. "The book of Isaiah is one of the original seven scrolls they found at Qumran. It dates back to more than a hundred years before Jesus, way before His time or His disciples." She squinted. "Out of all the biblical scrolls they've discovered, this one's the biggest and best preserved. The words we read now are pretty much the same as what people were reading over two thousand years ago."

A siren howled in the city streets below. Its wail threaded through the morning air, a reminder that ancient words and modern lives could coexist in the same breath. Jason ran a hand through his hair, his fingers snagging on a stubborn knot. "Perhaps more difficult for Xin was the Trinity doctrine."

Her forehead creased. "Definitely. It's beyond everyone's comprehension how three distinct persons could be the same God." Lifting her mug, she blew on her coffee. "The word Trinity doesn't appear in the Bible, but the Bible clearly teaches the concept. I've pondered it, and my conclusion is that we humans can't grasp the mystery."

Jason drew a slow breath. "We've talked about this before." He tapped the table—once, twice, again—to prevent his thoughts from scattering. "We're limited by time and space. The space issue has two distinct aspects. None of us is able to go to two places simultaneously and exist as two separate persons. Don't we sometimes wish we could be in two places at once? I hate it, but it's the truth."

She clinked her mug down. "Yeah. We debated this a while back."

"Space doesn't confine God. He can appear at multiple locations and exist in three persons concurrently." He picked up his spoon again and dug into the oatmeal. "Trinity and the hypostatic union reveal to us an important attribute of God. He is far beyond us."

"This teaching is so different from our human experience," she murmured, almost to herself, "that it must be a revelation from God."

A silence fell. The kitchen clock ticked louder with each beat until it felt synced to his pulse. "We all need confirmation sometimes." He stared into his oatmeal, the spoon useless in his hand. "Deb, pray for me." His eyebrows knitted together. He swallowed hard. "Vivian is ready to close the deal for the penthouse this morning."

"So fast?" Debra reached across and patted his arm. "Didn't she just sign the preliminary agreement last week?"

"Light speed when it's a cash transaction." He straightened up. "I'll accompany her to the final walk-through, then sign the formal agreement."

An hour later, his taxi climbed into Mid-Levels. The road widened beneath The Plaza. A silent queue of black sedans idled on polished basalt. He got off, and uniformed doormen opened the door for him.

Inside, light ran in shallow waves over a slate water wall. An enormous screen, the length of a city bus, hid a lounge. Beyond, a separate bank of elevators glowed a discreet gold sign: Penthouses—Private Access Only. The panel beside them offered biometric scans and key cards the thickness of credit bars. A wall display looped a serene video of a rooftop lap pool and a terrace with a fire pit.

Jason crossed to the onyx concierge desk. The broad-shouldered man behind it wore an earpiece and cuff links stamped with the building's crest. He offered the practiced smile reserved for all residents of The Plaza—the kind that said, "I don't care how much you spend. Nothing surprises us anymore."

Soon, Vivian walked in, followed by Abigail Tang, the seller's agent. A month earlier, Jason had only seen Abigail in company bulletins or on LinkedIn pages. Now, in an alternate version of reality, he exchanged conspiratorial greetings with her like old partners.

"Are you ready?" Abigail's heels clicked, and she guided them into the private lift. In the mirrored cab, the soft glow of cove lights traced their reflections as they rose in a hush.

The elevator opened on the sixty-eighth floor. Beyond the doors, floor-to-ceiling panes framed Victoria Harbour. Sunlight poured across a silk-and-wool rug while a faint hum from the concealed climate system kept the air cool and dry. Abigail drew aside the barely-there transparent sliding door to reveal the wraparound terrace. Its teak decking and pocket herb garden lent a green hush to the city's glitter.

They conducted a final walk-through. In the corridor, fluted oak panels hid a touchpad. With a tap, the lighting shifted to a warm gallery setting. The study, lined with bronze-edged bookshelves, looked east toward the ferries threading through Causeway Bay. The primary suite commanded a corner view, with a dehumidified dressing room and a freestanding tub angled toward the harbor.

They returned to the living room. Vivian turned to him, her expression unreadable. "Marvelous. I'm ready to sign."

"Excellent." Abigail nodded his way.

He patted his attaché case. "After the signing, Vivian will pay the balance by cashier's check, not by bank transfer, for privacy reasons."

Abigail gaped at him, then smiled. "We do accommodate these arrangements for our very best clients."

Vivian fixed him with a look that he remembered from form five, their fifth year of secondary school, when she'd sat in the last row and glanced up at him as he walked past. That was before she'd transformed herself.

After they returned to the lobby, her chauffeur drove them to Abigail's office in Central. With a technician's detachment, Jason arranged documents and guided his client to the necessary fields. Vivian's signature claimed ownership of the city's most prestigious square footage.

Abigail rose. "Congratulations, Ms. Jiang. If you have any friends interested in our properties, please let me know."

"Sure, I'll keep you in my contacts." Vivian picked up her Hermès Birkin bag from the desk.

As they walked out onto the street, Jason put on his face mask. "The penthouse is gorgeous. You'll be happy there."

She shielded her eyes from the sun. "With its location, the ground seems so far away. Life's problems too."

He changed his attaché to the other hand. "You could've bought something similar in Guangzhou. It might've been cheaper."

"How do you know I don't have one on my home turf?" Her tone dipped. "I want to keep my options open."

A call buzzed on her phone. She ignored it.

His gaze fell on her Patek Philippe watch. He'd seen ads in magazines targeting billionaires around the world. How much did it cost? A million? "So you'll spend more time here?"

"That depends on who wins." Her phone pinged again. She pressed it to her ear and shifted to Mandarin.

Jason listened. His body quivered, restless with a shame he couldn't quite name. Working in the real estate business with Uncle Brian for a year, he'd heard about mainlanders emptying banks into Hong Kong homes, but never experienced it. And Vivian—once shy, now formidable—stood at the crossroads of two cities.

Shortly after his client left with her chauffeur, Jason wandered to the nearby mall. Marble floors shone, and every shopfront appeared like a jewel box. Vivian's Birkin bag sprang to mind. How much did such a purse cost? With the commission he'd received from this deal, perhaps he'd buy Debra one.

He pushed through the glass doors of a Hermès boutique. A sales associate drifted over with a smile. As she fiddled with her silk scarf, he reached for the tag on a brown Birkin, fingertips skimming its pebbled skin. The number read HK986,000. Heat crept into his neck. He croaked a thank you and backed away, hyperaware of sweat at his collar.

The lighting at Coach beckoned him. Prices here didn't make his palms sweat. He found a periwinkle purse, soft leather with neat stitching. HK4,250. He imagined the way Debra's eyes sparkled when she was surprised.

"I'll take this." He removed a credit card from his wallet.

The associate boxed it in crisp tissue and slid over the receipt. He murmured his thanks. It wasn't a Birkin, not even close. But it was something he could give without flinching.

The city's luxury—so close, so elusive—stayed with him through his late lunch at a noodle joint.

When he returned home at dusk, the scent of roasted chicken floated through the flat, wrapping him in warmth. He inhaled, then exhaled, unburdening himself of the day's tension.

Dark hair pulled back, Debra appeared in the hallway. "Did everything go well?"

He loosened his tie. "We closed. I got my commission."

Her hands froze in midgesture. "They paid you already? Cashier's check?"

"Yeah." He reached into his attaché. "And I picked up something for you." He gave her the Coach bag, the glossy handles shining in the hallway light. "The rest is already in our joint account."

A smile bloomed across her face. "I've always wanted a designer purse. Coach suits me." She leaned in and pressed a kiss to his cheek. "Thank you, love."

He followed her into the kitchen and glanced at the calendar over their microwave—October 2022, its small squares blocked with words like *fellowship meeting*, *annual physical*, and *client*. "Vivian Jiang behaves like other mainlanders. It's the way they do business."

Debra frowned. "Did she mention her plan for moving money again?"

"No, why?" He braced against the counter. "She invited both of us to dinner this Friday to celebrate the successful transaction."

Debra pointed to her phone on the table. "Mom sent me some news. A guy moved billions earlier this year, and he was put in jail last week. Apparently, most of the money from the mainland is dirty."

"I'm only a Realtor." He rolled his shoulders, trying to look casual even as a tightness cinched his chest. "And I follow procedures."

She came around the counter and hugged him. "I know. Still, be careful."

Coffee. Warmth. A faint copper tang of worry on her tongue. He nuzzled her hair. "Of course I'll be careful. Don't worry."

"Perhaps I'm paranoid." She caressed his neck, rousing a row of goose bumps. "As long as she no longer talks about transferring money out of China, I suppose being her Realtor won't hurt."

Yeah, who could pass up the chance to pocket a commission of over two million dollars from just one penthouse deal?

His mouth found hers, and the conversation dissolved. She tipped her chin, letting him deepen the kiss, fingers threading into his hair. The familiarity quieted the noise that had been crowding his thoughts all afternoon. He drew her closer by the waist. She answered with a giggle against his lips. When they finally came up for air, he rested his forehead on hers. "Paranoid or not." He stole another brief kiss. "We'd better get ready for dinner."

His phone pinged. A message from Vivian with WeChat stickers of pandas holding moneybags said, "See you and Debra at Wynn's, 8 p.m., on Friday."

Debra whistled after he showed her the message. "Wynn's?" She drew out the name. "The place where the napkins are crisper than my résumé?" She squinted at the pandas on his screen. "Okay, the moneybags make sense."

He chuckled. "Vivian's treat."

"Do I need to practice saying 'sommelier' without sounding like I'm ordering a sandwich?" She wrinkled her nose. "Remember not to eat the centerpiece. And when something arrives under a glass dome of smoke, we nod like we expected it. Portions will be the size of compliments, but we will not cry. And whatever you do, don't ask for ranch."

He returned the phone to his pocket. "I'm putting 'skip ranch' on my reminder list."

She grinned. "Good. We'll pretend we always dine in rooms where the lighting costs more than our mortgage. Friday, eight. Let the pandas pay."

Friday arrived sooner than he'd expected. For the occasion, Debra chose a shimmery emerald-green cocktail dress and gold strappy heels. Jason went for classic black slacks, a white fitted shirt with silver cuff links, and a tailored charcoal blazer.

Inside Wynn's, the room appeared choreographed. Servers in jackets trimmed with gold-leaf accents hovered at the margins. The host guided Debra and Jason to a round table near a lacquered screen. Porcelain glowed at each place setting, chopsticks resting on jade saddles, the stemware bright. While they settled into the crescent banquette, Vivian strolled up in a blue silk cheongsam that skimmed her frame. A different Birkin hung on the crook of her arm.

"You're gorgeous." Debra rose to shake her hand.

Vivian's mouth tilted. "Older than the yearbook picture?"

"Oh no." Debra tucked a strand of hair behind her ear. "You look even younger and more beautiful."

Jason tried to flatten his napkin, then realized he'd already smoothed it three times.

Vivian took her seat, a ripple of perfume reaching him before her gaze did. The chandelier scattered light across her cheekbones as she glanced at the menu and then shut it with a decisive tap. "Abalone, Peking duck, braised wagyu," she told the hovering server. "And a bottle of white—something cold and clean." Her gaze locked with Jason's. "I always wanted duck at the year-end banquets in school."

"Yeah." Jason reached for his water and set it down again.

As they traded stories about teachers and bus routes and the old auditorium's broken air-conditioning, Debra's gaze flicked to the Birkin at Vivian's feet. Then she slid her Coach purse behind her back. "Jason said you two sat together at assemblies?"

Vivian waved. "Your husband was the top student in our class." Her tone dipped. "Unlike him, I always felt invisible, unless my classmates threw my schoolbag in the garbage. I was glad, though. It meant I existed."

Jason winced. Form five. While Vivian searched the trash for her English workbook, he stood in a corner and did nothing. Nothing cruel. Just nothing.

"In China, no one cares where you came from. Only how high you get. Here…" Vivian placed the green Birkin by her side. "Here we still remember who used to sit where at assemblies."

He laughed, for Vivian's sake, and his fingers closed around Debra's under the table. She squeezed his hand as if to press reassurance into him.

Vivian leaned forward, elbow on the linen. "Jason told me you're a PhD student at Chinese U working on vitamin D. The entire world is affected by COVID. Vitamin D is known to fight infectious diseases. Tell me about your research. How do you use AI to hack nuclear receptors?"

Debra's face lit up. "Traditionally, we target the protein's main landing spot. With AI, we're mapping out other side pockets that control it from a distance, uncovering new drug options that can quiet the signal."

Jason curved up his lips. "Deb's model predicted a new binding channel. She's proof-testing it in the lab. It could suppress VDR transcriptional activity in—"

Vivian tapped her glass. "Save some for the prospectus." She drummed manicured nails on her napkin. "I have three teams running AI for peptide design, but the progress is slow. Government contracts, lots of meetings, not like Hong Kong." She pivoted in her seat. "Debra, what's your next step? Will you file a patent?"

Debra blinked. "The university has filed a patent already. If we receive funding, we'll push for an IND application."

He arched an eyebrow. "Sorry, Deb. I forgot. What does IND stand for?"

"'Investigational New Drug.'" Vivian's smile broadened. Her voice dropped, taking on a velvet-edged gravity. "That's where the work becomes real. An IND is the border between the lab and the world. Filing means you believe in real impact—first in mice, then people." She circled her empty wineglass by its stem. "You're holding something nobody else has. Don't let it wilt away."

Crimson crept up Debra's cheeks. "It's a long process. So much red tape, and the funding—"

Vivian lifted a shoulder, and her diamond earrings flashed. "Funding finds the determined. The smart ones seek help where others wouldn't dream. Don't underestimate what you've built. If you run into walls, reach out to someone who knows how to slip around them."

Jason tracked Vivian's meaning, his heart thumping. "That's excellent advice."

Vivian's smile never wavered. "Debra, I look forward to seeing what you do next."

The server brought food, extra plates, and serving utensils for sharing. After he poured wine for them and left, Vivian raised her glass. "To bold ideas and execution. Cheers!"

Chapter Seven

Guiping, Guangxi, China
Winter 1847

The river curled behind the town's clustered streets. Light flickered, reflecting in the puddles left by the morning drizzle. Xin trailed Hong into Guiping, his heart thumping. Why such tremors? Anticipation or fear?

As they crossed a stone bridge, a figure appeared. "Cousin. You are returned."

Hong introduced them with courtesy. "Zhang Xin from Guangzhou. And this is my cousin, Feng Yunshan." He clasped the tall fellow's hand. "How fares our community in my absence?"

The corners of Feng's mouth crinkled up. He glanced about, as though weighing prying eyes, and gestured for the company to follow him down a narrow alleyway. "The God-worshipers have multiplied while you were gone. They come from hamlets and fields. Some are men whose lives have been struck by injustice. Others are women who have borne hardships in silence. The same truth draws all. We named our community the Society."

He paused, lowering his voice. "You may wish to know, cousin. Last week, a merchant from the city gave a generous sum. Yet, even with such kindness, our coffers are far from what we require if we are to expand our reach."

Zhang Xin released a quiet sigh. His fingers curled into fists. He had lived on charity before Roberts rescued him from the street. A passerby's mercy, the temple's steps, and an occasional meal from a vendor…

Silver sifted through everyone's grasp like river silt.

Hong's voice pulled Xin out of his gloomy reverie. "On that note, I have heard a rumor circulating in Guangzhou. Some years past, a notorious pirate buried his treasure near Hong Kong. Nobody has found the trove, though many have tried their luck with spade and pick."

Feng raised an eyebrow. "A pirate's prize? Such talk may be mere fancy." His smile returned. "Aye, faith is our guide as we seek both spiritual riches and the means to sustain our work. Should the wind blow fortune our way, we must be ready to seize the opportunity."

They passed beneath an arch to enter a modest courtyard. By a fire, two men crouched, one burly and the other thin. Both wore sun-faded indigo cotton jackets that fastened with knotted frog buttons to the right, the cuffs polished smooth by years of work. Their trousers were patched at the knees, and their rope-soled cloth shoes were dusted with chaff.

Xin's gaze weighed them as a carpenter would weigh timber. The wear on their clothes seemed believable, yet something in their stillness did not. They sat taut as a strung bow.

"Here stand our newest pillars, Brother Yang Xiuqing"— Feng inclined his head toward the broad-shouldered man, then the leaner figure beside him—"and Brother Hsiao Chaogui. Both hail from the fields with heavy labor. Their strength girds the Society."

Yang stood. "We are prepared to defend the God-worshiping community."

Hsiao also rose. "We have experienced only hardship. The Society provides us a path full of hope, and we will protect it till death."

Hong looked at them. "We are few, but with God's help, we will overturn the tyrant's throne. Tonight, we begin."

The flame crackled. Xin flinched. Unease licked up his spine with the same heat that nipped his calves. Were these field hands or blades honed for cruel work? Zeal, a sharp tool, cut the hand that wielded it. He shifted his feet, searching for cool earth, but found none.

Evening settled, heavy with humidity. He joined two dozen others in the market square. Air clung to skin, rich with the brine of pickled vegetables. At the square's edge, the tallest temple loomed, its black lacquer sticky with years of smoke, eaves scaled with green tiles.

Yang roared, "Smash the demons! Bring glory to the King of Heaven!" He surged forward.

The crowd moved with him. On Yang's count, they drove bamboo poles into the seam of the doors. Wood boomed. Hinges squealed. The right door gave first. Lattice panels shattered into slats.

Xin poured through the doorway with the rest. An offering table was heaved over. A clay censer shattered. Charms came down by the fistful. A drum by the portico took a kick and sagged. His body trembled as he reached for an ancestral tablet. A woman held on to it. "Pray, do not break it. Our ancestors will not forgive us."

Around him, relics crashed to the floor. Furious feet thudded over a hundred generations. He hesitated. His mouth went dry. Then, with a grunt, he wrenched the wooden tablet free and hurled it to the earth. It shattered. The woman's howl dissolved into silence. She collapsed.

Oil from a toppled lamp spread in a slick trail. Flames licked up and chewed at the silk hangings. The mob rushed out of the temple. In the center of the square, someone started a fire. Soon, Xin followed the others and tossed effigies, carved wood, and gilded animals onto the heap. Smoke rose with a bitter perfume.

"Can things broken here ever be mended?" A gentle voice rang out amid the chaos.

Xin pivoted on his heels. Amidst the shadows and embers stood a teenage girl—perhaps fifteen or sixteen—with an oval face, her cheeks flushed from the heat. She wore a martial artist's outfit, the tunic torn at one sleeve. Her bright eyes shimmered with unshed tears. Loose strands of black hair escaped from a simple braid that grazed her shoulder.

Their gazes locked. He stepped closer.

"If we are to be made new, maybe pain is the price." She spoke again, then pressed a piece of paper into his palm, and disappeared back into the crowd.

Xin tucked away the slip and continued to feed icons into the inferno. Night deepened, punctuated by the distant clangor of gongs. When the last idol was burned and the crowd scattered, he wandered down to the river's edge.

Moonlight slithered over the currents. Roberts's calm sermons about forgiveness sprang to mind. How strange. The same God stirred peace in one place and conflagration in another.

The night air, thick with the scent of charred incense, drifted around him. Xin returned to the narrow abode he shared with seven other men. The hour waned into a sullen hush, except for snoring from the pallets inside the chamber. He crouched on his mat near the far wall, withdrew the slip from his tunic, and brought it close to the oil lamp. The characters were written with uncommon neatness, each stroke deliberate, betraying discipline and purpose. "He that mends the broken world is blessed, for by sorrow the soul is cleansed."

At the end of the message, two words *Miao Lan* gleamed.

Is Miao Lan her name?

Her oval face and question sprang to mind. Xin reread the sentence. Could the ruins be redeemed? He folded the slip, stowed it in his tunic, and fixed his gaze upon the moonlight at the edge of his pallet. Repeating the words—*blessed*, *soul*, and *cleansed*—he willed himself to slumber.

For the next three days, he roamed the riverfront lanes and asked around the market for the girl. A woman eyed him over her shop counter. "Miao Lan, you say? Many girls answer to Lan, but none here with such a family name as Miao. You'll not find her in these parts. Perhaps she is not from here at all."

Hope drained away like lamp oil from a cracked reservoir. He thanked the woman and stepped once more into the street.

A band of soldiers marched by, boots drumming and muskets slung. He slumped his shoulders and pressed onward. A man wearing the Qing military uniform blocked his path. "You there! Halt."

Xin's heart hammered. "Sir, I am only passing through."

The man surveyed him from head to toe. "We need stout lads for the emperor's banners. Name and village!"

Xin swallowed, hands balled in his sleeves. "I am from Lanchi," he improvised, "and a cripple." He limped back and feigned a wince.

Another soldier grunted, "He looks built enough to me."

The first fellow waved a list. "We have quotas, and no time for malingering. Strip your clothes. Let's see your legs."

Xin scanned his surroundings. To his right, a woman toted a laundry basket past the alley's mouth. "Oh, sir. I need to fetch my pouch, for it holds my medicine."

Without waiting for a reply, he spun and darted into the alley.

"Stop! Seize him!" came an angry roar.

He plunged past the hanging laundry, dodged a startled dog, and ducked beneath an awning. Behind him, bootsteps thundered. He slipped through a narrow breach in the wall, scraped his body raw, and tumbled onto the rear lane.

Soldiers called out to one another, their shouts growing faint as they carried down the distant lanes. He touched his brow to the cold stone and drew several heavy breaths. Unlike his brother, he had thus far eluded conscription.

In the afternoon, he returned to the temple's charred ruins. Splintered beams littered the ground. He fingered the slip of paper in his sleeve, the paper now creased many times over. From afar, a peal of laughter reached him.

Could it be Miao Lan?

He hurried after the sound. It faded away. In the hush that followed, Xin stood alone. The river rippled on, heedless of sorrow. With slow steps, he made his way through the twilight, uncertain of what awaited him. Her name and her writings remained kindled against the darkness within him.

The following week, government patrols swelled along the outskirts. News swept through the community. Hong's cousin, the patient giant Feng Yunshan, had been clapped in chains by Qing soldiers.

Dusk paled the sky to ash. The congregation huddled beneath a canopy of willows.

A youth dashed up, carrying a strip of paper. "Alas, our brother Feng Yunshan was subjected to a public procession through the county seat and coerced into making confessions."

A hot sting rose behind Xin's eyelids. His mouth went dry. In his mind's vision, Brother Feng was trussed in a cangue, jeering faces pressed close, gongs beating time to his shame.

Hong clenched his fists. The other leaders, Yang, Lady Wei, and Hsiao, gathered at his flank.

Xin shifted toward them without meaning to. The camp's dust drifted into his nostrils. What would the leaders do? He'd tear through the yamen doors if he could. Yet he halted his steps and thinned his lips into a line.

Then Hsiao's eyes rolled skyward. With a shuddering breath, his voice boomed forth—not his own reed-thin tone, but unearthly as rolling thunder across the hills. The sound lifted the hairs on Xin's nape. The ground tilted, and a wind slid cold across his face.

"I'm your Lord, Jesus. I see your sufferings. Verily, the hour is near. The shackles laid on the righteous shall burn before my fire. Do not fear the oppressor, for the Sword of Heaven is drawn." Hsiao reeled, arms outstretched. "Did I not promise freedom to those who thirst for righteousness? Rise! Purify the land of idols and all who offend me."

Hsiao's proclamation battered through Xin's chest, each phrase a bell struck in his bones. His fingers clenched until the nails bit his palms. He gawked and gasped, a sound breaking out of him as if pried from his ribs. Around him, his comrades wept. A woman fell to her knees. A farmer's fists struck the earth. An old man wiped tears from his cheeks.

After Hsiao's trembling subsided with his head bent low, the urgent decree still hovered above the river.

Hong moved forward. "This is guidance from on high. Our suffering is seen. Falter not. God's vengeance stands near."

The flames in Hong's gaze steadied Xin. Fear and reverence twisted together until they were indistinguishable, a single rope he could grip. He lifted his chin. Whatever the hour demanded—fighting, bleeding, burning—he would meet it.

Above them, the stars twinkled in the night sky.

Silence fell anew when Hong raised an arm. "Our faith unites us, but faith alone does not open prison gates. The world is foul with silver that buys justice for the cruel and chains for the righteous. Bring forth your offering, and together, we shall ransom our brother's liberty."

Coins crowded the collection bucket, and Xin cast in everything he possessed. The clatter of his last coppers sounded like a farewell. Hope drew taut within him. If heaven counted every copper, might heaven also count him?

On the morrow's eve, they gathered again. Low greetings passed from lip to lip. Xin, pockets empty and soul tender, hid behind an aged willow. He pressed his spine against the ridged bark until it marked him.

As the wind drifted off the river, Yang Xiuqing trudged up to the willow where Xin stood. Yang's frame shuddered. His eyes rolled until the pupils fled. When he spoke, in a voice not his own, a chill crawled the length of Xin's arms. Yang roared, akin to dreadful drumbeats. "I am Yahweh, your heavenly Father! Let everyone bow before my son, Hong Xiuquan."

Xin's heart stumbled, then raced. Tears pricked. Dread and yearning mingled anew until he could no longer tell them apart.

All fell to their knees under the spell of the deep, solemn tone. Xin's legs softened before he chose. He folded, forehead to earth. In the dust, he whispered, though he could not tell to whom, "Accept me."

After the trance, Yang sagged to the ground.

Reverence gripped the community once more. Xin's chest tightened.

Hong rose and cast his gaze over the riverbank congregation.

"My brethren," he intoned with a grave steadiness, "the Father has spoken through Brother Yang. The idols are cast down. Our way is set, though the emperor's dogs prowl ever nearer."

The crackle of torches cut sharp lines across faces moist with sweat. Xin shot to his feet and emerged from behind the tree. "Who among us shall shrink from this calling, having heard the Father's command? Not I, not while the weight of our brother Feng's chains presses on my heart!"

A ripple of agreement passed through the crowd, murmurs swelling to bawls.

"No more fear!"

"We are the Father's children. Deliver us!"

Within days, by silent courier, the money entered the magistrate's ledger. One dusk, Feng Yunshan stumbled back into their gathering. Cheers shook the night's hush. Feng, his wrists still rubbed raw, clasped Hong's hand. "For God, I would bear tenfold more."

The riverbank thronged with believers. Hong, the teacher, stood as heaven's chosen king.

Xin no longer doubted. Purpose girded him. Money smoothed the wheels of their movement, widening its path through hungry villages. What if he could find the legendary pirate's treasure? With such wealth, would their reach extend even farther?

Chapter Eight

Cheung Chau Island, Hong Kong, China
Autumn 2022

The evening air turned cool above the moon-flecked sea. Jason sat in the breezy dining room, gazing through open French doors over the dark surf. The aroma of sizzling beef wafted from the kitchen. Debra brought out a tray piled high with food, her cheeks flushed.

His mother-in-law reached for her teacup. "Look at you, Jason." She sipped her tea. "Who'd have thought real estate would pay you better than all that government work? We are so proud." On her lap, Mateo squirmed, holding his sippy cup.

Jason's chuckle came out thin, a nervous scrape, and he rubbed the back of his neck to chase off the heat climbing his collar. "Only for one deal. Most days, I'm still chasing buyers who vanish like wind." He glanced at Debra. Her fingers brushed his under the table, and the knot between his ribs loosened.

Uncle Brian jabbed a slice of wagyu beef with his chopsticks. "Let's not be modest. Jason just closed the penthouse of the year for Miss Vivian Jiang. Tell us again, how much commission?"

Jason recited the number and scratched behind his ear. "Not enough to buy this beach house from Grandpa, though he'd never sell it." The joke tasted bittersweet. He cleared his throat. "Vivian was impressive. She knew what she wanted and made decisions faster than anyone I've met."

Uncle Brian whistled. "State-owned money. Bottomless pit. If you play it right, you could amass wealth beyond anything we ever imagined."

Under the table, Debra's thumb stroked his knuckle, a quiet thrum that said, "I'm proud of you." Then her smile faltered. "Are they the kind of clients we want to serve? Aren't you worried about the risks?"

"I'm careful, Deb."

Mom lifted a hand. "Hong Kong isn't what it used to be. Our freedoms fade day by day. That friend, Vivian Jiang, looks pretty and powerful. But does she conquer the world out of fear?"

"Let's not judge, Maggie." Uncle Brian's tone turned cynical. "Those with connections in Beijing play by a different set of rules."

Debra took Mateo from Mom and ruffled the boy's thick black hair. "I want us to stay grounded and not let all the materials change who we are." Her gaze swept from Jason to the Coach purse in a corner.

Mai Po's murky wetlands surfaced in his mind. Hours spent cataloging migratory birds, the quiet thrill of holding a wild heron, his team chatting as they tested for contamination… Then circumstances beyond his control drove him to resign and seek other paths. He caught his uncle's gaze across the table. "Sometimes I miss the wetlands. At least there, the only thing you had to bribe was a raccoon dog with peanuts."

Debra passed Mateo to him. The baby wriggled in his lap.

"Raccoon dogs? Aren't they related to foxes? I didn't know they eat peanuts." Mom arched an eyebrow. "Seriously, it's been over a year since you resigned from your government job. Didn't your collaborator in Canada have a wetland conservation job for you? When will the immigration paperwork be completed?"

The word *resigned* thudded in his chest. Jason's arms tightened around Mateo. He stared at his tea and frowned. "Not for another while because of COVID."

Uncle Brian raised his teacup. "To the raccoon dogs and to our honest Realtor. May his conscience be as clean as his sales record."

They toasted. A salty breeze fluttered through the linen curtains. The sunset traced molten gold across the pale sand along the beach outside.

Debra touched Jason's knee beneath the table, a wordless reassurance he craved. She glanced from her mom to Uncle Brian. "Since we're all reading my dad's manuscript about the Taiping

Heavenly Kingdom, I have a question for you. Both Jesus and Hong Xiuquan claimed to be God's sons. Yet they faced different responses from the crowd. Why so?"

Uncle Brian straightened. The lamplight touched the silver at his temples. "Ah, what an intriguing question." He folded his forearms on the table. "Well, consider the cultural background. Jews held a fierce belief in one God. A Jew claiming to be the Son of God would be guilty of blasphemy. Such a claim was a direct challenge to everything they held sacred. For many, the idea was not just hard to accept—it was impossible. The consequence was death."

He paused to sip his tea, and Mom continued for him. "Our culture is different. In traditional Chinese society, people believed in many gods and spiritual beings. So when Hong Xiuquan claimed to be the son of God, sent to establish a heavenly kingdom to replace the corrupt Qing dynasty, his message resonated with people. Inspired by his vision, large numbers rallied to support his cause."

Jason bounced Mateo on his lap, making the baby giggle. "When I first read the Bible, I was amazed by Jesus' bold claims. As a Jew, Jesus knew His teachings defied Jewish tradition and would lead to His death. Was He crazy? Only someone out of His mind would insist on such things, yet His words carry authority." His gaze swept over his family. "Think about the Sermon on the Mount in Matthew. Not even Confucius taught like that. The only explanation is that God truly became human in Jesus. And, even more incredibly, as Jesus predicted, He rose from the dead, proving He is God."

The conversation soon turned to revolutions, faith, and the question of what had turned Xin into a zealot.

Debra lifted her teacup. "It's interesting." The steam curled around her face. "In one of the chapters, the rumor about the pirate's buried treasure resurfaces. I can't help but wonder if the plot will develop in the direction of the famous pirate chief, Cheung Po-Tsai."

"Right. This one is a continuation of the previous manuscripts about Cheung Po-Tsai." Mom leaned forward, her eyes twinkling over the rim of her cup. "Brian and I are almost done reading. Do you want me to tell you what happens?"

Debra shook her head, a smile on her lips. "No spoilers, please." She sipped tea, then set her teacup down. "Let me find out for myself."

Uncle Brian grinned. "You'll see. The second half is full of twists. Your dad pulled off his best trick there. I almost missed the clue about Liang Fa."

"Oh, that…" Mom started, then clamped a hand over her mouth.

Debra shot her a mock warning glare. "No hints. So far, the name Cheung Po-Tsai hasn't appeared. Perhaps it's another of Dad's red herrings."

"After reading this manuscript, I started to think your dad wrote it alongside the other two. It must have happened after he accepted Christ as his Savior." Mom tipped her chin toward Debra. "Although he probably could have finished writing the one about Cheung Po-Tsai's wife, he ran into a dilemma. Either he kept his promise to Auntie Lindsay, his publisher, to write a secular book, or he breached the contract."

Debra's jaw dropped. "So you think he left that one for me to finish and gave me a hint about Robert Morrison?"

"Yeah. He trusted you'd infuse it with a Christian perspective. Since he didn't write the last part, Auntie Lindsay could only blame you if it didn't sell well." Mom tapped the table. "By the way, we haven't seen Lindsay in a while because of COVID. Now that the pandemic's eased, maybe we should pay her a visit."

When Mateo started gumming a napkin, Jason freed it from the boy's chubby fingers. "It makes sense and explains why he had these left unpublished. I can't wait to keep reading."

A comfortable silence fell over them. The orange glow outside faded to dusk, shadows lengthening in the room.

Uncle Brian reached over and patted Jason's arm. "You ought to share the gospel with your high school classmate, Vivian Jiang."

Jason furrowed his brows. "I've been thinking about it." He glanced out the window at the last traces of sunlight. "Tell you what. Vivian invited me and Deb to a yacht party next Saturday. Deb has to go to the lab that day and can't make it. Do you want to come with me?"

✳ ✧ ✳

Victoria Harbour glimmered beneath neon lights as Jason stepped onto the swaying gangplank with Uncle Brian. The three decks of lit-up glass loomed ahead, its hull glossy as lacquer. Next to the entrance, two young fellows in tailored suits greeted guests.

"This *Blue Sea* is incredible," Jason whispered, nerves fluttering in his stomach. The cuff links made him self-conscious. Other than to Wynn's, he hadn't worn them since his wedding two years ago.

The other guests drifted onto the yacht, speaking Mandarin, Cantonese, and English.

Inside the salon, rose perfume wafted around. Blue-and-white porcelain bowls overflowed with lychee. Champagne glasses sparkled on silver trays.

"Jason! Brian!" Vivian swept across the floor, a vision in scarlet silk, her hair twisted high. "Welcome. I have so many friends for you to meet."

She gripped Jason's hand, an enormous diamond ring glittering on her right middle finger.

A clatter sounded on the spiral staircase leading up from the lower deck. Loud laughter preceded a woman in a tailored navy cheongsam, diamonds glinting at her ears. Two young men in designer tuxedos flanked her, each with an arm looped through hers.

Vivian's chin dipped. "Ah, the evening's entertainment arrives. Gentlemen, meet Sandy Yang."

Sandy paused just long enough for the spotlight to catch her, then flashed a smile. "Miss me already, Viv?" A Mandarin lilt rolled from her tongue as she extricated herself from the grip of both companions. "Jason, right? Viv told me about you. I'm Sandy. This is Leo, and that's Ricky. They both think they're my boyfriend. Isn't that cute?"

Leo, the tall one, exhaled a boozy breath. "Only until you find a better offer, babe." He swayed, clipped a server's elbow, and nearly knocked a tray of crab dumplings into a hedge of lilies.

Ricky's glare cut through the chatter. "Maybe if you could hold your liquor, she'd keep you this time."

Sandy snapped her fingers. "Don't start, boys. Let's make tonight boring for these nice people." She winked at Jason. "Vivian collects ambitious men. You look ambitious. Or scared. Hard to tell."

Vivian's lips tightened. "Sandy, why don't you and your escorts find the bar and let—"

"No, no," Ricky cut her off, voice rising above the music. "Let's fight it out now. Leo stole Sandy's phone and is reading her WeChat." He jabbed a finger at Leo's chest.

A ripple of attention swelled. Heads turned. A girl's laughter died midpeal. A couple near the bar angled their phones up, hungry for a clip. Perfume and black vinegar drifted together. Waitstaff flowed around the forming ring with trays held higher.

Heat crept up Jason's neck. His grip slicked on his cold glass. He set it on a nearby table.

Did this happen often at this sort of party?

Sandy's scowl dropped the temperature a degree. "Give it back, Leo. Now."

Leo hiccupped and raised the phone skyward. A few gasped. One camera flashed.

Vivian hissed. "Sandy, please. You're embarrassing me."

Sandy bared her teeth, almost a grin. "Viv, everyone needs a little humility, especially in Hong Kong." Her gaze slid to Jason. "Connections. And protection from your own mistakes."

Uncle Brian chuckled. Different languages braided into a hum that pressed on Jason's eardrums. He stepped back, drawing Uncle Brian with him. The crowd parted a fraction, then surged again.

With a dancer's move, Sandy snatched the phone out of Leo's raised hand. "Done." She tapped the screen dark, then slapped Leo's shoulder.

Vivian forced a laugh that didn't reach her eyes. The circle loosened. Conversations restarted in relieved bursts.

After the guests carried the spectacle off, Vivian tugged Jason and Brian aside in a whisper. "We all have our dramas. Just stay sharp. Don't take your focus off what matters."

From the deck above, music surged. Jason exchanged a glance with Uncle Brian before Vivian guided them up into the throng of guests. She made a quick introduction. "Jason and Brian Guan, DreamAchieve Realty. This is Xu Dawei. You might have heard about him and the MyriadMed Group. He's buying up half of Central."

Sandy approached and waved her obsidian nails. "So you're the one who closed Viv's penthouse. She's making a statement.

These days, you have to be bold to stay ahead in Hong Kong real estate, yes?"

A bell rang. Servers emerged carrying lacquered trays of Peking duck and abalone in the shell.

Vivian grabbed a duck wing. "Jason is trustworthy. That's rare."

The yacht lurched and left the pier. Central's skyline receded, a cutout of jagged light against the velvet sky.

Sandy leaned in. "Don't be shy, Jason. Networking here isn't only for business. It's about building protection. You never know who you'll need. Sometimes a casual dinner can prevent ten years of trouble." She tilted her head toward the two men in the corner. "Over there are a mainland exec and a well-known lawyer."

Before he could respond, she drew Vivian away.

Uncle Brian grabbed an entire tray of shells from a server. "I love abalone. What a feast!"

In front of them, the exec slipped a business card into the lawyer's palm—the motion secretive, new habits from China.

Jason nodded. "It's wild, Uncle. I feel like we're at a poker game sorted by sharks."

Uncle Brian bit into an abalone. "This is where deals happen, favors owed, and secrets traded."

Jason forced a smile. Secrets traded. The words scraped at his nerves.

Vivian resurfaced and patted his arm. "I want to introduce you to Mr. Joe Niu. He's interested in buying property in Hong Kong. Joe, meet my friend, Jason Guan, the best agent in town."

Joe, round-faced, with diamond cuff links and a northern accent, grabbed Jason's hand for a firm shake. "Vivian speaks highly of you. I might need help to acquire a small asset. Nothing public, you understand."

The man's touch sent a spark through Jason. From Uncle Brian again, Jason caught the faintest hint of a nod. Was it a warning or encouragement? Either way, the game was on. He straightened, matching Joe's pressure. "I'm happy to assist, Mr. Niu." He spoke in an even tone, despite the thrum under his ribs. "I value discretion."

"Good. Please call me Joe." He gaped at Jason. "Often the safest place for a secret is right where everyone can see it."

A shout erupted from the lower deck. Glass shattered. The music faltered.

Vivian pressed a palm to her forehead. "Are Sandy's two suitors at it again?"

The boat moved farther from the city lights. Victoria Harbour unfurled into the night, a ribbon of glistening silk.

Uncle Brian put down his plate with a sigh. "This is Hong Kong, a place that never seeks peace and tranquility."

Chapter Nine

Guiping, Guangxi, China
January 1851

The sky diffused an amber light over the hills. The footfalls of countless pilgrims converged upon the narrow valley. Zhang Xin moved among them, struck by an awe he dared not name.

Never could he recall a greater multitude. Believers came from Guangdong's stony villages, from Liuzhou's thresholds, down from the ragged ridges of the Gelao and into the heartlands of Hakka. Men carried shovels on their backs, and women with plaited hair cradled infants at their bosoms.

"'Tis the day of his birth," mumbled a voice near Xin. "Hong, God's second son."

The assembled lifted their throats in chorus. "Praise the true Lord. Praise the new dawn and the end of sorrow. The Kingdom of Great Peace shines in the east. Behold our king, the Son of God!"

The melody drifted toward a tent, resplendent with red silk. At its mouth sat Hong Xiuquan, clad in yellow garments with characters denoting "Heavenly King." Beside him hung five lanterns painted with the characters for justice, peace, virtue, righteousness, and love.

Xin's throat tightened, eyes stinging with unshed tears. All his memories of hunger, of beatings, and of dark alleys in Guangzhou seemed to lift from his bones, dissolved by the shouted hope. Following others, he kneeled and touched his forehead to the soil.

Yang Xiuqing strode forward and thundered in a voice that shook the frostbitten air. "Brothers and sisters, the spirit moves within us. Let us be as one. Idols shan't corrupt the land. Our deliverance has arrived."

The first drum spoke low. Then another answered, and soon the earth seemed to beat. Cymbals flashed and clashed. Wooden clappers worried the cold like teeth. The sound ran along the bare terraces and came back from the dark limestone peaks.

Xin's heart hammered with the drums. Was this possible? A land made clean of idols, the hungry filled, and the humbled lifted up. He stood at the birth of a kingdom, its purpose wide as the wan winter sky stretched over the black-toothed hills.

The sun sank to the horizon. Hong stood up from his throne. "Children of God, today we gather not to exult one man, but the will of heaven. I envision a realm where fathers need not sell their daughters to repay debts, nor is a woman forced to be a concubine of a man thirty years her senior. You have trusted not in me, but in that vision."

A great cheer erupted. Xin stretched out both arms. The kingdom was no longer a dream, but a reality. He laughed, and somewhere inside the laughter, a sob shook free. A hymn rose, stitching disbelief to belief. By the time the torches guttered and the square emptied, joyful tears drained his soul.

The next evening, he sat under the willows by the river. The faint resonance of hymns from yesterday still echoed in his mind.

Light footsteps approached. He jerked up his head. Before him stood a young woman with plaited dark hair.

He sprang up, breath catching after so many barren days of searching. "Miao Lan?"

The maiden dipped her chin. "Have we met? How do you know my name?"

From the fold of his tunic, he brought a small paper, thinned and softened by much handling. His fingers shook as he offered it. "You gave me this when last we met. Your words have kept me company."

She read the note. Her lips turned upward. "I am pleased it did you some good."

The murmurs of the nearby crowd gathered strength. He ignored others and fixed his focus on her. "May I ask you something that has troubled my thoughts? When you gave me the paper, you said, 'Could what is broken here ever be mended?' What did you mean?"

She fell silent for a moment, then spoke in a low voice, her words almost drowned out by the noise. "You have such an excellent memory. Was it the day we committed the idols to the flames?" She sighed. "My baba often remarked that an idol is only wood and paint. Yet, to consign them to the fire…"

Xin placed a palm on his chest. "Although some among us believe 'tis the way to begin anew, I did feel uneasy on that day."

She fiddled with her braid. "We sought to cast aside superstition. Will burning those items grant us the freedom we seek, or only invite other demons?"

Her candor drew him closer in spirit. "It consoles me you felt so. I feared I alone harbored doubts."

She looked up at him. Their gazes locked beneath the lantern's golden sphere. "Doubt is a faithful companion to those who think. Do you still have them? Our king has proclaimed the birth of the Heavenly Kingdom of Great Peace."

Xin lingered over her question. So much had happened, such as the fervent throng in the assembly, the banners vibrant with celestial script… "I—I confess, sometimes I do. Our cause is righteous. Yet my faith fluctuates."

The shadows played about her face as if to reflect his turmoil. She tilted her chin toward the night sky. "'Tis human nature. Even my baba demurs in private. Recently, Heavenly King summoned him."

"Summoned by our king?" Xin's eyebrows shot up. "For what?"

"Aye. Baba's skill with staff and saber is sung through all Guangxi." Lan inclined her head. "Heavenly King declared that unless our soldiers are trained by a master who knows both discipline and courage, we would no more be a great host than a rabble. My baba was elected to shape the army in the arts of war and defense."

Her words, spoken with a grave composure, weighed on Xin's soul. Around them, the air was rich with the mingled scents of damp soil and trampled grass. He stood still. Pride touched him, that he might be numbered in so weighty a cause. Fear too, lest his hands prove unequal when steel and shout came near. He bowed, scarcely trusting his tongue. When they parted, he carried her father's name as a man might bear a lamp through the night.

In the following days, Lan told Xin about villages left behind, of rice and rain, of scars that pulled tight in cold weather, and of pay come due. The watch gong answered the crickets whilst smoke from the cook shed crept under the eaves. A coal-red moon hung above the hills. He whispered a promise no ear would hear. "I shan't turn my face from danger when called."

Training began in earnest. Xin and other newly enlisted soldiers assembled before dawn. Master Miao strode amongst them. A man in his late thirties or early forties, tall and broad-shouldered, with sinewy arms and a seasoned warrior's confidence, he possessed a pair of striking, luminous eyes like Miao Lan's. Raising an arm, he shouted, "You believe heroism springs from a moment's fury? Nay. Discipline is the true root of victory. Stand as one! Move arm over shoulder, shields touching. Remember, the kingdom's fate depends on unity."

They learned of stratagem—how to feign retreat to draw out the enemy, how to guard supplies, and when to raise banners so all might rally. Xin's body ached, but the camaraderie of those sweating at his side strengthened his resolve. "God be my help. I shall advance undaunted."

✳ ✧ ✳

The horn on the last day of training gave them leave. Mist lifted from the paddies and curled along the dikes. The low roofs of the town clung to the water's edge. Cooking smoke drifted from the bamboo groves, sweet with millet and garlic.

Passing a knot of youths wearing long, messy hair, Xin nudged Lan forward and jested, "No more that Manchu-imposed odious queue."

Her lips quirked. She tapped two fingers on her chest in a silent salute before letting a smile slip free. "The queue is a chain to the old habits. And look at the women. They stride in trousers. Their shirts hang loose and free, without the gilded ribbons of Qing fashion. Nothing to hinder their movement."

The dark hills, the river's breath, and Lan beside him… Xin drank it in, and a swelling pride made the chill air taste sweet. Here, in the early spring fields outside the town, even the hair on his head declared a new season. He muttered, "We can all march and fight."

"The skirts are for the old world too. We need more than beauty nowadays." Lan chuckled. "Some women even walk barefoot to remind all that foot-binding is banished. No more crippled daughters. Our feet carry us forward. They must be strong."

His breath stalled as heat pooled beneath his ribs. In a few short weeks, freedom revealed itself in ordinary things.

Lan shifted her empty basket from one hand to the other. "My sincere thanks for accompanying me. The herbs we gather can tend wounds on the battlefield."

"Indeed." He shielded his eyes from the morning sun. "Have you heard the rumor about a pirate's buried treasure?"

The river glimmered like jade. Even in early spring, the weather turned out mild on this sunny day.

Lan squinted, the playful light in her gaze fading away. "Baba says the Heavenly Kingdom needs supplies. If we are fortunate in our foraging, we shall put whatever we collect today to good use. As for pirates and treasure, 'tis fancy spun by idle tongues." She cast her glance over the meadow. "Though, if such treasure exists, it would do much for our cause."

Side by side, they roamed the wilderness. She instructed him on the virtues of various remedies—gentian root to abate fever, honeysuckle to calm anxieties, and elderflower to soothe inflamed throats. In turn, he recited verses from Confucian sages imparted to him by his baba. Before long, their discourse shifted to recollections of earlier days. Xin lowered his voice. "Since my fifteenth spring, I have had no kin. Grief and solitude were my only companions."

Lan laid the basket on the ground. "My mama passed away when I was eight years of age." Moisture glistened in her eyes. "Thereafter, the world became subdued. Each shadow seemed to lengthen when I no longer had her with me."

The sunlight lit her countenance in hues of gold and copper, revealing a faint scar at her temple. How many other injuries did she bear?

"People say time mends grief," she murmured. "Yet I believe we merely face it in a different fashion."

Xin reached for her sleeve, then thought better of it. "With another soul to share the burden, its weight lessens."

For the first time since Mama's death, the hush inside him stirred, akin to a frostbitten field catching a warm wind. Lan's presence replaced his loneliness with something new.

She picked up the basket, and they pressed onward. Occasionally, their hands met. He dared not tell her about the emotions within him.

Did Miao Lan care about him too?

They reached a swollen brook where stones lay half hidden in the foam. He paused. "Shall we not turn back? The water runs high."

Lan surveyed the peaceful surroundings. "If there are herbs on the other side, we must risk it." She stepped sure-footedly onto the first stone, her basket held high. "Follow me."

He rolled up his trousers and followed onto the slick stones at her bidding. The river nipped at his ankles, a chill sharpening his senses. She slipped and cried out. His arms moved before thought. Her weight hit him, and his breath caught as she settled against his heart and giggled. The world narrowed to her warm body against his, as if history had led to this moment.

"You are always ready to help." Crimson colored her cheeks.

Braided with a tenderness, he swallowed. "I would never fail you."

His voice rasped with everything he didn't dare say.

She straightened up, her fingers lingering on his arm, as if reluctant to break the silent spell that enfolded them.

Do not go. Let me be your stay when the earth trembles.

Yet he held his tongue and followed her.

On the far bank, under an old camphor, wild orchids peered from the moss. She pointed toward the vibrant flowers. "Those are the best for lowering a fever. Let us gather them."

Down on their knees, they harvested the flowers. Their hands brushed again. Xin's heart thumped when her fingers paused on his.

She drew back and broke the enchantment. "Why did you join the Heavenly Kingdom?"

"I sought a realm where none of us need ever bow to cruelty." He turned up an orchid and pressed it into her palm.

She dropped it into the basket. "A noble soul may get wounded—"

Heavy footsteps rustled in the thicket. Four Qing soldiers appeared. Their gazes fixed on Miao Lan.

"Ho!" The tallest bared yellow teeth. "What fine catch do we spy? A rebel and his pretty whore. Lay down those herbs, girl. Come oblige your betters!"

Xin sprang to his feet. "This lady is no one's spoil. Go your way."

A silent glance passed between him and Lan. He widened his stance. Miao Lan set the basket down and crouched to pick up a thick fallen branch.

The rogue jeered. "Move aside or die where you stand. Today, we take what's owed to us."

Lan snapped the stick in two, passing half to Xin. They fell in step, backs pressed together. She whispered, "Aim the jagged end toward their acupoints."

In Xin's peripheral vision, a stout foe lunged at Lan. She raised her stick and stabbed the man's wrist. He howled, dropping his sword. Using her momentum, she spun and crushed her elbow into his jaw.

A soldier charged Xin. He ducked and followed the footwork from Master Miao's demonstrations. The tip of his branch struck the attacker's ankle. The man collapsed.

Two more assailants rushed toward them together. One slashed at Xin with a dagger, while the other seized Lan's sleeve.

She targeted the man's shoulder acupoint with her branch and numbed his grip before flipping him overhead into the reeds.

Xin blocked the dagger with his stick, then jabbed the man's exposed wrist. The fellow dropped the weapon. In a smooth motion, Xin twisted his arm, forcing him to his knees.

The soldiers scrambled in the mud. "Sorceress!" spat the tallest. "We'll be back—with more men next time!"

Lan grabbed her basket, turned, and dashed away.

"You saved us." Xin trailed her, his breaths ragged. "With your courage and your baba's teachings."

She gaped at him. "We saved each other, Zhang Xin. Would you promise to always walk these fields with me?"

He raised a hand. "Wherever you walk, Miao Lan, I will follow."

The uncertain, muddy path stretched ahead, yet in the shared understanding between them, he no longer felt lonely.

Together, they disappeared into the reeds, their shadows cast as one beneath the rising sun.

Chapter Ten

Hong Kong, China
Autumn 2022

The fall air sharpened overnight. The usually humid corridors between the Mid-Levels's towers thrummed with a chill. Jason arrived at the base of the Celestial Residences building, his navy suit crisp.

After the yacht party, both Sandy Yang and Joe Niu had contacted him for property showings. He arranged to meet them on the same day because they expressed similar interest in luxury apartments in Mid-Levels.

Sandy Yang's message had appeared guarded. "Want to look at properties, perhaps a notch below what Vivian bought."

Her WeChat bubble pulsed with a lipstick emoji. Jason slipped his phone into his pocket as the lobby's gilded doors parted for him.

The concierge greeted him by name. Sandy was already waiting, one stiletto heel tapping against the vein-cut marble floor. She wore a white suit, a blue Birkin bag on her arm. Long dangling earrings grazed her shoulders.

"You're early." Jason guided her toward the gold-plated elevator.

She arched an eyebrow, smiling just enough to count as polite. "Of course. Time is valuable. Vivian says this is one of the best addresses—enough privacy for important guests. Is that true?"

He pressed the button for the thirty-eighth floor and cleared his throat. "Absolutely. No paparazzi, not even for celebrities."

"Hmm." Sandy pursed her lips, flicking away her gaze.

The elevator moved in silence. When it opened, he led her down a hallway perfumed with orchids, the kind only a weekly shipment from Japan could provide. He inserted the key card into the lock. The door swung inward, revealing white marble. Light and panoramic views of the harbor tumbled in through floor-to-ceiling windows.

Sandy came in and didn't gasp, but her eyes widened after she paced through the foyer.

"Nice, although I've seen better in Shanghai." She dipped her chin. "Good for entertaining and for avoiding attention." She retrieved her phone from her bag and snapped a few photos, as if to confirm the reality for someone else.

Jason guided her into the kitchen. "Three thousand square feet." He drifted toward the large island, fingers skimming the cool quartz. The stainless lip of the sink caught the light. So did the sheen on his palms. Tour patter came easily. The little thud under his ribs did not. "Harbor's wide open. No neighboring towers to block the view."

Sandy followed. Her floral perfume wafted around. She put her phone beside a potted bonsai. "I saw the layout from my online search. What I want to know is how many units here have changed hands in the last year and whether they have been flagged for, um, unusual transactions."

A beat. Jason's pulse ticked in his throat. "I understand your concern. Hong Kong's property market is scrutinized." His smile held. His mouth was dry. "There are ways to stay under the radar. I could connect you with—"

A dry, humorless breath escaped her. "Don't make the offer unless you're sure. Look, I'm only asking because… well, after what's happened recently, I don't need more trouble." The pendant lamps cast a halo around her head. She clicked her heels and returned to the living room. "You and Vivian are old friends, right?"

Jason trailed her. "Yes. High school classmates." The words opened a small door in his mind—shy Vivian in a tiled corridor, the smell of rain on concrete, the way she'd always averted her gaze.

Sandy set her Birkin on the coffee table. "Did you ever wonder why Vivian, a nobody from Hong Kong, no connections in China, moved up so fast?"

The question landed hard. His gaze slid to the harbor view. Of course he'd wondered. Who hadn't? "She's resourceful. Ambitious." He hesitated. "She's also lucky, I suppose."

Sandy released a sharp laugh, more of a bark. "You think luck gets a woman into those prestigious places, Jason? Please." She tipped her head to one side, her narrowed gaze assessing. Then her shoulders sagged, and her haughtiness dissolved into exhaustion. "Where we are, men loom at the gate. You can't enter unless you have something they want. The clever Vivian figured that out."

Jason kept quiet.

She sat down and retrieved a slim cigarette from her bag, rolling it between her fingers. "Her boyfriend, Du Jin-Dong, controls Guangzhou. He doesn't care about business skills as long as you make him feel important."

A knot formed in Jason's stomach. The name had made the rounds in the news. The guy had talked about how Guangzhou continued to take the lead in reform, innovation, and high-quality development, all under the guidance of China's outstanding leader, Xi Jinping. Du had even pointed out that Guangzhou consolidated its position as China's economic engine, fostered cutting-edge industries, and promoted sustainable growth amid COVID-19.

It seemed obscene that his former classmate, the shy girl with the nervous giggle, was Du's mistress. "How do you know so much?"

Sandy's lips pressed together. She stood up, opened the sliding glass door, and walked out to the terrace. "In my circle, everyone knows how you move up. You do things for them—clean up their messes, hide their money, sleep in their beds. Vivian plays it better than anyone."

Jason followed her out and peered down at the harbor again. Toylike ferries crawled, their wakes stitching white lines across the dull water. "And you?" He waved away the whiff of cigarette smoke. "Are you playing the same game?"

She snorted. "No. I have my family's money and need to keep it safe in Hong Kong." The words were clipped, polished, like she'd practiced them.

"Is it not safe in China?" His tone light, he stole a glimpse of her face, searching for any crack in the lacquer.

Sandy ignored his question. "I'll call you about this apartment." She ground her cigarette out on the railing and flicked it into a nearby bin. "Don't tell Vivian we've talked."

As they returned to the lobby, Sandy's secrecy pressed against his chest. He watched her leave. The morning sun stung his eyes.

Part of him wanted to call Debra, to hear her clean, untroubled voice, to ask her which chapter of her dad's manuscript she was reading. Last night, they discussed a scene in the manuscript where Zhang Xin met Miao Lan again, and the two were on the verge of falling in love. Also, the theme of the pirate's buried treasure threaded through the story. Deb had asked him what it would mean for Zhang Xin and Miao Lan. He'd kissed her and replied, "I suppose we'll read on and find out."

Instead of dialing her number, he let the screen dim in his palm.

Not now. Stay sharp.

Lunch with Joe Niu was minutes away. He'd offered to treat Joe at the nearby Four Seasons Hotel, one of the few hotels in Mid-Levels.

The hotel lobby swallowed him in cool, perfumed air. Polished marble mirrored a ceiling of glass and light, and a spill of white orchids arched over a table.

Joe stood in a corner. "You're late."

Although not a big man, he carried himself with the force of gravity.

A twitch needled Jason's neck. He pasted on a smile. "Traffic." If he let the barb hook him, he'd bleed. He steered Joe toward the restaurant.

Service moved quietly around them while they picked at lunch, more ritual than meal. Jason took the set—soup, a small fish, and rice. Joe asked for steak and steamed greens. They spoke of the weather, roadworks, and nothing that mattered.

When the tea cooled, Jason signed the bill. "Ready to view the property?"

Joe slipped on his jacket and rose.

Jason guided him up Bowen Road into The Paramount's gorgeous lobby. Sunlight cut through the tinted panes, painting stripes across the marble floor.

The central air diffused Joe's heavy cologne. His paunch was buttoned into a designer charcoal-gray suit. While his silver-framed sunglasses perched atop his buzz-cut head, he tipped his chin at the uniformed doorman. "Not bad. What is the price per square foot in Chinese yuan?"

Jason did a quick conversion. The Realtor's script rolled off his tongue. "About ninety-eight thousand. This building is popular with mainland investors. Close to Central, with awesome views over Victoria Harbour."

"Ninety-eight thousand?" Joe whistled. "Pocket change for my friends. Did Vivian tell you about me?"

"She said you're in logistics and entertainment?"

Joe's eyes narrowed. "Vivian rarely says much. That's how she succeeds. Have you two been friends for long?"

"Since high school," Jason answered in a flat tone.

The elevator opened. After they stepped in, Joe touched a mirrored wall. "Vivian is a legend." He folded his arms. "Folks underestimate her. Not many women survive in our world unless they're tough, superstrong."

Jason pressed button 28. Advertising images flickered on the only unmirrored wall—a fitness center with pools and rooftop gardens.

"Vivian has changed a lot." He focused on the rising numbers.

Joe released a low laugh. "She knows how things work, who has the power, who wants what. Everything is about our desires, isn't it?"

Jason remained silent, letting his client's babble fill his ears. At floor 28, Jason unlocked the door, and they glided into luxury.

Joe wandered through the living room. "Vivian is clever." He ran a hand over the teal sofa covers. "Still, nobody runs a group like hers just by being clever."

A cold weight settled on Jason's shoulders, but he maintained his neutral face.

Joe's voice dropped lower. "Her man, Du Jin-Dong. What a character. He's old enough to be her father. Divorced three times, has a parade of girls in every city. Vivian pleases him and gets her rewards." He inspected the gorgeous harbor view. "She's the only one who has kept him interested for this long."

Leaning against the panoramic windows, Jason forced a smile. "She's very focused."

"Focused? Hah!" Joe placed a palm on the glass. "I'd say ruthless. She has a reputation for cheating, lying, and sleeping with anyone she needs to. She'd slice up her own mother for the right deal." His phone pinged. He checked it and tapped a few messages. Then his speech turned more careless. "Did my words shock you? Vivian said you Christians view things differently. Don't take me wrong. She's a survivor. All of us survive whatever way we can. There's no rule. Only opportunities and danger."

Jason gazed down at the harbor and stifled a shiver. The city sparkled under the sky, indifferent to the fates it shaped and shattered.

So timid Vivian from form five transformed herself into an influential man's mistress, trading her dignity for unimaginable power. What drove her to such choices? Yeah, she could afford her Birkin bags. Was she happy?

Joe stowed the phone away, all business again. "Show me the bedrooms. I want to see the bathrooms too." He winked. "Vivian loves big tubs."

"Of course." Jason guided him forward, fingers tightening around his folder. "Come this way."

The day wore on. Conversations and viewings blurred into one another until sunlight slanted gold through the windows in the third bedroom.

After Jason ordered an Uber to take him and his client to Central, they parted, and he took the ferry home. His mind churned and replayed every harsh bit of gossip Joe and Sandy had shared. Did they survive by any means necessary?

How could it be true? Vivian in a penthouse bathtub and tangled in Du's bed, the senseless chasm between the person he once knew and the woman described with such crudity…

What were those so-called opportunities they'd talked about? What dangers lurked behind each of their choices?

When he stepped into the apartment, the warm, clean scent of dish soap wrapped around him. Debra stood at the sink and clattered dishes in the suds, gospel music humming in the background. She glanced over her shoulder and smiled. "How were the showings?"

He set his keys on the counter with care, as if any sharp sound might rattle something loose inside him. "Strange."

She dried off and waited.

He pressed his thumb into the center of his palm until it hurt. "Sandy and Joe talked a lot about Vivian. About how she climbed to her current position."

Debra's mouth formed an *O*. "What do you mean?"

His jaw tightened. He swallowed. "They said she slept with her bosses. Now she's with this official, Du Jin-Dong. He's powerful and has numerous girlfriends. Vivian is just one of his mistresses."

The gospel melody sounded too cheerful, the room too clean for what he'd just said.

"And what do you think?" Debra edged around the counter and grasped his shoulders. The smell of detergent lingered on her fingers. "According to the news, Du Jin-Dong appears to be a capable official."

"Yeah, not easy to reconcile the images of Du and of Vivian." He peered beyond her into the dim comfort of their flat. "In the old days, she was nervous, eager to please everybody. Hard to imagine her as the ruthless, powerful manipulator."

Debra stepped away to switch off the music. "Jealousy can twist people, especially when someone rises above them. Perhaps Sandy and Joe resent her success. It's easy to spread rumors about a person you wish you could be."

His gaze followed her lovely profile. "Maybe you're right. I feel relieved I'm only helping them buy properties."

"I'm glad to hear that. We shall pray for her instead of judging." She returned to his side and hugged him. "Didn't Uncle Brian encourage you to share the gospel with her? Let's pray that she'll soon accept Jesus as her Savior."

He wrapped his arms around her, grateful for the anchor she offered in a senseless world. "You know... I hadn't had my nightmare for a while, but last night, it returned. The same cold, suffocating feeling. Maybe I'm under more stress than I realize."

Sandy's and Joe's remarks about Vivian coiled through the shadows. Was there any truth in their words?

Chapter Eleven

Yong'an Prefecture, Guangxi, China
Autumn 1851

Near the moss-clad walls, the morning sun strove to pierce the mist. The fog rested in every hollow, desaturating the world to muted grays. Through the haze, figures in worn and mended uniforms moved quietly.

Xin advanced, casting an anxious glance to his right. His hands clenched so tightly his knuckles ached.

Miao Lan kept pace beside him. Her rebellious hair had slipped free of its braid, black strands fluttering across her cheek. A faint smile tugged at her lips. "Xin, you walk as one whose boots are filled with stones."

He tried to laugh, but his lips refused to cooperate. "I have never…" He released a cough. "I have never been in a battle before." His voice trembled despite his effort to steady it. "Each step feels heavier than the last."

Her gaze held his, steady as a drawn blade. "Do not fear. The reports our agents have brought are plain. The Qing army is ill-drilled and short of supplies. With resolution, we shall succeed."

A shout rang out. Captain Feng Yunshan leaped atop a broken stretch of masonry, his sword flashing above him. "Brothers!" His words cleaved the fog. "The heavenly vision descends upon us! This day, we seize Yong'an in the name of God's son. Stand fast. Let justice shield our cause!"

A murmur ran the length of the line. Xin bowed his head, shaping with parched lips a silent prayer, and tightened his grasp upon the ash-wood haft of his spear. "Do you believe we shall prevail?"

Lan pressed her sleeve close against his arm. "We have journeyed too far to turn back now. Do not forsake your faith." Her nearness put some courage in him.

From the shrouded slope, a bell tolled. Along the ranks, hats of straw and dented helms gleamed, and flags stirred upon a faint wind. Drums spoke to the left. A gong answered.

Xin lifted his spearpoint toward the wall. "There, upon the battlements, the Qing emperor's men."

"They are afraid." Lan swept her blade through the air in a bright arc. Her mouth was firm. "We shall reduce them to ghosts."

The far wall rolled out smoke, and the first cannon gave tongue. The ground leaped. Xin flinched, heart pounding as the earth ahead exploded in jagged bursts of dirt and flame. A hot gust stung his cheek. Men in the foremost file pitched backward in agonizing silence amidst the roar.

Around Xin, the world turned into a thunder of iron. He uttered another hoarse prayer while the bell tolled again.

"Forward!" Captain Feng's cry broke over them. "Forward! For righteousness!"

Xin's knees trembled. For one black instant, cowardice beckoned him to turn, to flee into safety. Yet if he ran, would he ever cease running?

Lan surged past, her braid dark against the smoke. "For God's sake, do not falter!"

Her shout struck him like a stone. He set his foot forward into the sucking mud.

The ladders thudded against the wall. He paused at one's base, Lan above him. "If"—his voice trembled—"if we should be parted, Lan, pray remember me, not merely as a comrade, but as one who bears affection for you dearly."

She lifted her steel sword. The sheen along its edge caught the gray light as she glanced down at him. "We shall meet again. If not in this life, then in heaven."

The heave of bodies drove them upward. Damp rungs bit into his palms. His breath roared in his ears. At the crest, men from both sides collided. Steel rang, shields slammed, and the air trembled with war cries.

"Lan!" Xin called, panic rising.

"I am here! Stay with me!"

An imperial swordsman lunged at her.

Lan snapped her forearm up, knocking his cut aside with the flat of her sword. She stepped in close and bound his weapon to the guard. A twist drew his wrist open. She slid her sword along his blade, turned her hilt, and drove her point into the gap beneath his arm. With a smooth motion, she wrenched free and pivoted.

The man collapsed behind her.

A soldier rushed Xin with a downward chop. He caught it, the impact shivering up his body. With a quick sweep, he cut across the man's thigh above the knee. The defender cried out and pitched to the stones, clutching his leg. Xin moved past him, unwilling to look back.

Their ranks thickened as more comrades poured over the ladders. The defenders faltered. Some flung down shields and ran for the alleys. Cries of surrender rose above the clash of steel. From the ramparts, the old banners loosened and tumbled. The victors surged forward together, pressing through the last makeshift barricades.

Captain Feng grasped the city's banner in his fist. "Yong'an is ours!"

Xin sucked in a breath. Sweat trickled down his temple. His vision blurred. The battered rooftops spun around him. Dead and wounded from both sides littered the street.

Was this a victory? Did he kill the man today or only injure him?

Lan rushed to his side, her brow beaded with sweat. "We have come through."

A jagged laugh burst from his lips. His legs threatened to give out. He blinked, swallowing back tears. "Did we...? Is it really ours?"

The gates succumbed. The banners of Taiping, inscribed with characters of Heaven, drifted through the streets.

Children peered from behind their mothers. Elders looked on with hollow eyes. The people gathered in the square.

Captain Feng mounted a cart. "People of Yong'an! The days of oppression are ended. The Heavenly Kingdom brings you peace. You are brothers and sisters to us."

Xin stared at the bloodstained stones. "What have we become?"

Lan lifted her face to the sky. "We are the ones who carry hope into the morrow."

✳ ◇ ✳

Time flowed on, a ceaseless river that carried weeks into months. As winter settled, the scent of smoke became a daily companion. Yong'an changed, transformed by the slow, inevitable turn of the season.

Amid these shifts, Xin's bond with Lan deepened. On a morning veiled in frost, Miao Lan stood at his side, her hair unbound. "Xin." She gazed at him, her voice carrying an uncertain tremor. "During the breach, you spoke to me as though the end might find us both."

He shifted, his hands awkward at his sides. "Did I?"

"You asked me…" She stepped closer, her trousers brushing his knee. "If I would remember you, not as a comrade but as one bearing affection. Was it sincere, or some fever born of battle madness?"

Heat crept up his neck and bloomed across his face. He fumbled for a poet's words, yet stumbled upon his truth. "Lan," he whispered. "In the battle, beneath death's shadow, my heart could not lie."

She turned away as if to contemplate his meaning. "Would you say it again, in peace as in war?"

"In peace, in war, my heart remains as it was." He reached for her arm, then halted, fearing to overstep the boundaries of respect and modesty instilled in him by a lifetime.

A single tear slipped down her cheek. She caught his roughened hand before he could pull away, her grip anchoring him. "Then you must promise, Xin. Should I fall, do not forget me."

His breath hitched—a wave of terror, of hope, of everything he had not said. He drew her to his bosom. "Lan, I swear by all the heavens above us. I will never forget you."

Crimson colored her cheeks. She put a palm on his chest. "Shall you, in accordance with our custom, speak to my baba?" Her voice was scarcely above the wind that rustled the leaves. "If your promise to me endures, let us be bound with his blessing. No storm may unmoor what we have found."

The weight of tradition filled the hush between them. Xin's mind raced, grappling with the enormity of what Lan had asked. At last, he nodded.

With dusk's pale light filtering through the encampment, he steeled himself and trudged along the coarse gravel path to the tent of the Miaos, his heart a wild drum. Within, Lan's father sat enthroned behind his tea tray, the vapor rising in delicate spirals.

Xin pressed his forehead to the mat, bowing lower than he ever had. "Esteemed Master Miao, I stand before you with humble intent, seeking not to offend but to honor. I beseech your permission to wed your daughter, Lan, in the sight of all."

A grave stillness stretched. Xin lifted his head. Master Miao's thick brows drew together, his lips thinning into a narrow line. "Xin," he uttered at length, "you come before me with nothing. You possess neither family ties nor standing nor fortune to bestow. By what right do you presume to claim my daughter in marriage?"

Each syllable struck him with the chill of a winter rain. Xin licked his dry lips. Still on his knees, he searched for suitable words. "Though I am lacking in wealth and noble lineage, my devotion is true. I vow—"

Miao released a snort. "Devotion?" He leaned forward, his stare cold. "What value is devotion when the belly aches and the roof leaks? You speak of empty vows. Do you think I raised my daughter to live in squalor, clinging to a pauper for scraps of hope?"

Xin forced himself to meet Miao's glare.

The master's voice jumped. "You mistake kindness for weakness and boldness for worth. Do you know how many have sought Lan's betrothal? Sons of high merchants, young officials, each offering more than you could in a lifetime. Yet you come as if your pleading alone could sway the mountains."

While Xin remained quiet, Master Miao's mouth curled into a sneer. "Unless you can conjure gold from air or prove to me your worth beyond what I can see, leave my sight at once."

"I understand. Thank you for your time."

Xin rose and wandered along the village's perimeter, each step weighed down with the master's words. Light lingered among the ruined walls. He returned to his tent.

The next day at dusk, he ventured to the willow trees, their branches trailing along the narrow stream's bank.

His heart pounded. Would Lan come as promised? Or would her father's disapproval separate them for good? He waited, breath shallow, fingers twisting in the hem of his sleeve.

Soft footsteps sounded on the mossy path. Lan appeared, her eyes shining in the dim light. She reached for his hand. "You saw him?"

Xin nodded. "He would sooner see me gone than grant us a chance."

Her jaw clenched with the quiet steel for which he loved her. "My father is not the world," she muttered. "He cannot decide our fate."

Xin shook his head, shame mingling with desire. "He is right in pointing out that I have nothing—no bridewealth, no name."

She squeezed his hand. "You have an honorable soul and a fierce determination. That is worth more to me than all the gold."

"If we find a way," he exhaled, "would you still—?"

She leaned in, pressing her cheek to his. "Always."

Above them, a wind swept through. He rooted his feet firmly. Whatever storms they might encounter, his resolve was forged in fire.

Xin sucked in a breath, emboldened by her nearness. "I have learned something, Lan. On the market this morning, I chanced upon a newcomer from Guangzhou. He talked about the pirate's treasure—Cheung Po-Tsai's hoard. He said it lies somewhere near Hong Kong."

Lan's eyes widened. "Cheung Po-Tsai? Is it true, then? Not just a fable for children?"

Xin swallowed against the pressing doubt. "The fellow said he spoke to an aging man who had sailed with the pirate chief in his youth. This old man's tongue was loosened by rice wine, and he told of passages concealed by tide and stone, where a great chest was secreted. Gold, jade, and jewels swaddled up against the damp. It sounds fantastical." He paused, the magnitude of hope threatening to choke him. "I believe there is some truth in the new information. The man gave Cheung Po-Tsai's name and a riddle he had received from the old sailor, who claimed 'twas composed by Cheung himself."

Lan's fingers tightened on his. "Tell me this riddle. If fortune favors the brave, let us seek it together. Your future, our future, may hide in one of those caves. And if all else fails, at least we have tried more than most."

The rustling leaves whispered secret tales. Xin released his hold on her and retrieved a piece of paper from his tunic. "Here it is." He recited it together with Lan. "'To be found inside the ancient script, the words proclaim: "Seek ye out of the book of the Lord, and read: no one of these shall fail." Within a language eastward born, where wisdom's roots bind faith to pages worn. Tarry not. Another lies in wait with secrets more profound.'"

Lan knit his brow. "This term 'eastward born' might refer to some ancient script from the Orient. Chinese, perchance, considering the mention of Cheung Po-Tsai."

Xin's palm lingered at his chin, then pressed to his lips as though to steady a quickened breath. "Indeed, your musings chime with mine. Yet this talk of a 'book of the Lord'…" His voice sank to a hush. "It seems ill-suited to our customary writings."

Trumpets sounded in the distance, summoning them back to their tents. Xin folded the paper and tucked it away. "This riddle remains impenetrable. Let us hope none other should chance upon its solution, for time is not a luxury we possess."

Chapter Twelve

Kowloon, Hong Kong, China
Autumn 2022

Jason guided Debra toward Uncle Brian's apartment. As soon as they knocked, the door flung open, and Deb's mom beamed at them. "There you are! I was thinking you'd bailed and left us with this mountain of food."

"Don't let her guilt you," Uncle Brian called from the kitchen. "She loves drama."

Jason smiled and handed over the pork knuckles Debra spent the afternoon preparing. "We wouldn't miss our weekly dinner together."

"The tea's almost ready." Mom ushered them to the dining table. "Sit."

Uncle Brian, clad in a polo shirt and khakis, emerged and planted himself on the window seat. While he poured jasmine tea, Mom set out an array of dishes—stir-fried greens with garlic, fish steamed with ginger and scallions, a pot of sweet-and-sour soup, and, in the center, a platter for Debra's prized pork knuckles.

As they settled into their seats, a squeal echoed from the nearby playpen. Mateo stood up, clutching a wooden spoon like a trophy. Mom scooped him up and placed him in a high chair. The baby's tiny fingers reached out for his sippy cup.

"He's our little food critic." Uncle Brian chuckled. "And he's already mastered the art of mess-making."

They all laughed as Mateo babbled and patted his own plastic table.

The mingled aromas of ginger, scallion, and garlic wafted in the air.

"So, Jason. Your high school classmate." Uncle Brian ladled soup from the pot into his bowl. "Have you heard from her friends needing homes?"

Debra gave Jason's knee a gentle squeeze beneath the table.

He hesitated, nudging a chunk of fish across his plate. "Nothing happened. Both Sandy and Joe ghosted me after several viewings." He shrugged. "Maybe they aren't ready."

Mom twisted the lid off a jar of pureed sweet potatoes for Mateo. "What's your take? Did you get any read on those prospective clients?"

Mateo's eyes sparkled when she offered him the first spoonful.

Jason's lips pressed into a thin line. He speared a piece of pork knuckle. "They're all from the mainland. It seems everyone wants to get their money out, in case—"

Uncle Brian, midchew, waved his spoon. "In case the crackdown comes. Or Beijing tightens the leash."

Jason looked away. Vivian's laughter and her words, "You're safer on the outside," broke into his thoughts.

As if sensing his unease, Debra patted his knee again and diverted the conversation. "Have you finished reading my dad's manuscript about the Taiping Heavenly Kingdom?" She glanced at her mother. "Mom, you're the history buff among us. Do you know what the Chinese government's official line is about that troublesome period?"

"After 1949, the new government needed heroes for their story, so movements like the Taiping got rebranded." Mom fed Mateo another spoonful. "Instead of rebels, they became early revolutionaries. That's what students read in most textbooks these days. They emphasize the antifeudal, anti-imperialist elements."

Mateo put his finger into his mouth and dug out some yellow puree.

Uncle Brian wiped the baby's hand with a paper napkin. "The Communists wanted a historical arc, something to show their 'people's revolution' had roots. That's why they described the Taiping as a sort of proto-revolution. Never mind the wild religious angle or the chaos they brought."

How ironic. China, with its hardcore anti-religion atheism, endorsed the Taiping Heavenly Kingdom deeply rooted in religion, albeit a twisted form of Christianity. Jason rubbed his temples, the intense thrumming behind them irksome. "So you're saying the Party cherry-picked what was useful and ignored the rest?"

"Exactly." Mom's brow creased. "If it fits the master narrative, it gets included."

Debra leaned forward. "Isn't that what every government does? Use history to claim legitimacy."

Uncle Brian poured fresh tea for everyone. Steam rose from Jason's cup. Was any story—national or personal—ever the whole truth? Perhaps Debra was right. What Sandy and Joe told him about Vivian could be rooted in their jealousy.

Setting down the baby-sized spoon, Mom pinched the bridge of her nose. "The Taiping was notoriously bad. They tried to make a new dynasty in the name of salvation with new laws and a new calendar. Chaos came gift-wrapped."

"Imagine having 'the Heavenly Peace' printed on your business cards, Jason." Debra giggled. "Would your clients trust someone so unorthodox?"

"Hey, say whatever you want. Some pay extra for unorthodox," he retorted.

Uncle Brian sipped his tea. "The Taiping leaders thought reinventing the world would save them from their sin and the system's rot. But it bred new monsters."

"Uncle, you sound like a philosopher." Jason ran a finger over the rim of his cup. Vivian's face flashed up anew. How ruthlessly she'd reinvented herself. Was there a kernel of truth in Joe's and Sandy's comments about her? Then every ornament she wore was both proof of victory and an added bondage.

A distant siren wailed.

Debra stood and reached for the teapot. "Society changes, but some things don't. Sin, fear, hope. I bet Hong Xiuquan started a new calendar to erase the past. It didn't help."

"This brings to mind Nicodemus visiting Jesus at night." Jason fidgeted. "The Bible teaches the hope of starting over with a different approach. Pastor Wong's sermon last Sunday touched on the theme of transformation."

"That's the difference. The Taiping folks wanted to wipe the slate clean themselves. They thought new rituals would fix the old heart." Uncle Brian kissed the baby's cheek. Mateo giggled, his tiny fingers curling around his dad's thumb. "The Bible says only God can renew us."

Debra poured more tea. "You mean 'born again'?"

"Yes." Uncle Brian straightened his shoulders. "Jesus told Nicodemus, 'You must be born again.' By God's Spirit, not by obeying more rules. Religion is full of people trying to save themselves. Christianity is God saving us, giving us a new heart." His eyes narrowed. "Jesus changes us from the inside out. In contrast, Hong Xiuquan, for all his zeal, tried to force the world to be holy from the outside in."

The siren faded. Jason's heart hummed with his favorite Bible verse, "If anyone is in Christ, he is a new creation; the old has gone, the new has come."

"Transformation could never be imposed. It has to start from your soul." Debra put down the teapot. "It sounds so simple, but—"

"But it isn't easy." Mom spooned another bite into Mateo's mouth. "Maybe that's the issue with Hong Kong too. Although we all want change, nobody trusts the offers from the government or the protest leaders." She looked up. "We talk about a new heart. I just wish our citizens would listen to one another."

A muscle twitched in Uncle Brian's jaw. "After China took over in 1997, Hong Kong has changed so much. As a Realtor, I look at the listings often. It shocks me that luxury places go to companies, not individuals. You never know who the real owner is."

"Since China's economy took off"—Debra clinked her teacup onto the table—"people are buying up everything, including the history."

Mom stopped feeding Mateo to pat Debra's arm. "Folks lose themselves in that world. My boss's cousin got jailed for being a small part of someone else's scheme."

Uncle Brian exhaled hard. "I remember hearing you say that, Maggie." He pursed his lips. "It's tempting when the money runs that deep and dirty. Power corrupts, yes. The desperation underneath also changes a person. Some men do things for security, not greed."

"Speaking of that, Zhang Xin was desperate to find the pirate's treasure, not for security or greed. He thought, with wealth, he'd obtain Master Miao's approval to marry Lan." Debra rested an elbow on the table. "In Dad's last manuscript, the riddle was hidden in a book the pirate chief gave to Liang Fa. Now, it surfaced in a different way. I suppose Cheung Po-Tsai could have shared his riddles with others, including the old sailor, his subordinate."

Uncle Brian's fingers touched the rim of his teacup. He shifted in his chair. "Wait until you read the rest of the story. Xin found the second riddle and the map—"

"Please don't spoil it." Debra scratched her forehead as if easing an itch. "Back to our original topic. Peace won't come from laws or police, nor from shouting louder than the next person." She peered out the window. "It comes from mercy, from when people see each other as more than sides in an argument."

Mom sighed over Mateo's gurgle. "Most of my friends think our best hope is to leave. A US or Canadian passport, a new beginning. Sometimes I wonder if that's giving up or just common sense."

Uncle Brian turned to Jason. "Any new developments with your application to move to Canada? Have you heard from your former collaborator—what's his name—about the paperwork?"

Caught off guard, Jason almost tipped over his teacup. "Dr. John Baker. Yeah, I got an email from him yesterday. Because of the pandemic, it'll take longer to complete the application. He says that with the backlog, it may not happen this year."

Debra reached for his hand. "It'd be nice if you could return to your field and work on wetland conservation with Baker in Canada."

"I'd love that to happen." He tightened his grip on her fingers. "At the same time, I worry about you. If we move, you'll have to start your PhD research all over again."

"I may be able to transfer the program to the University of British Columbia." Debra smiled. "Professor Li said his friend there is also working on the vitamin D receptor and will welcome me."

"Ah." Uncle Brian helped himself to another of Debra's pork knuckles. "Immigration backlogs, moving across the Pacific Ocean, uncertainties about research… Remember, they don't control your future. God does. You may end up in Canada, or you may stay here. He'll walk with you always."

Jason didn't answer. He watched Mateo's eyelashes flutter as sleep crept over him.

Debra tucked a loose strand of hair behind her ear. "I hope you're right, Uncle."

"New beginnings aren't just a change of countries or governments. It's what God does best. And that's something no border, no politics, can take away." Uncle Brian's tone firmed up, like someone who had known both exile and homecoming. "Let's talk more about the Heavenly Peace. They had some wild stories, especially the Eastern King, Yang Xiuqing, the dude who claimed God the Father literally spoke through him."

Debra's eyes widened in mock awe. "Ha. He went into those trances and started channeling the Old Man Upstairs and giving imperial pronouncements."

"Exactly." Jason swirled his tea. "He'd go all stiff, and suddenly the voice of God would thunder from him, telling Hong what to do, punishing officials, and exposing traitors. Kind of convenient."

Mom snorted. "That was how they operated. Never mind evidence. Once God spoke through Yang, the verdict was set."

"Execution followed. No appeals. No mercy." The words came out rougher than he'd intended. Jason sighed. "A short road from vision to violence when leaders claim divine hotline access. Hard to argue when God Himself interrupts."

Uncle Brian picked up Mateo from the high chair, laid him down in the playpen, then covered him with a blanket. "Historians say Yang started abusing that power, faking divine messages to settle scores, enrich himself, and even humiliate Hong Xiuquan. And nobody dared question, because, well, who wants to call God a liar to His face?"

Debra chewed on her lip. "If he was faking, why didn't the Almighty God strike him down? You'd think there'd be some lightning bolt, some big warning shot from above."

"That's an interesting question." Mom leaned closer. "God doesn't always work like we expect. Sometimes, He lets people run with their lies long enough to show everyone where it leads. What happens next is more important."

Jason's fingernail clicked the teacup rim. "Right. I remember from my high school history class that the movement fell apart after all the pretending and power games. The Taiping vanished from history." He stared into the tea. "Call it what you want. To me, that was punishment. Direct. Powerful."

Uncle Brian's eyes glinted. "Exactly. God's judgment isn't immediate. In His time, the whole rotten house collapsed. You can't build a kingdom on lies."

Mom let out a slow breath. "Although Yang didn't get a thunderbolt, the consequence was severe. The ruins of Nanjing, the end of the dream for millions, and the warning echoing even now… We can't put words in God's mouth for our own gain."

As the last spoonful of soup was savored, Jason rested his gaze on the city beyond the window. Neon webs stretched across Kowloon's towers, masking old scars beneath fresh light.

The laughter of his family felt fragile. With everything happening, was he just another face in a crowd that history was about to swallow?

Chapter Thirteen

Yong'an Prefecture, Guangxi, China
December 1851

Xin rose from his thin mat, then paused in the near darkness, ears straining for unusual sounds. Outside, the city awoke to his comrades standing guard over the spoils of their victory over Yong'an. Smokiness tinged the predawn air.

He had not seen Lan for four days. His heart beat in rhythm with the surrounding uncertainties. Had Master Miao forbidden her from leaving their tent?

Footsteps sounded. "Xin, come out."

Xin donned his robe and left the tent without disturbing the others. Outside, Little Bao—a beggar boy he'd shared food with the night before—glanced around, then pressed a scrap of paper into Xin's palm. Without another word, Bao melted into the shadows, disappearing down the path.

The note bore the slanted, careful characters of Lan's hand. "At dusk, by the north well."

He hid it deep in his sleeve. The day could not move swiftly enough.

By noon, drums from the Taiping garrison beat time for them to gather. The temples, once sacred to local gods, now rang with hymns to the heavenly Father.

Under the winter sky, the crimson-and-gold banners of the Heavenly Kingdom streamed aloft in a sharp wind.

All eyes turned toward the center of the market. From the Taiping ranks, the captains—Yang Xiuqing, Hsiao Chaogui, Feng

Yunshan, Wei Changhui, and Shi Dakai—rose, waiting for the verdict that would seal their destinies.

A hush rippled outward as the Heavenly King stepped forward. Xin kneeled among those gathered. He cast a glance at the fellow soldier by his side. "Will he call our names?"

The man whispered back. "Whether he does or does not, we have already chosen our path."

Xin tried to smile, yet anxiety pinched it short. "What if—?"

The Heavenly King began to speak. All fell silent. His arm rose, his sleeve catching the weak sunrays. "Brave officers and loyal brethren, by God's mercy and the sword of justice, Yong'an is delivered from darkness. Let there be order that righteousness might flourish anew."

His gaze swept over the multitude. Xin's heart thumped. What would the king proclaim?

"Merit shall be rewarded," the king intoned like a bell. "Yang Xiuqing, your faith and virtue are the marrow of this cause. You are thus acclaimed as East King, with the title of Nine Thousand Years."

Yang Xiuqing dropped to both knees. "May I serve with unwavering loyalty, a humble servant to this great cause."

One by one, the king raised up four more kings—Hsiao as West King, Feng as South King, Wei as North King, and Shi as Wing King.

The crowd murmured at the titles.

Xin squinted up at the proclamation. The word *king* clanged around in his head. "Kings. Five of them to share the rule." He released a humorless laugh. "Share what? We've taken one town. Yong'an and its cracked wells. Where are their territories? Are they kings of the market stalls?"

The man beside him cocked his head, perhaps having heard more than Xin intended to say. "Yang Tao." He introduced himself. "A title is a fine thing, light on the tongue, heavy in the wearing."

As the declarations ended, Xin arched an eyebrow. "Why did the king want to share his power with five others? Can faith hold so many swords in the scabbards?"

Yang Tao patted Xin's arm. "Only God knows."

The Heavenly King lifted the final scroll. "Thus, shall the Taiping Heavenly Kingdom carve for itself new civil, military, ceremonial rules. Let the Heavenly Calendar commence, for each day won from tyranny is a blessing returned to the land and its people!"

A great gong echoed out over the hills. The world, so long stained gray by despair, seemed daubed in fresher colors or perhaps painted in a hopeful illusion.

"Aye," Xin muttered again, "mark this day. Are these new kings any less fallible than the Qing tyrant?"

The crowd surged with exhilaration, their every shout and cheer grating on his nerves. Ought he not to partake of their happiness? Why did foreboding surge within him?

Beneath the faded clang, he drifted apart from the tide of celebration.

Evening fell. He trudged to the north well where stones clustered by an old wall. He had not waited long before Lan, draped in a midnight-blue cloak, appeared.

"Xin?" she whispered.

He peered through the gloom and reached out until his fingers found hers. "Lan." The chill in the air could not compare to the ache in his chest. "I have missed you beyond all words. Four days have crawled by as four years."

Overhead, a cloud drifted across the moon.

She tightened her grip on his hand. "My baba grows stricter. Yet my heart is steadfast."

Something rustled in the well shaft. A tremor ran through him, cold as the stone at his feet. "Do you trust me, Lan?" Xin spoke in a low voice and pressed closer, craving her warmth.

Her luminous eyes looked up at him. "More than any other soul. Still, I fear what future awaits us if Baba continues to disapprove."

Xin's breath caught. The thought of losing her clawed at him. Desperate and determined, he drew her into his arms. "I must gain his respect," he vowed. "Somehow. Whatever it takes. I swear it."

Lan bit her lip. "But how?"

He reached into his tunic and withdrew a piece of paper. Under the silvery moonlight, the riddle seemed almost alive. "If only we could interpret this and find the pirate's treasure. Once I bring your father this legendary hoard, he will honor me."

She swallowed hard. "It eludes our understanding."

Xin tucked a lock of her hair behind her ear. "Together, we shall solve it and secure our happiness. Of this, I am certain."

"Aye." Her lips, already released from her teeth, now curled into a faint smile. "Let us, for the moment, lay this matter to rest. Pray, tell me—what is your opinion of the recent events concerning the five kings and the emergence of the new orders?"

He beckoned her toward the nearby wall. Unrest stirred in his soul. "I have pondered my time with Reverend Roberts. Something he said rang in my head."

Lan remained quiet, her brow creased.

"Roberts said, 'The Christ I serve calls not to earthly kingdoms nor fields of slaughter.'" He leaned against the wall. "According to him, God's kingdom is not one claimed by bloodshed. The endeavor for a heavenly order in this world must beware of men's ambition."

"I comprehend you." Her eyes narrowed to mere slits. "The king—indeed, all our kings—speak much of new statutes, of the Heavenly Calendar, of a grand restoration to Eden. I wonder who among us shall be made to bear the cost."

Xin twisted his fingers together until his nails carved crescents in his palms. "The rules bid us to shun opium, wicked thoughts, to cleave to purity beyond reach. 'Tis good to seek virtue. Yet—" He faltered, as though the word snagged on a thorn. "Is the decree sufficient to drive away the darkness? In chasing the light with such fervor, we may carve shadows deeper than before."

Lan's voice dipped low. "When mercy is dethroned by censure, those who stray are doomed."

"Indeed." He flinched. A shiver crept up his spine. "The king says God desires holiness." He pressed a fist against his chest. Weariness lay heavy on him. "But who can bear such constant scrutiny? It threads through my prayers and finds me wanting." He let out a brittle laugh that died at once. "We cast off the yoke of one emperor and forge another in righteousness' name. At what point does zeal become a chain?"

"This Heavenly Calendar is meant to render all things sanctified." Lan leaned into him, her palm flat on his chest. "Our farmers tie their lives to the traditional calendar for planting. Does heaven's reckoning fill the paddies? Will a date inscribed by edict bring rain or sun?"

Xin managed a thin smile. "Roberts once told me that men mistake the kingdom for its trappings—days, customs, rituals. He claimed true heaven grows from within, not fashioned by laws."

Her shoulders slumped. "We are forced to follow without question or be accused of faithlessness." She drew a step back. "What will you do, Xin?"

He exhaled, caught between bitter laughter and a sigh. "Shall these changes make us better?" His gaze met hers. "Perhaps paradise is not won by decree, but by love."

The moonlight caught gold in her hair. She grasped his hand again. Their fingers tangled. "Zeal shan't snuff out love."

For one brief heartbeat, she tilted her face up, so close the warmth of her exhale tickled his skin.

Should he touch her lips with his?

Before he could proceed, she withdrew a pace. "I shall send word of our next meeting through Little Bao."

She slipped into the night, footsteps fading into the hush.

✳ ✧ ✳

As their discourse still echoed in Xin's mind, a crisp wind whipped in from the river. East King Yang Xiuqing rushed into the center of the assembly's circle. His body convulsed. His eyes rolled back. He thundered, his voice not his own. "Hear your heavenly Father! Let every soul submit before my son, Hong Xiuquan! We must root out the traitors."

All present dropped to their knees. Xin pressed his forehead hard against the earth.

The bells tolled. He lifted his head. His comrades in arms stood in two neat files, their sashes fluttering beneath the banners.

Upon the makeshift dais, the appointed judges conferred. Before them, three men kneeled, wrists corded behind their backs.

A square-bearded official read aloud. "These men are accused of betrayal. They worked with the demon Qing, betraying the Heavenly Law. Their words and actions sowed poison among the brethren. We must judge them now, or leniency will let the rot spread."

Xin's breath stuttered in his lungs. "Surely these are not strangers." He searched the faces and recognized Old Yao, the potter he had met in Guiping, Guangxi.

93

Yao tried to rise, only to be forced back by the grip of a young soldier. His cries rang out in the winter air. "Mercy! I am no traitor. My only crime was to shelter a wounded nephew, not knowing he wore Qing livery. Do you all believe I could betray our king?"

The judges turned stony faces, and one of them pronounced the verdict. "Treachery shall be punished."

No assent arose from the crowd, only averted gazes.

The chief judge gestured, and the executioners, draped in white, emerged.

Xin's body shook. Was this the paradise promised to them?

The soldiers forced Old Yao to kneel further. The sword rose, and the world narrowed to the glint and fall of the blade. Red blooms spread over the ground.

A gasp broke from the throng. The other two men fell next, their pleas unheeded.

Afterward, the crowd dispersed. The banners overhead now appeared like a warning written in blood and gold.

Two days later, Xin met Lan by the river at night. "Did you see? No matter how holy the decrees are, the sword sharpens its own law."

"I knew Old Yao. He was my baba's friend for years." Moisture shimmered in Lan's eyes. "Heaven is not made manifest in this place. Not in these deeds."

He mumbled, more to himself. "Alas, a new kingdom with ancient tears. Where do we turn?"

Silence fell between them, shaped only by the river's gentle gurgle. His hand found hers. The moonlight painted a silver path along the current. Her fingers lingered in his. The world paused. His sorrow ebbed in her presence. They stood, bound by hopes unspoken. Before they parted, she promised to send word of their next meeting soon.

Back in his tent, slumber eluded Xin. A line from the riddle haunted him. "Seek ye out of the book of the Lord, and read: no one of these shall fail."

He had encountered those words before. But where and under what circumstances? Perhaps in the battered wooden trunk in Roberts's parlor, crowded with books and ragged papers. Among them were several translated volumes of the Holy Bible by Liang Fa.

Hadn't one of them contained that very phrase? Yet which book might it be? And why would a pirate cite a Bible verse in his riddle?

Chapter Fourteen

Hong Kong, China
Autumn 2022

The elevator glided up. Jason checked his reflection in the mirrored panels, smoothed his hair, and tugged the lapel of his navy blazer. The bottle of Château Margaux he'd selected gleamed in its gift bag. Vivian's housewarming party tonight would be a golden opportunity to procure new clients, and he intended to make the most of it.

The doors parted on the penthouse floor. The sleepless city stretched out under the milky moonlight. Victoria Harbour seemed to whisper a simple truth that it never belonged to anyone.

While Jason stepped over the threshold, a woman in white gloves—Vivian's housekeeper?—accepted the wine, then disappeared out of sight. Muted jazz music and the subtle perfume of tropical lilies permeated the atmosphere.

He searched for the crowd. Yet the living room was empty, except for the hostess standing by the floor-to-ceiling windows in an emerald silk dress that clung to her voluptuous figure. Where were the bankers, lawyers, and tycoons?

Vivian turned, lips parting in an almost grin. "Jason, you made it. Welcome to my lair."

Her shiny ebony hair was swept back, exposing her delicate neck. She moved with unconscious authority, spine straight, jaw angled as if daring anyone to underestimate her.

"Congratulations." He shook hands with her. "You have a gorgeous place with a spectacular view."

She approached a crystal decanter on a side table. "I should. I paid enough for it. And thank you again for helping me buy it."

She gestured to the sofa. "Sit, please. Let me get us a drink. I've just opened a bottle of 1990 Sassicaia. Only the best for tonight."

His conscience tickled. He rubbed his chin. This was business, wasn't it? He settled on the edge of the designer couch, half expecting the doorbell to ring and a dozen guests to pour in. But the apartment remained silent.

Vivian reached for the two glasses on the coffee table and poured the wine. "To new beginnings." She offered a toast. Her gaze met his as if issuing a challenge.

He clinked his glass against hers. "To your new castle."

She released a throaty laugh. "You think I'm a queen?"

"You act like one." He braved a grin. "You'd have terrified my high school self."

She swirled her wine. "High school. Feels far away, doesn't it?" Her laughter faded. "It still surprises me how we have changed. And you, the top student, would be my only former classmate at my first real home in Hong Kong."

Jason's heart skipped a beat. "Where are your other guests?"

She shrugged, the silk slipping on her collarbone. "I only invited you. These days, I'd rather spend time with people who knew me *before*. No pretense. No games."

He took a cautious sip. The wine was extraordinary, velvet on his tongue. More intoxicating was the electric pull asimmer underneath her words. Yeah. Vivian wrapped her loneliness in bravado.

Her dress shimmered emerald in the light. She poured herself a little more and sank into the sofa's curve. Her knees brushed his. Her night-jasmine perfume wafted into his nostrils. "I want to ask you something, Jason." She set down her glass. "Since you're the only person in this city whom I can trust."

The room closed in on him. He flashed on Debra's beautiful oval face and the comfort of their shared prayers, then refocused on Vivian. "Sure. Anything."

She tucked a loose tress behind her ear. Her eyes shone with a restless sparkle. "Have you ever gotten tired of following rules?"

His pulse quickened. He shifted his knees away from hers. "Depends on who's making them."

Her chuckle sounded practiced. "I spent all my life playing by other people's rules. My parents', the Party's, men's. In business, in politics, and in bed." She let the sentence dangle, her intent unspoken but crackling between them. "What about you? You seem good at saying no. Still, everyone has a price. Or at least, a dream they wish they could buy."

Jason forced a smile. "Some things aren't for sale."

"Are you sure?" She reached out, her fingertips tracing his wrist. "You could become very, very successful. With the right partner. The right risks."

He swallowed and remained quiet.

"I've been thinking"—her words turned deliberate—"about starting a business on the Hong Kong side. A company, maybe. You'd be the CEO. I bring my contacts, and you bring your skills. We could make a killing. Real estate, consulting, venture capital for biotech start-ups. There's so much money, so many folks wanting to move money out of the mainland into this city." She leaned closer, her lips brushing his ear. "You don't have to answer now. Just consider it."

She drew back and locked her gaze on his.

His chest throbbed.

"Partners who trust each other and ask no questions. They understand what the other needs." She picked up her glass once more and pressed her thigh against his. "No more shame."

He sucked in a breath, her scent seeping into his lungs. His mind flickered to Debra and her gentle touch as she prayed for him that morning. *Don't overreact. This is work.*

Vivian placed a palm on his knee, her fingernails tracing tiny patterns through the fabric of his pants. "Ever since high school, your gorgeous eyes have enchanted me. You always saw good in people. Even in me, when nobody else did."

Heat crawled up his neck. His whole body thrummed. He wanted—what did he want? *I'm married.* The urgent words shouted at the back of his mind, a brittle dam against the current pulsing in his veins.

Every muscle screamed a warning, but raw desire pressed. He'd never felt so exposed or so alive.

"We'll be great together," she murmured. Her lips moved toward his, the lamp glittering behind her.

A sudden shrill pierced the thick air.

He jerked away, nearly spilling his wine. With a shaking hand, he fished the phone from his pocket. The screen glowed. Pastor Wong. Was it a slap or a deliverance? He released a light cough. "Sorry, Vivian. Let me take this." He stepped into the hallway. His legs trembled, heat and chill tangled inside of him.

"Jason!" Pastor Wong's voice boomed through the line. "Just wanted to check. You and Debra are coming to Dawn Island this weekend, right? The folks there are waiting for your testimony. They admire you."

Jason steadied his breath. The silence beyond the hallway grew tense, pressing at his eardrums. He licked dry lips. "Yeah, of course. Thank you for calling."

"Are you well?" The pastor's tone softened. "You sound troubled."

Jason's pulse thudded in his throat. He pinched the bridge of his nose and pressed the phone tighter to his ear. "Life's complicated, Pastor." He swallowed. "The enemy is good at dressing up temptations. Sometimes they camouflage as opportunities."

Pastor Wong paused, then prayed for him—right there, a wash of words about strength, discernment, holiness.

When Jason hung up, he faced his reflection in the corridor mirror. Sweat beaded his brow. He lifted a silent prayer to thank the Lord, composed himself, and returned to the living room.

Vivian was refilling her glass. "Everything okay?"

He tried not to look at her lips, the hollow at her collarbone, and the outline of her curves beneath the thin silk. "Have you heard about the Dawn Island Gospel Drug Addiction Treatment Centre in Hong Kong?" He cleared his throat again. "The program there recognizes the need to go beyond just addressing the addiction itself. Volunteers like us take the time to understand the person's history, substance use, and mental health status. Based on that, we create a personalized treatment plan."

Vivian sank deeper into the sofa, one foot curled beneath her. "The gospel again, huh?" Tease edged her tone. "Ever wonder if you're missing out on fun, always being the decent Jason?"

A nervous chuckle slipped out. He stared down at his hands, knuckles white where they gripped his phone. "It's more about not wanting to ruin what I've been given." He glanced up, the confession raw.

Vivian's smile faded. She motioned for him to sit down. "You don't have to be so uptight."

"Actually, I'd better leave right now." He patted his pockets as if he'd just remembered a task. "I forgot I have to prepare for my talk. Thanks for the invite, anyway."

Her face dropped. Then she gave a practiced shrug. "Of course. Can't let your fans down."

He hurried toward the exit. "Thanks for the wine. Next time, Debra and I will invite you to our place."

As he fled, the sweet scent of her penthouse clung to him. Inside the elevator, he leaned his forehead against the cool wall, the insistent thud of his pulse in his ears.

When he reached his apartment, the tide of self-reproach had receded, leaving a gritty residue of relief. He unlocked the door and stepped inside.

"Hey, honey," Debra called from the sofa, the tablet on her lap. The smell of garlic and ginger hung in the air. She'd taken the free night to experiment with a new wonton recipe, or so she'd texted. Her brow scrunched. "You're home earlier than I expected."

Jason loosened his tie. "Yeah, I guess I am." He dropped his bag and slid in beside her.

"How did it go?" She put the tablet on the coffee table. "Did you meet more clients interested in buying properties?"

Should he tell her what had happened? No, it'd hurt her feelings and bring questions he wasn't ready to answer. "Not really."

She glanced at him, then at the tablet. "I was reading Dad's manuscript about the Taiping Heavenly Kingdom. It dawned on me that Yang Xiuqing and Hsiao Chaogui became ji tong for God and Jesus."

"Ah, *ji tong*, spirit mediums." He slung an arm across her shoulders. "I've read the chapters too."

She nodded. "Back then, most Chinese believed in spirit mediums. Yang's role as God's spokesperson and Hsiao serving as a ji tong for Jesus would have strengthened the loyalty of their followers."

"Strange, right? How people look for something sacred, someone to embody the divine. It blurs the line between faith and performance." He kissed her temple, grateful for the distraction from his tangled thoughts.

Debra twisted a strand of hair around her finger. "I keep imagining what it must have felt like for Xin. If I had been there, I probably would have been awestruck as well. At the same time, Xin was educated and a thinker. He harbored doubts all along."

With a silent sigh, he pulled her into a tight hug. "We tend to crave tangible things, images we can see and touch."

"Yeah. From the beginning, humans have longed for something to hold on to as proof of God's existence. That's why Aaron gave in to the Israelites' request and made a golden calf, a physical representation of the God who brought them out of Egypt." She nestled into his chest. "Our desire for certainty may end up leading us astray."

"Huh." He tried to focus. Yet, his mind tripped back to the velvet hush of Vivian's living room and the heat of her nearness. He stared at Debra's lovely oval face.

"Are you okay? You seem distracted." She frowned at him, then shrugged. "Anyway, the whole idea of ji tong… It makes me think about how belief shapes everything. Marriage, trust, even what we're willing to risk."

He swallowed, voice rough. "Faith is complicated. Maybe more than we admit."

"You always say that." She grinned. "Want some leftovers? I saved you a plate."

"Love to." He carved out a smile.

As she rose and moved to the kitchen, he palmed his forehead. What he didn't say—Vivian, the wine, the subtle gravity of temptation—sat heavy on his shoulders. He muttered a prayer under his breath, thanking God for His protection. The familiarity of his home and his wife's love steadied him.

She returned and gave him a plate with a pair of chopsticks. "You still don't look like your usual self."

Jason's gaze met hers. If only he could unburden himself. "Long day." He began to eat, his appetite mechanical.

Debra carried on with stories about history and about faith, change, and hope. He listened, letting her voice ease the quiet ache he'd brought home with him.

Chapter Fifteen

Yong'an Prefecture, Guangxi, China
April 1852

Heavenly Kingdom banners bobbed above the weary visages of retreating soldiers. Zhang Xin, in his threadbare sandals, shuffled onward. Every shift of his foot drew a wince as woven straw scraped flesh already rubbed raw.

A hoarse voice from somewhere up the ragged column commanded, "Keep moving."

The command rippled through the lines, and the surge of uneasy bodies pressed him deeper into the procession. Panic fluttered at the base of his throat, the ghost of Yong'an's walls still tight around his ribs.

He fiddled with the tattered red sash knotted about his waist and muttered, "Still holding together, at least."

"Are you talking about your clothes or your body?" Beside him, Yang Tao, Xin's comrade, grumbled. His cheeks were hollow, his lips cracking white. "My stomach is emptier than a temple after a plague. Where is heaven?"

Xin offered a chuckle that turned into a cough. The reversal of the battle's outcome and the current siege of Yong'an by Qing forces stung. "Since the New Year, they have been strangling us. No carts get through. No rice. Even the rats have learned to hide."

"Rats tasted better than the boiled leather." Yang snorted. "And the pox—did you hear Old Wen wheeze himself to death last week? I thought his lungs would climb out of his mouth."

A youth with a fever-spotted face stumbled by. Xin reached out on instinct to steady him, then pulled back, guilty at his own fear.

He shivered. Roberts oft repeated a proverb about heaven's path being narrow. Now, the Qing had thrown an invisible ring around them, and it had tightened until every breath scraped.

A bugle squealed ahead. An officer astride a bony mare turned in the saddle. "Hear the word! By command of the Heavenly King, we must break the siege and move to Hunan, then on to the Yangtze valley."

Murmurs broke. Hunan? Yangtze?

The officer shouted, "The river routes will carry us to resources enough to fill a hundred bellies. Grain. Salt. Powder. Souls waiting to be saved, and soldiers waiting to be sworn. Keep your ranks and live to see it."

"Resources?" Yang rubbed his belly. "I should start with a crust of yesterday's bread."

Xin's chest tightened. Hunan. He had never been there, yet the syllables cooled his tongue. The Yangtze rose in his mind as a silver spine with green terraces. They could escape dust and hunger. "The king says heaven is close." He released another mirthful chuckle. "Guess we'll see soon enough if his vision holds stronger than the sinews in my legs."

The day yielded to twilight. Near the Jintian Ferry, the army found temporary rest. The low-burning campfires started, and unsteady shadows leaped across the men's gaunt faces. The river sang its ceaseless song. Only the occasional rasp of blade against whetstone or the groans of the wounded troubled the hush.

Xin's gaze strayed toward the glow from a nearby fire. Miao Lan bent over a man's mangled foot, binding the wound with such limited cloth as could still be scavenged in desperation.

Master Miao was nowhere to be seen.

With swift resolve, Xin hastened to her side and dropped to one knee. "Have you exhausted your supply of bandages?"

She responded with a shrug. "Every day brings new injuries and fewer supplies. I have done what I can. He will walk when the sun rises. He must. We all must."

Her steadfastness was a balm he could scarcely name. The order in her movements brought transient solace amid the chaos. "And are you—" He regarded her with a half smile. "Are you well, Lan?"

She dabbed a final measure of salve on the soldier's wounded flesh, then cast Xin a sidelong glance. "I am as well as any living amid the ruin." She pointed at the river. "The men whisper of defeat."

Xin studied the ink-black water. "My faith grows thin too, like rice soup stretched for too many mouths. Still, I cling to it, stubborn as an old ox."

She sighed. "Heaven is ever a promise, but seldom a shelter."

Her hand brushed over his shoulder. They rose together. The world beyond them receded. The soldier lapsed into fitful sleep. Somewhere near, a solitary voice began a muted hymn.

Xin's fingers trembled as they entwined with hers, desperate to savor the truth of her presence. He led her behind a nearby boulder and leaned closer. His breath stirred a stray lock of her hair, her subtle jasmine scent dizzying him with longing. "Lan, I have missed you so much..." He faltered, his tongue heavy with words he practiced in solitude but never dared to speak aloud.

Cold dangers warred with sudden joy. He searched her face, tracing the curve of her cheek with his gaze. Her nearness comforted him. He drew her into his arms as if the air itself conspired to press them close. The tenuous space between them crackled with all the feelings he had fought to suppress. When she rested her head against his shoulder, his breath caught. He closed his eyes, letting himself become the axis of her trust and tenderness.

At length, she mumbled, "Upon further reflection regarding our circumstances, I am persuaded that, should you succeed in discovering the pirate's treasure, my baba would give us his blessing."

"Indeed, I, too, have deliberated this matter at great length." Xin released a sigh. "This riddle of the pirate vexes me. I recall a passage I once encountered in a translated volume of the Bible whilst with Missionary Roberts. Now that everything depends on its solution, I wonder which volume 'tis in and where I can find it."

A tense silence settled. He turned away, searching for answers in the darkness.

Across the water, a faint glow betrayed the massing of the imperial foe. Lanterns marked the positions of the Qing soldiers. A countless host gathered with menacing intent. Their weapons glinted orange in the baleful firelight, the iron mouths of their cannons yawning in the gloom. Now and again, an officer's sharp command surged above the whisper of reeds.

"The encirclement tightens." Xin touched the bark of a nearby willow. "Word has reached us that more Qing banners gather upstream. The enemy means to crush us before another moon can pass."

"The Heavenly Army must break free." Lan drew away from him. "Or our heaven will vanish into the earth. We will not perish here. The rich valleys lie in Hunan."

Her courage lit a brief fire in him, though it could not quell his hunger nor the ever-present ache of anxiety.

They leaned into each other, reluctant to part.

An insect flew toward them. Lan brushed it away and touched his sleeve. "Be careful." Her gaze flickered around the surroundings. "I'll send you a note when 'tis safe for us to meet again."

With heaviness on his chest, he stood motionless while she slipped away, her figure soon swallowed by the darkness. He withdrew into his tent and wrapped himself in his cloak. Would they break through the Qing's siege? Might he die on the banks of this sorrowful river?

Before dawn, the alarm shattered the silence. "To arms! Qing devils approach!"

The camp leaped into panic. Lanterns blazed. Xin sprang up and scrambled for his weapon.

Along the battered roads, he trudged with others in South King Feng Yunshan's group. The air thrummed with uncertainty, every crossroads haunted by the scent of burning fields.

Xin glanced at Yang Tao. "Which way to Hunan? Where does salvation lie?"

The march paused. East King Yang Xiuqing emerged before them, eyes wide and glassy. He raised his arms skyward, then thundered with powerful resonance. "Listen! Your heavenly Father is speaking. Destroy demons and save the people."

Beside him, Hsiao Chaogui also entered a trance and spoke in an altered voice while pointing northeast. "I'm Jesus, your Lord. En route to Hunan, we must take Quanzhou first. The Father will deliver the town to us by the end of the month."

The crimson and gold banners of the Heavenly Kingdom once more fluttered into motion. Feng perched high in his sedan chair. Xin pressed onward, one hand tight on his sword.

As they reached a hill by the river, a crack split the air. Gunfire rang from the Qing camp. Horses reared. A shell burst. In the chaos, Feng's sedan lurched, and he slumped forward.

Xin staggered up the narrow path. The pungent tang of gunpowder hung thick. Pain twisted Feng's face. Blood spotted his robe. Yet he caught Xin's arm. "Fear nothing. Protect the Lord's son!"

"Hold on." Xin pressed down hard on the wound, breath hitching. "Please—hold on."

The gongs rolled from the rear.

"Shields up!" a captain ordered.

Men surged down the slope. The river lay wide and brown. Reeds bent and whispered.

"Low water!" someone cried. "Fear not. Cross and fight. The Qing has only a few guns."

A squad waded ahead, driving bamboo stakes into the mud to mark the safe path. Hymns rose. Men sang over their shoulders. God's second son moved beneath a torn white banner. Xin kept the banner in sight the way a sailor keeps a star. He and Yang Tao carried Feng's sedan into the water. Cold seized his shins. Mud sucked at his sandals. He gritted his teeth. "Steady."

"Fear nothing," Feng whispered again.

A gunshot rang out again. The river's surface rippled. "Down!" someone yelled.

Xin dropped together with Yang. Arrows hissed past.

More men from their army hit the shallows. Qing soldiers fled before the wall of wet men and pikes. The Taiping formed and shoved the gap wider.

"Make way!" Xin shouted as he and Yang shouldered Feng's sedan chair up the bank. An arrow narrowly missed Xin's arm. Feng sagged, but kept his eyes open, murmuring prayers.

At last, they broke through the Qing siege. Xin and Yang bore Feng to safety. Yet unease gnawed at Xin. Was the enemy's retreat only a feint? How long before the Qing closed ranks again?

✳ ✧ ✳

Quanzhou, Guangxi, China
April 1852

For eleven days, prayer marked their march northeast. Each night, Xin and Yang kept vigil outside Feng's tent. At dawn on the twelfth day, Feng breathed his last. The mourning drums fell hard. A tremor rippled through the line. Orders passed down in desperate gasps. "Revenge! Let none escape!"

From every side, the Taiping converged. Drums beat with fury. Warriors, galvanized by the fallen king, carried scaling ladders to Quanzhou's stone walls, while others formed teams to ram the ironbound gates with heavy logs.

The smoke of burning thatch drifted above the rooftops. Within a day and a night, the old bulwark crumbled. Quanzhou's doors opened, and the pent-up vengeance of thousands surged in.

Xin stumbled over bodies in the breach. Screams mingled with the clash of steel. Axes and knives gleamed. Shouts, driven beyond reason, tore from raw throats.

No mercy befell the town's citizens. Taiping soldiers wrenched mothers from their children, their blades flashing. In the market square, an old man pled for his life only to be cut down, his cry swallowed by the roar. Flames crawled across the huts. Light revealed sprawled corpses—merchant, beggar, child—indiscriminately slain. The invaders spared no one.

A peddler fell to his knees before Xin amid toppled baskets of dried persimmons. "Please—"

"Kill him," the cold command rang out.

Xin's grip trembled as he raised the sword. The man's pleading gaze met his. He faltered. Then, with a desperate cry, he thrust the weapon forward. The steel struck flesh, warm spray flecking his cheek, and the peddler crumpled to the bloody stones. Xin stepped back, the coppery stench of blood thick in his nostrils. Nausea crept up from within. He had believed himself prepared. He had carried the weapon, recited the hymns of brotherhood, and hurled curses at the old world. Yet, as he stared into the corpse's glazed eyes, his stomach lurched, and he recoiled.

He stumbled out of the carnage and staggered forward. At the water's edge, he dropped his weapon, bent over, and retched until nothing came but dry sobs.

A small voice pierced the stillness. "Are you all right?"

Startled, Xin jerked up his head. There stood a boy, perhaps ten years of age, beneath a willow. He wore a torn tunic, his visage streaked with soot.

Before Xin responded, soldiers' torches broke upon the bank. "Someone by the river!"

A cold jolt shot through him. Without thinking, he grabbed the boy's arm and dragged him into the reeds.

Mud sucked at Xin's feet. Cold water rose above his shins. Concealed in the shadows, he held his breath as footsteps thundered along the riverbank—Taiping searchers scouring for those who fled.

After his comrades departed, the boy looked up and whispered, "Are you not one of them? Why did you help me?"

Xin choked out, "I know not."

The lad regarded him. His hands twisted together. "My name is Wang Hui. My home lies outside the town. If you have nowhere else to go, my parents may give you shelter."

Xin hesitated, uncertain whether greater peril lay ahead or behind. But in the boy's gentle candor, he divined something unspoiled amid the wreckage. With a nod, he followed Hui.

They trudged through lanes half choked by broken tiles and dead lanterns. Beyond the outskirts of Quanzhou, a hut hunched beneath the tangled boughs of mountain laurel and camphor trees. On one side, a rickety lean-to shed sheltered a stack of shriveled firewood and a few clay jars. Wang Hui slipped through the crooked gate and motioned for Xin to follow.

Within, the scent of dried chrysanthemum and mugwort drifted in the air. A slim woman of middle years hurried forth from the curtained recess. Faint lines at brow and mouth marked her oval face, while her dark eyes shone with a brightness. Her long hair, threaded with silver, was bound at the nape in the manner of those accustomed to swift motion.

She cast her gaze on her son. "Hui, I bade you not to enter the town today. Must you always tempt fate with so little heed for your own safety?"

"Mama, I meant no disobedience. Only…" The boy ducked his head. "Did you not teach me acupuncture so I could help others? There may be injured people I can assist."

An exasperated huff escaped before she pressed him to her chest. "Your heart is too quick to spill out, child. The hour is ill-chosen for such an act. Else, your kindness may cost you more than it must. Still, better well-intentioned folly than cold indifference."

Wang Hui detailed what had happened.

At his words, she turned her focus on Xin. "I am Ying Si-Fen, Hui's mother. Thank you for saving my son's life. Come, drink tea with us."

Xin glanced around the room. On one wall, swords long and short hung beneath yellowed scrolls with faded brushwork. Low shelves lined the corners, crowded with ceramic jars, each labeled with names such as tiger bone, ginseng, and angelica root. Bundles of dried roots and medicinal herbs dangled from rafters overhead, spreading knotted silhouettes on the earthen floor.

As Xin settled on a low stool near the hearth, from an inner chamber emerged a square-jawed man garbed in the austere black-and-indigo robe of a kung fu master. He introduced himself as Wang Jun, the boy's father, then gaped at Xin's long, unkempt hair. "Are you one of the Taiping? I have heard of the massacre. Why did you spare my son?"

The boy's mother approached and offered Xin a ceramic cup brimming with tea, steam wreathing her face in a gentle halo. "Drink, and drive out the chill."

Xin accepted the cup and bowed his head. "I am a wanderer seeking heaven on earth. For that, I followed Taiping. Yet today—" He choked. Moisture rushed behind his eyelids.

Wang Jun placed a hand on Xin's arm. "Many lost souls wander these roads since the rebellion. You brought back my son. For that, my house is yours tonight."

An old man, spare as a willow switch, entered the chamber. A long white beard flowed down his chest like a silvery cascade. His eyes, clear beneath bushy brows, shone with a gentle but penetrating light, as though seeking the very marrow of Xin's being. "Heaven on earth? Which heaven do you seek?"

Xin hesitated, the rim of the cup trembling below his lips. "I–I sought a land without suffering, where all men might be equals and hunger is no more."

The man stroked his beard. "There is only *one* everlasting heaven. Its gates are opened through the grace of Jesus Christ, not by any earthly rebellion. Did our Lord not say, 'My kingdom is not of this world'? Those who trade violence for hope reap only sorrow."

Xin dropped his jaw. Had he not heard those same words from Roberts?

Ying Si-Fen guided the venerable man into a chair. "Zhang Xin, permit me to introduce my uncle, Liang Fa. It may astonish you to learn that Hong of Taiping first drew the spark of his great endeavor from my uncle's writing."

Xin stared, almost uncomprehending, at the aging author seated before him. *Liang Fa*? His mouth went dry. *Was this the man whose tract had sown the seeds of a nation's upheaval?*

The shadows in the chamber shifted. Xin's thoughts hastened in wild tumult. Did Roberts not mention that Liang Fa had toiled alongside Morrison to translate the Bible into Chinese? Might he own the translated tome that contained the very phrase of the pirate's riddle?

Chapter Sixteen

Kowloon, Hong Kong, China
Autumn 2022

The text message arrived on a Friday, among the digital dust of a dozen notifications. Jason paused in the middle of scraping cream cheese onto a slice of toast. A crimson envelope icon glowed at the top of the screen, and beneath the sender's name, an ornate *V* gleamed gold. "Jason, something exciting. Dress for a surprise. Four p.m. Monday—Vivian."

A prickle ran down his spine. His hand shook as he set down the butter knife. What was she up to now? Against his will, the memory of their last encounter surged up. Her rich perfume and half-whispered words had aroused him. He'd wrestled with a dark thrill ever since.

He swallowed, mouth dry, thumb hovering over the message. Appended below, an address he recognized, a gallery reserved for high-profile openings.

Before he swiped it away, Debra leaned over, an eyebrow arched. "Vivian again?" She swirled the dregs of instant coffee in her mug. "Is this another of her events? Nothing seemed to come of the yacht party or the housewarming party."

He mustered a nonchalant chuckle. "Just an exhibition this time. Art and free wine, I suppose."

Yet his pulse quickened. Less than ten days ago, he'd been driven into a corner, the city's lights glittering like a thousand fireflies behind Vivian's porcelain face. If Pastor Wong hadn't called him, would he…?

He pushed his plate aside, uncertain of his hunger. Perhaps it would be different this time. After all, a public event with roomfuls of art and socialites should be safe.

Debra's mouth twitched into a lopsided half smile. "Hope it's more fruitful than before. Maybe you'll walk out with another fat penthouse commission. Mid-Levels again, huh?"

"I hope so." He maintained a steady gaze and drew her into his arms. "When we got married two years ago, we didn't have our honeymoon because of the pandemic. If I earn another fat commission like the previous one, we ought to plan our dream holiday. France, Italy, the hills and vineyards."

She brushed a finger over his knuckles. The glint in her eyes seemed to pierce right through him. Was it concern, affection, or something far more complicated?

For a moment, neither spoke. Did she sense the nerves beneath his surface?

Debra kissed his cheek. "Go and bring back stories. I'll stay home, unless you have other plans for Monday evening."

He leaned in, desperate to memorize the taste of her lips, the steady anchor of her presence. Properties, lucrative deals, and wealthy clients all faded into insignificance. Only Debra was real. Only her.

"Deb, you bewitch me." The admission trembled with his aching desire for her above the crowded ambition of his life.

She pressed her body against his. "I want you. Today. Tomorrow. And now," she murmured.

The golden morning light poured into the room. He caressed her oval face, voice husky. "I'm yours, one hundred percent yours."

Her fingers explored him, the heat grounding him. When he trailed kisses along her shoulder, she arched into him. Each sigh, each whispered promise was shared only between them.

All too soon, reality pulled them from their private world. The next two days fled by with family gatherings and Sunday worship. On Monday, an Uber dropped him off at Mid-Levels. The gallery, a colonial remnant grafted onto glass extravagance, jutted out over the slope like a ship half launched. His footsteps echoed on the marble steps. The foyer smelled of lilies and varnish. A single staffer in black led him down a hall flanked by canvases. He caught glimpses of Victoria Harbour through enormous windows.

Vivian stood at the far corner, a vision in crimson silk. The delicate white gloves she wore, as if prepared for a baptism more than a party, caught his attention and brought back the sensation of her fingertips tracing his jaw last time.

She turned. "Jason, you're punctual."

A nervous laugh snagged in his throat and came out as a whisper, "No crowd?"

No laughter, no other guests. Only an unseen piano unraveled lonely chords.

A shiver crawled up his spine. His skin prickled beneath his shirt. Was this another trap?

Vivian smiled. "Guests will arrive soon. We have an hour alone, just you and me." Her gaze flicked over him. "Nice suit, neat tie, every bit a proper gentleman."

His mind spun. Why had she asked him so early? What did she want? His heartbeat sped up.

She extended her hand. He shook it, the satin glove frictionless. His pulse drummed a warning that he couldn't suppress.

Vivian uncorked a bottle of Bordeaux and poured it, the red glimmering in the brass lights. "This is aged. Do you love old things, Jason?"

He took the glass. The cool stem bit into the web between his thumb and forefinger. The wine climbed the bowl in slow, dark sheets. It tasted layered, a pleasure that demanded surrender. "It depends. Some traditions are worth keeping."

"So loyal. You're a good Hong Kong citizen. Never more British than the British, never more businesslike than your uncle." She released a chuckle. "The world's moved, hasn't it?"

Good citizen. Her words pinned to his skull like a name tag. Heat rose to his ears. Was it from the wine?

She sank onto a velvet bench, then gestured for him to sit. "Did you ever play in the harbor as a boy? My father took me there once. We tried to skip stones, but he said the water was never the same after the British left. Too many secrets under the glitter. Even the fish act differently now."

He sat, careful not to let his knee brush hers. The velvet gripped his trousers. He lifted the glass to his face as a shield. "You moved to China."

"Where else would I win?" She sipped her wine. "Please remember. My offer stands." Her voice dropped to almost a purr. "You run a company for me. I'll supply the capital."

She set down her glass. Her gloves skimmed the stem as though fearful of staining it with her touch. "You'll be more than a gentleman, Jason. You'll become very rich." She edged closer. "Will you join me?"

Her nearness drowned him. The scent of her perfume, the gentle curve of her neck, the quiver of anticipation in her poised smile… A jolt coursed through his veins.

Through the thin glove fabric, her thumb tickled the sensitive skin inside his wrist. She leaned in. "You are the most trustworthy guy I've ever met. I trust nobody else. Not here, not up north. That's why I need you."

His breath hitched as if the world had shrunk to the space between their two bodies. Outside, the sunrays flickered on the water, indifferent, exquisite.

She tilted her head. "Do you ever wonder? You behave like a gentleman. But what does it buy you?" She drew out the words as though trying to summon the answer from him.

The room grew dense, heavy with passion. He wanted to stand again, to keep moving so nothing could attach. Instead, he remained motionless.

"You can cash in all that decency. Be rich, respected, and safe." Her gloved fingers slipped upward to toy with the knot of his tie. "Desired, even." She breathed out the last syllables.

The floor slanted beneath his feet, nudging him toward her. "I'm not…"

She cut in. "You're not afraid, are you? Don't you crave what everyone wants?" Her lips brushed his earlobe in a slow, languid tease. "Partner with me. We'd be an unstoppable team."

A current pulled him from the solid ground of vows and principles. Vivian's scent filled his lungs. Beneath his skin, insistent heat thudded, shattering his resolve.

He bit the inside of his cheek. Desperate restraint held him back from the edge. But that edge was shrinking as Vivian pressed closer, her breath hot at his ear. A small voice whispered in his soul, about Debra, about sin, about God. Each warning clawed at his conscience, begging him to run before it was too late.

He remained seated. "Vivian," he managed, "I—I can't. I'm a married man."

The protest sounded flimsy, more plea than command.

She chuckled. "Everyone hungers for more, Jason. Why pretend you're different?" Her arms wrapped around his neck, fingers sliding into his hair. His skin turned electric. "Say yes. Be my partner. We'll give it our all and aim for the win. Don't worry about what others think. No one is going to find out."

Her tone curled around him, imbued with promise and peril. His heart hammered, his reason dissolving in the haze of her presence. She leaned toward his mouth, so close he sensed the faint tremble of desire between them. One of her hands moved down to his thigh. Her fingertips traced intricate circles that blossomed outward at a hypnotic pace. Each motion issued a silent invitation to step across a boundary he'd drawn for himself long ago.

Lust for the forbidden crashed through his body. The gallery's open expanse seemed to collapse until the world funneled down to the last fragile line separating choice from surrender, faithfulness from temptation.

Before he could cover her lips with his, flashing fluorescents painted the marble with crimson and ice blue. A digital voice echoed down the hall. "Emergency! Please evacuate immediately."

He froze.

A distant crack, like gunfire, reached them. Vivian's eyes widened. She whirled toward the window. "What—?"

A second noise, the unmistakable thunder of helicopters overhead, cut through. Floodlights swept in wide arcs through the floor-to-ceiling glass.

Jason ducked by instinct.

Vivian hissed. "Who called the police? They're not supposed to…"

The alarm's din swallowed her breathless words.

The doors opened, revealing gallery staff, a security guard, and a few early arrivals.

Jason stood, but Vivian seized his arm. "Please stay."

He tore free. "I must leave now."

The helicopter spotlight slid away. He ran to the lobby. His shoe slipped on the polished floor. He dodged another security guard and nearly bumped into a fire extinguisher on a marble pedestal.

Outside, a small crowd rushed out of the building, the world wild and real.

The cold air seared his lungs with each desperate breath. He descended the steps two at a time, adrenaline pulsing, head full of Debra and the Lord's mercy on him.

Behind him, the sirens faded, their banshee wail giving way to the city's familiar din. Horns, shouts, and the distant hum of early evening traffic swallowed up the evidence of what he'd almost done. What he'd almost let himself become.

As taxis barreled past, Jason leaned against a wall, laughing, shaking, his suit rumpled. He was free, clean, unscathed.

Or was he? The word *unscathed* snagged on his conscience. What if the Lord hadn't intervened? What if he'd given in to Vivian, to desire, to the lure of wealth? Would he have recognized himself in the morning? Or would it have shattered the threads of his faith, marriage, and self-respect?

He fumbled with his phone.

Debra answered on the second ring. "Are you okay?"

Breathless, he grinned. "Yeah. I am now."

She let out an audible sigh. "You sound different."

How much should he say? The truth pressed at the cage of his teeth. He'd encountered darkness and escaped, skirting the line he'd sworn never to cross. "I'll tell you the story when I get home." His throat closed up, and he released a shaky cough. "Deb, when I see you, remind me who I am and why I married you."

He hung up before she answered, leaving suspicion in his wake. What game was Vivian playing? How many pieces had she already moved into place?

Chapter Seventeen

Quanzhou, Guangxi, China
April 1852

Gentle snores from the Liang Fa's chamber drifted into the parlor. Xin curled up by the hearth, his mind hovering at the fragile partition between memory and slumber.

Soon enough, he plodded onto the cobbled lanes of Quanzhou. The air carried the iron tang of blood. Beneath the fleeing townsfolk in tattered sashes, the streets flowed red. The banners of Taiping fluttered amidst the ruin.

Lan appeared, her hands outstretched, her frightened eyes wide. "Xin, where are you?" She called again. "Xin, do not leave without me."

A tide of refugees swept her slender frame away. He fought through the throng, cold sweat prickling his brow. Yet the press of bodies, a sea of souls destined for doom, pushed him back.

Then the gunfire resumed. He glimpsed the flash of sabers. Lan reappeared. A fleeing soldier struck her waist with a weapon. She fell, her pale face etched with a silent plea.

"Lan!" Xin shouted, and his lungs filled with acrid smoke.

He reached her too late. Blood spattered the hem of her gray tunic. The city burned behind her. A temple collapsed as if heaven mourned.

Xin dropped to his knees. "Nay—"

The visage of Liang Fa loomed above. "Those who trade violence for hope reap only sorrow," he intoned, his words echoing through the emptiness.

Xin awoke, tears staining his cheeks. Yet Lan's lifeless face lingered. The war-torn world beyond the small shelter waited in eerie silence, save for his weeping.

The cock's broken crow heralded dawn. Xin, his sleep denied, shoved aside the reed-mat door with more force than he meant. The humid air closed around him, sticking to his skin. As he ducked beneath a battered red lantern, he stole a glance heavenward. Under the camphor tree's boughs sat Liang Fa, a sober figure amidst the day's birth.

Liang looked up. "So, you, too, are robbed of sleep? Dawn finds more mourners than celebrants these days."

Xin hugged his arms close, a vain attempt to compress the agitation into manageable form. "The night is full of accusations. I find no solace in dreams."

Liang Fa rose and stepped forward. "In youth, I mistook fervor for divine sanction too. What did it earn me? Ashes of hope and the dull ache of what I could not mend. But if we forsake faith, what light abides to banish the dark?"

Xin's thoughts faltered. He shook his head hard, still haunted by the cold specters of ruined Quanzhou and Miao Lan's visage. Was she safe, or—? "Our country is rife with sorrow and pitiless acts. Fields burned, villages emptied by sword or famine, mothers torn from babes. Does God behold our plight? Does He hear us in our affliction?"

Liang Fa beckoned him into the hut. "Affliction, young man, is the very lotus upon which virtue rests. Have you reflected, perchance, on the story of Job? He whom God tested, yet whose trust in the Almighty did not break."

After Liang lit a candle, he prepared tea and poured the amber liquid into two small cups. The scent of oolong drifted between them, grounding Xin.

Liang set a cup before Xin. "Job lost children, health, and wealth. In his deepest affliction, he demanded answers from the Almighty. He wept, he raged, yet never did he cease to address his God."

Xin's hands trembled as he wrapped them around the cup. "God responded to Job. What if, for us, there is only silence?"

Liang shifted on the wooden stool. "Faith is built not from receiving answers, but from God's presence." He intertwined his fingers. "I, a poor Christian servant, have seen trial and danger. The Qing has hunted me, my brethren, even the Englishman, Robert Morrison, who translated the Scriptures into our tongue. For years, we have been driven to secrecy, threatened with prison, and forced into exile, merely for proclaiming the good news. Many a night, I prayed behind shuttered windows, uncertain if dawn would bring the soldiers."

A shudder traversed Xin's frame, as if the very darkness beyond the window pressed inward with malignant intent. Little did he suspect the full measure of trial Liang had borne in pursuit of his convictions.

While Xin remained silent, the old man continued, his eyebrows knotted. "Though the law forbade us and the emperor's minions pursued us, still the Lord abided with us." Liang's voice remained steady with the force of assurance. "Then the war broke out with the British. After Qing signed the treaties with foreigners, the gates were thrown open to the missionaries." A strange light twinkled in his eyes. "Even the course of kingdoms and the march of history are under our God's sovereign sway."

Xin clenched his fists at his sides. "If suffering is meant to test our virtue, what about people who die without ever learning? Most country peasants haven't heard a word about Christ or Confucius." He stared into a dark corner. "Do their hardships lead to being saved, or are they lost forever?"

"Those are no idle queries." Liang reached out to touch Xin's arm. "My child, tell me. When your mind alights upon the image of the cross, what is it that you behold?"

Disconcerted by the unexpected question, Xin rubbed his chin. "I see Jesus suffering and dying on it."

Liang inclined his head. "And what more?"

Pursing his lips, Xin searched his memory. The story he'd learned under Missionary Roberts rose and scattered. "There were two thieves, one on each side, and Roman soldiers stationed about."

Liang withdrew his hand and folded it in his lap. "Ah, if that is the sum of your vision, then it becomes clearer why you have forsaken Missionary Roberts's path to follow the Taiping."

Xin looked up, frowning. "Why is that?"

The question sounded sharper than he intended. Had he missed something vital?

"When I consider the cross, I perceive myself crucified there instead of Jesus Christ." Liang swallowed, his voice low but firm. "I am the reason for His agony. 'Tis my sin, my very self. He took my place. I am the cause of His death."

Outside, a bell tolled, faint and mournful. Inside, the tea between them steamed with a fragile promise of hope against the shadows. A knot tightened in Xin's chest. The discourse only deepened his confusion. Perchance, he should pursue another matter?

He drew a steadying breath. "Forgive my candor. Years before, when Robert Morrison, your friend, sought to bring the Holy Word to China, did any of his company have the name of Cheung Po-Tsai, who once ruled the seas south of Guangdong?"

Liang pressed his lips together. "Aye, Cheung Po-Tsai. The Qing stationed him in Macau after he surrendered. We became friends. He presented me with a volume of the poems by Li Bai, a Tang dynasty poet, and I passed it on to Ying Chun, Si-Fen's father."

Xin inclined forward. "Did Cheung Po-Tsai assist in the work of translating the Holy Bible?"

"He may well have. Yet I cannot say with certainty, since I was absent from Macao for a time." Liang's tone turned reverent, as if invoking a name at an altar. "'Twas through me that he first made the acquaintance of my mentor, Robert Morrison."

The candle's flame wavered. The small light fought for its shape.

"Strange to find outlaws among saviors." Xin returned his attention to Liang. "Do you recall, among the translated volumes, the verse, 'Seek ye out of the book of the Lord, and read: no one of these shall fail'?"

Liang's eyes widened. "Aye. A verse from the book of Isaiah, though I confess I cannot at this moment recall the precise chapter."

A flutter rose in Xin's stomach. His voice quivered. "Is there anything that speaks to his having left a riddle?"

The old man flashed a faint smile. "Only a man with great need or great ambition would inquire thus. What are you seeking in the pirate legend?"

While Liang's question lingered, footsteps sounded on the worn boards, accompanied by a ripple of laughter. Xin exhaled at the interruption.

Ying Si-Fen entered, carrying a large tray, her silk robe cinched around her waist. Beside her strode Wang Jun. Their son, Wang Hui, bobbed forward.

"Uncle," Si-Fen greeted Liang, "you have risen early again."

Wang Jun gave a respectful bow to Liang and a querying nod toward Xin. "Pray, forgive us if we intrude."

"None at all, Master Wang." Xin rose and bowed in return.

With deft hands, Si-Fen arranged pickled tofu and vegetables beside steamed buns. The domestic tranquility of this secluded house, so distant from musket fire and the burnished terror of recent despair, infused Xin with a strange longing. Would he and Lan, if she were alive and well, one day possess such a refuge with the solace of teacups and distant birdsong?

Wang Hui gaped at Xin's every gesture in the unstudied way of a boy drawn to new friends.

At Wang Hui's side, Wang Jun ruffled the hair at the boy's crown. "Do not forget your manners."

After Liang offered a blessing upon the meal, the family ate and engaged in gentle conversation regarding the recent disturbances and conjectured as to what course the Taiping might next pursue.

Xin's attention flicked to the swords on the wall. He hesitated, pressing his fingers together. The thought slipped out before he could control it. "I notice your collection of weapons. Are you practitioners of the martial arts? Pray, forgive my curiosity. I have lately received some instruction myself."

Si-Fen's lips curved up. She sipped her tea. "My husband and I learned swordplay from my father. In calmer years, 'twas more sport than necessity. Still, we are ill-prepared for the recent event. I thank the Lord our dwelling lies so well concealed as to escape the notice of the invaders. However skillful we may be, we cannot withstand a zealous army." Her gaze darted to her son. "Hui has taken a keen interest. He tutors with his father each morning, and we allow him the wooden sword."

"Indeed." Wang Jun heaved a sigh. "I wonder whether the Taiping army has moved on. If so, we ought to go into the town and seek those in need of our aid."

"It'd be prudent to avoid any encounter with them." Si-Fen nodded. "Let us wait till we take counsel with our brethren in the faith."

"Mama?" Hui rocked forward and glanced at Xin. "If it pleases our guest, may I practice swordsmanship with him?"

Wang Jun's brow arched. "If our guest consents."

Xin set down his chopsticks. "It would be an honor. I confess that in recent months my training has suffered much from all the disturbance." His words fell with a tinge of sorrow, a remembrance of fire and flight.

Wang Jun reached for the two wooden swords in the corner. "Hui, remember to respect our guest. Each strike is a question, each parry an answer."

Hui's eyes sparkled as he followed Xin outside into the sun-dappled courtyard. Light and shadow danced through the tree branches. The family moved beside the doorway to watch.

Hui bowed in proper form. Xin returned it. In that instant, the age and status between them evaporated.

They circled each other. Hui struck first, feet shifting with an unexpected swiftness that belied his age. The blade arced. Xin, surprised, met it with a parry.

"Excellent footwork," the boy's father praised.

Encouraged, Hui advanced. His movements undulated from side to side, as if emulating the form of a certain beast. Perhaps a cobra? His gaze sharpened and hovered over Xin's vital acupoints.

Xin lowered his body to shift his center of gravity, muscles coiling in anticipation as he searched for the gap in his opponent's intent. Yet Hui twisted his blade beneath Xin's guard, a move full of audacious improvisation.

"Watch out!" shouts escaped the onlookers.

Xin yielded ground, his skills dulled by weeks of hunger and trauma.

With a swift sweep, Hui lunged.

Xin moved back so fast he almost lost his balance. Only his reflexes let him block Hui's fierce attack. They stepped apart for a moment to catch their breath and size each other up.

Hui narrowed his eyes and darted right. His sword tip grazed an acupoint on Xin's waist, enough to call a point, but not harm.

Xin dropped his weapon. "You have bested me."

The courtyard burst into applause.

Putting his hands together, he bowed to Hui. "I am honored to bear witness to your prowess."

Crimson colored Hui's cheeks. He gave his sword to his mother. "You let me win."

Xin bowed again. "Nay, Hui. You pressed your advantage with a keen spirit."

They returned to breakfast together. Outside, the bell tolled once more, a reminder that every day was a new chance, no matter how haunted its beginning.

Wang Jun took the last sip of his congee and rose from his seat. "Xin, we are obliged to visit our faith community and ascertain more of the matter. I pray you make yourself at ease in our home. My wife has prepared fried rice for your lunch. And do not attempt to rejoin the Taiping. They would account you a deserter and put you to death."

"Aye. I understand." Xin's heart quickened. Might heaven grant him the chance to search the house for the book of Isaiah? Within its pages, would he discover the clue to the pirate's buried treasure?

Chapter Eighteen

Kowloon, Hong Kong, China
Winter 2022

Jason looped his arm through Debra's, and they left their favorite barbecue duck joint. Sunlight dappled the pavement in amber pools as they strolled through the cool afternoon air. The scent of barbecue still clung to them. "Deb, where are you in reading Dad's manuscript about the Taiping Heavenly Kingdom?"

Debra exhaled into the cold air. "Before we left, I was reading about the unexpected meeting between Xin and Wang Jun's family, including Liang Fa."

Sliding his free hand into his coat pocket, Jason brushed a crumpled receipt. "Ha! I'm ahead of you in my reading. I remember that was after the Quanzhou massacre, right?"

"Correct." She nudged a pebble with her shoe. "It's strange. The Taiping was so extreme, so violent, but parts of their revolution, such as banning foot binding and allowing women to become soldiers, were progressive for their era."

He retrieved the receipt for a peek. Right—dim sum with a mainlander last week. "Be prepared. Dad's story is about to take a dramatic turn."

"Don't spoil it for me." Debra took the piece of paper from him. "Lunch with a client last week? Anything solid coming out of it?"

"No news yet." He stuck the receipt back in his pocket, then surveyed the cluster of gleaming skyscrapers across Victoria Harbour. Vivian's penthouse flickered through his thoughts. Since the gallery party, she hadn't contacted him. He exhaled hard, almost a laugh.

Praise the Lord for His mercy and protection.

This was how it needed to be. The boundaries he'd set must have taken hold. Good thing he hadn't divulged anything that might hurt Debra. There was no reason to, unless Vivian decided to make another move in her game. "Human nature is full of contradictions. I'm thankful for the Almighty's presence among us. Without God, humankind would have plunged into ruin of our own making."

"Yeah, history is in God's control." Debra pulled him to a stop beneath a lamppost. "Can you imagine being a woman in the 1850s? All that hope, and all that risk. One foot in the old world and one in the new. Nice to learn more about Ying Si-Fen. In Dad's last manuscript, she was a heroine through and through."

He gaped at her oval face. So lovely. How could he even consider another woman? Paul Newman's famous quote sprang to mind. For sure, when a man had steak at home, he wouldn't dream about hamburgers. "The world still seems teetering like that. Move forward, then snap back."

"Well said." Her head tilted. "The Taiping movement started out religious, revolutionary. For a short while, everything tipped upside down—more equality, at least in theory. But old habits crept in. Nothing's simple."

Jason took her hand and traced his thumb over her wedding band. His mind flicked to Vivian's smile. What was she up to? Did she find someone to work with? His phone buzzed. He loosened his hold on Debra and clicked it open. An inquiry from a mainland buyer looking for office space in Sheung Wan. He promised to text the caller the place and time for them to meet and hung up.

A different ringtone trilled. Debra fished her phone out of her purse and answered it. "It's Professor Li," she mouthed, then switched to speakerphone.

Jason drew her to a bench in a quiet corner inside the Star Ferry Terminal.

"Debra, I received a rather interesting call." Professor Li sounded amused. "A woman named Vivian Jiang reached out to me. Is she your friend?"

Debra's shoulders stiffened. "She's Jason's high school classmate."

Professor Li chuckled. "She offered funding, Debra. Quite a lot of it. She mentioned your name and said she wants us to collaborate on studying the vitamin D receptor using artificial intelligence. I did a quick online search about her. Her company, Sinogene Pharmatech Holdings, is a state-owned enterprise. Well-funded and expanding fast."

Jason arched an eyebrow. So, Vivian was up to something. She'd changed her tactics.

"I didn't expect this at all." Debra fidgeted. "Did she say more?"

"That's the gist." Professor Li paused. "It's about your project. She seems familiar with our protocols. Did you give her access?"

Creases formed on Debra's forehead. "When she invited Jason and me to dinner, she asked me about my research. I gave her a brief introduction. That was all."

"The money's tempting. And the university is always encouraging us to get out of the ivory tower and engage with the 'real world,' but I won't do anything unless you approve. Let's discuss more about it when you come to the lab tomorrow."

The line clicked dead.

"Wow, Vivian meant it when we met with her last time." Debra gripped her phone tightly. "Not sure what she has in mind."

The low drone of the city rushed in. Jason stared out at the harbor. "She moves fast."

Debra gaped at him. "What do you mean?"

He hesitated. The charged edge of Vivian's laughter echoed in his memory, the sly way her knees brushed against his, her fingers caressing his thigh… He wanted to bare it all, but the confession stuck in his throat. He pressed his lips tight. "Just a hunch. She seemed interested in what you're doing."

"Professor Li made it sound like—" Debra gave him a sidelong look. "She knew technical details I hadn't mentioned during our dinner together. Did you…?"

His jaw tightened at her unfinished sentence. "Are you implying I told her?"

"I didn't say that. But people slip sometimes, especially with an old friend." She searched his face. "It feels off."

A knot formed in his chest. "You think I gave her your confidential information over coffee?" His tone sharpened.

She stood up. "I don't know what to think anymore. I don't know her motives. And I don't know why she's suddenly everywhere."

He rose as well, stretched to his full height, and stared down at her. "I could ask you the same about your lab. About all those late nights and—" The unfair thought twisted, but it was out now.

A muscle trembled in her jaw. "Don't deflect."

He put his hands up as if to ward her off. "I didn't tell her anything, okay?"

She remained mute.

Silence expanded between them, broken only by a ferry horn from the water.

At last, she shook her head. "Let's just go home."

He wanted to reach for her again, but she kept her arms crossed over her chest. The familiar closeness between them slipped away.

❋ ✧ ❋

Days passed in an uneasy quiet, each conversation between them shorter than before. Then Debra informed him that Professor Li had set up a meeting with Vivian for them all.

The following Tuesday, he and Debra took the train to a dim sum restaurant in Sha Tin, a town near the Chinese University of Hong Kong.

"So, this is the famous joint near Chinese U?" Jason sat and surveyed the settings. "Professor Li has good taste."

Debra nodded, fidgeting with a linen napkin. "Let's see what Vivian has to say."

Professor Li strolled in and slid in beside them. "Good afternoon. Have you ordered yet?"

"Only tea." Debra dropped the napkin on her lap and poured tea for him. "We'll wait for Vivian."

Almost on cue, Vivian entered, clad in a Chanel suit. She dropped her Birkin onto the floor before taking the last remaining seat. From the next table, four women gawked at the blue leather bag with a subtle Hermès logo, unable to hide their envy.

"Thank you all for coming." She smiled. "I hope you don't mind—I took the liberty of requesting the chef's special for us."

"Of course not." Professor Li sipped his tea. "So tell us more about your proposal, Vivian."

She steepled her fingers. "I meant what I said about funding. My company has an interest in AI and wants to invest in translational research. Your lab's work on the vitamin D receptor is exactly what we're after." She nodded to Debra. "Especially your ideas about using deep learning to map receptor-ligand interactions. With the right resources, you could get results in a fraction of the time."

Jason studied her over the steam curling from his tea. "You already seem familiar with the details." He set the cup down with deliberate care, his hands visible on the table between them as a silent barrier. "How?"

Vivian's lips curved. "Debra mentioned Chinese U had filed a patent. Easy. All I needed to do was pull it out."

A server arrived with plates of lotus root and sautéed snow pea shoots. Debra glanced at Jason and Professor Li, then returned her attention to Vivian. "Are you planning to take over our IP?"

Vivian chuckled. "Not at all. I want to partner with you. We bring funding. You and Professor Li form a new company and license the patent from the Chinese U."

Professor Li tapped the table. "We are cautious about academic freedom."

Another server brought abalone dumplings, xiaolongbaos with crab roe, wagyu beef puffs, and foie gras spring rolls. He set down the dishes. "The imperial bird's nest will be served later."

"Sure, thanks." Vivian waved and focused back on Professor Li. "Totally understood. My legal team will talk to the university's office."

Debra's cheeks flushed crimson. "What's my role in the company?"

"Up to you and Professor Li." Vivian picked up a dumpling with chopsticks. "Or, if you wish, Jason can join as director."

Jason glanced at Debra. For a second, the hullabaloo of the restaurant faded to her oval face, her brow creased as if hope wobbled somewhere between fear and intrigue.

She swallowed her mouthful of beef. "And you? What will be your role, Vivian?"

"Esther Fok, an attorney and a member of my team, will serve on the board with you." Vivian cut the dumpling in half. "Doesn't the university always encourage scientists to become entrepreneurs? Here's your opportunity."

A slow tingle ran down Jason's spine. He exhaled. "How do you protect your investment?"

"Besides Fok being a part of your board, we'll sign a standard declaration of trust between us." Vivian's eyes glinted. "A common practice in Hong Kong, breaking no rules." She raised her teacup. "Well? Are you in?"

Action hung suspended. The city's shimmer reflected in Vivian's ruthless optimism. The future had slipped free of all obligations except for its own desires.

They ate and talked about science, politics, and the names of streets only locals knew. Each topic skirted possibility, coded in half jokes and sideways glances. Beneath the easy laughter, the undercurrent held.

After they finished the imperial bird's nest, a server arrived with their dessert, the egg tart. Debra stirred her tea. "When do you need a decision?"

"No rush." Vivian put down her chopsticks. "But the sooner we start, the sooner we make an impact."

Professor Li's lips crinkled up. "Well, if it is a partnership, I wouldn't mind seeing how it evolves."

Vivian raised her teacup again. "To new science and good food." She placed her teacup back on the table. "We have to complete a few things before anything else, of course."

Professor Li squinted. "The usual?"

Drawing a thin leather folio from her bag, Vivian opened it to reveal a short stack of documents. "Confidentiality is step one. I've brought draft nondisclosure agreements for everyone sitting here and others on your respective teams. You'll want your counsel to confirm, but the terms are fairly standard—no sharing unpublished results, commercial details, or any aspects of the proposal until we're ready."

Jason knitted his eyebrows as he read the first page. "And what about the university's requirements? They're pretty strict on IP."

"That's where due diligence comes in." Vivian waved. "Your legal team, my advisors, and Professor Li's office can all do a thorough review. Nothing moves forward until everyone is satisfied with the structure and risks."

Debra sucked in a breath, as if her hope now tangled with new anxieties. "So, after signing the confidentiality agreement, what happens next? A letter of intent?"

With a small nod, Vivian leaned forward. "Or a memorandum of understanding. Either way, it clarifies expectations on both sides. The document isn't binding, but it gives us something straightforward to show our lawyers and compliance teams."

Professor Li adjusted his glasses. "Compliance checks too? Even if it's private at the start?"

"That's the way." Vivian took a bite of the tart and swallowed. "We all do background checks. On each other, on prospective partners, and on other relevant issues, including university requirements."

Jason huffed, overwhelmed. He met Debra's eyes, finding love and trust in them. A knot twisted in his chest.

Should he bare the truth about his previous encounters with Vivian? What game was she playing?

Debra folded her napkin. "Fair enough. We'd want the same protections if the roles were reversed."

With a quick grin, Vivian slid the folder across. "Please take the weekend to look over the documents. We'll set up a meeting with everyone's legal team soon."

Professor Li raised his fork. "To paperwork, then. The only obstacle to real progress."

Laughing under her breath, Vivian tapped the stack. "And the first sign of success."

The new enterprise they'd begun sketching took on the first contours of reality. They clinked cups and finished the dessert in companionable silence.

On the train, Debra slipped her arm through Jason's. "I'm sorry I doubted you the other day, honey. Vivian dug up the details of our project by studying our patent. She seems excited about what we're working on, don't you think?"

His grip on the handrail tightened. He stole a glimpse of Debra's profile. Her kindness, her warmth, and her dedication to science… Tenderness mixed with fear swelled in his chest. "Vivian is determined." He searched for a suitable phrase. "I'm not sure she knows where the boundary is. Not just with science."

She tipped her head, lips thinning. "Yeah? You think she'd try to take credit for our work?"

He managed a strained chuckle. "No, not exactly. There are other ways people can disrupt a partnership, even if it's not their intention. We should keep our guard up."

"You're right." Debra squeezed his hand. "I guess in this field, you never figure out what someone's after."

If only he could come clean and tell her about his tense moments with Vivian.

The train slowed at their station.

They stepped onto the platform, the future uncertain.

Chapter Nineteen

Quanzhou, Guangxi, China
April 1852

The hut grew silent, save for the occasional creak of floorboards shifting under Xin's feet. Dust floated in the late morning sun. His heartbeat thrummed with nervous trills. He inhaled, then pushed open Liang Fa's chamber door. His gaze fell upon the battered chest in a corner. Did the preacher keep his belongings there?

Xin's fingers twitched with restless indecision.

"An honorable man never begs or steals…" Baba's words surfaced as if he stood alive before him. Did Confucius utter such wisdom?

He wrinkled his brow. Bible verses echoed in his conscience. "Thou shalt not covet thy neighbor's goods."

How many times had Roberts's gentle voice intoned those sacred teachings? Now, in the lonely morning, they rang all the louder.

Xin pressed his fist to his lips, steadying the desperate flutter of his spirit.

Another vision, Lan's beautiful oval face sweet as spring rain, intruded. She'd squeezed his hand and whispered, "You have an honorable soul and a fierce determination. That is worth more to me than all the gold."

His breath trembled. To search his host's possessions, even for a pirate's riddle promising treasure—was it not a betrayal of all he had been taught? His skin prickled, but… What would become of him and Lan if he let this chance slip away?

He hovered on the precipice, his feet rooted as ancient pines, unwilling to cross the threshold. His gaze fell on the chest again. Amidst the light spots on it, the glazed eyes of the helpless peddler, whom he had run through with his sword, emerged.

In comparison with such a merciless deed, what was an act of theft?

Xin lowered his head in silent apology and stepped forward.

The once brilliant lacquer that bedecked the chest's surface had yielded to the merciless passage of years. He lifted the lid covered with delicate carvings. The trunk opened to reveal a veritable trove of books and journals with their edges curled, maps grown brittle because of age, and a collection of enigmatic artifacts.

A dagger, its hilt studded with gems, gleamed. He took it up, the metal cold in his palm. His lips crinkled up at the incongruity. "This, I daresay, would seem more fitting as a pirate's booty than as part of Liang Fa's collection."

Sunrays streamed in from the window, casting long banners across the floor. He relinquished the dagger, letting it settle atop the other contents. He reached for a book and ran his fingers over the title in elegant calligraphy, *Good Words to Admonish the Age*.

Anguished recollections surged up. The day Roberts had given him a similar volume, the inspiration it sparked in the Heavenly King to start the Taiping movement, yesterday's massacre...

He exhaled hard. What if Liang had never set his pen to such momentous purpose? What other path might history have chosen, had the book never found its way to the Heavenly King?

A remote bell tolled, stirring him from his melancholy. He set aside Liang's work and looked at the remaining manuscripts, each one bearing the quiet weight of years. At length, he rested a hand on a substantial volume, its cloth cover faded to a twilight blue, the word *Isaiah* embossed in English above its Chinese counterpart. He flipped through it and discovered a swollen page in the thirty-fourth chapter. Someone before him had already cut along the margin and split it apart. There, wedged close like a sin, hid a slip of foolscap.

Xin retrieved it and devoured the characters.

Seek where spirits roam on moon-pearl sands,

> At the dragon's breath, an entrance stands.
> Climb with courage to the watcher's crest,
> Face northward for your quest.
>
> There the hidden trove shall lie,
> Sheltered from storms beneath the pirate's sigh.
> Gaze toward waters embracing ancient stone,
> A book's gleaming secret shown.
>
> Legends slumber yet dare be told,
> Lies the treasure, resplendent in jewels and gold.
> Beware the curse, its silent stare,
> For shadows weave death's snare.

He read it again.

"Now, I comprehend the first riddle's intent," he muttered under his breath.

"Within a language eastward born where wisdom's roots bind faith to pages worn" must have referred to the Chinese translation of the Holy Bible, and "Tarry not. Another lies in wait with secrets more profound" signified the presence of a second riddle.

The verses in the current riddle pulsed with unraveled mysteries. What did they mean?

The wind bellowed beyond the thin pane, as if sorrowing for the chieftain who once ruled the tempest-tossed shores. Xin sat on Liang Fa's cot and brushed a finger over the opening line.

"'Where spirits roam on moon-pearl sands,'" he recited aloud. Could it be a certain place by the sea, swollen with tales of marauders and the ghosts of lost fortunes? The hair on his neck prickled.

Oh, how he wished Lan were at his side. With her keen intellect, the riddle would doubtless have yielded its meaning in short order.

He traced a finger along the next cryptic clue. "'The dragon's breath' might allude to an entrance of a coastal cave, hidden among jagged cliffs." He tightened his grip on the paper. "'Climb with courage to the watcher's crest.'" His brow furrowed. Was it a wayfarer's signal to seek the highest lookout over the restless ocean expanse? And what of "Face northward for your quest"? Did the treasure lie that way?

"'Sheltered from storms beneath the pirate's sigh.'" His voice quavered with newfound hope. He drew a deep breath. Surely, a quiet enclave existed, where legends were secreted away.

He rose and paced the small room. "And does 'gaze toward waters embracing ancient stone' describe some outcropping by the water?"

A knot formed in his stomach. Taken together, the hints pointed to a peak facing the north, shielded by the cliffs, and inside a cave. Xin sank once more onto the cot. He must procure a map to ascertain the location.

His skin tingled. He hastened to the chest and sifted through the maps within. One by one, he drew them forth and spread each upon the cot to study by the golden glow. At length, he chose three.

The first chart, a coarse oil-stained sheet, depicted a tract of jagged rocks ascending from the sea. Clustered in silent vigil against the monsoon, the land tapered into slender isthmuses fringed by palms and wild hibiscus. Along the edges, some cautious soul had drawn faint red lines. Perchance a warning about perilous tides and invisible undertows.

The second, of a finer quality, appeared to have been inscribed by a scholar's methodical hand. Boulders arched over a sheltered ocean cove. The neat script bordering the shadowed bay warned, "Avoid the undertow and trust instead in the guidance of the stars above."

The last was the oldest of them all, its once dark ink faded almost to gray. Along the shore, a curious procession was limned in the pallid light. Their dress and bearing bespoke not common travelers but lawless mariners. Most notable was a faint sketch of a lone wretch standing with arms flung wide, perchance in desperate supplication or in sinister invitation.

Xin rolled the three maps tight, slid them into his satchel, and stepped into the morning light. His recent dream of Miao Lan clung like smoke. The street smelled of river silt and damp stone. A shutter banged. A cock crowed. Was she safe? Did the Taiping host remain in Quanzhou? If so, was it prudent to venture within its walls, or should he heed Wang Jun's counsel and keep aloof for a time?

And if he found her, would she cast her lot with him in search of the pirate chief's gold?

Alas, he must steal about and learn what he might.

He lengthened his stride. Near the outskirts, iron boots clattered, and angry shouts shattered the calm. Four Qing soldiers, helmeted brass catching the light, appeared. Xin froze under their notice. One of them, a broad-shouldered fellow, shouted, "Stop, you! What is your business here?"

Xin's mind reeled for escape, yet his feet would not move. A strange recognition troubled his soul. He might have been looking at his mirror image.

The soldier, perhaps in his midtwenties, possessed a sturdy, square jaw and an upright manner. His almond-shaped eyes carried a glimmer at once wary and resolute under thick, well-defined brows. The straight nose lent quiet balance to a countenance marked by dignity.

The man also stared. Then he stepped closer. "Xin?" His whisper carried a tremor. "Is it—can it be you?"

"Zhang Hao?" Xin's throat tightened.

His elder brother, his own flesh and blood. The world contracted into a slender space, a brother, long lost, discovered anew beneath blade and command. Faint recollections arose, childhood laughter, Baba's tales spun by firelight, the comfort of Mama's soup...

A stout soldier, his craggy face bearing a scar, spat and raised his sword. "Long, messy hair. Must be a refugee from the Taiping. Nobody can save you from the emperor's justice."

Zhang Hao's eyes flashed under the battered brim of his soldier's cap. In a lightning motion, he drew a dagger hidden inside his cloak. The blade caught the sun as he plunged it into the scarred fellow's exposed neck. Crimson flowed forth in a terrible rush. The man gurgled like a slaughtered pig, his weapon clattering to the ground.

The second soldier, young and sickly pale, fumbled for the spear strapped along his back. Before he raised the weapon, Zhang Hao brought his foot upward in a fierce arc that struck the youth beneath the jaw. A crack sounded as blood and shattered teeth burst from his mouth. He collapsed, limbs splayed, his fate sealed by Hao's merciless blow.

Above them, an indifferent bird chirped from a tree branch. The last of the three soldiers tried to flee, his boots slipping in the gore. Zhang Hao seized the abandoned sword and, with a practiced strike, cleaved the man from shoulder to waist. A grotesque spray of scarlet stained the earth, seeping toward Xin's feet.

For a brief interval, naught but the gasp of the dying and the fevered cry of a magpie above disturbed the solemn stillness. Xin's heart pounded, each thud loud. All around him, blood mixed with dirt, evidence of what his brother had done.

Zhang Hao's jaw tightened. Yet his chin trembled. "Xin, why are you here? Speak quickly. Where are Baba and Mama?"

The question struck Xin with the force of a blow. "Baba and Mama…" His lips fumbled, his gaze flicking to the corpses before fastening on his brother. "They departed this world soon after you were seized for service."

Hao looked past Xin as though searching some distant hope in the gloom. "Alas, I feared as much." His shoulders sagged. Then he straightened again. "And you? How have you endured? This world devours the lonely."

Xin sucked in a quick breath. "I have done what I must." His voice quavered as he gave a brief recount of the years. "'Tis a hard season, but now I have found you—"

Hao hacked a rough cough into his crimson-stained sleeve, then lifted his head. His battle-worn eyes still held a lingering ember. "I have doomed myself already. Whatever befalls me, you shan't sink with me. Promise me, Xin. Leave the Taiping. Swear you will cling to life, not ruin."

Xin's stomach twisted. Images of the defenseless peddler, whom he had pierced with his sword yesterday, seemed to reflect in Hao's haunted gaze. He swallowed down agonized emotions—fright for the hardened men he and his brother had become and grief for the innocence neither of them could reclaim.

Hao knows not that my soul is already fouled beyond saving.

A chill wind swept around, carrying with it the faintest hint of plum blossom. Before Xin replied, Hao trudged away with the stiff gait of a man who dared not linger.

"Hao, pray, wait for me!" Xin's cry broke as he flung out a desperate hand.

Hao turned, his voice clipped. "I cannot tarry here, nor can you, lest ruin be our joint fate. We must alter our appearances so our foes know us no longer. Come. We depart at once."

Amid the scarlet ring of slaughter, the brothers bound their fates together once more.

Chapter Twenty

Kowloon, Hong Kong, China
Winter 2022

Vivian's proposal refused to leave Jason's mind. The initial due diligence had been completed. Anxiety haunted him throughout the process. Every passing day, he ached to bare his secrets, to confess everything to Debra, to stop it. Yet, for fear of hurting her, he'd kept quiet. Tomorrow, the team, including Professor Li, would meet again to finalize the terms.

While the city's lights pulsed like a distant warning, he helped clean up after dinner. "Deb, have you finished reading the chapters about the impact of the Quanzhou massacre on Xin in Dad's manuscript?"

"Yeah." Debra wiped the dining table with a paper towel. "The event changed him. His moral yardstick shifted. In desperation, he moved against everything he'd been taught and stole the maps from people who showered him with kindness."

Jason stacked the plates, each clink sharp and unresolved, echoing the disquiet in his chest. "After Quanzhou, Xin's soul darkened somewhat. Although he still wrestled with the question of why humans suffered, he hadn't yet summoned the courage to confront the far more difficult truth that his own actions had contributed to the pain."

A shiver ran down his spine. He couldn't help but remember that night—the guilt that twisted his insides when he stood on the edge of betrayal, the weight of temptation pressing down on his resolve. Most chilling, though, was how easy it had almost happened. Like Xin, with one slip, he'd have let everything he believed about himself shattered. The abyss would have closed him off from tenderness and trust forever.

Debra paused, her hand suspended in midair. "That's the hardest part, isn't it? Most of us shy away from admitting we shape much of the suffering around us." The drain gurgled, as if in reluctant agreement. "I wonder how Dad resolved the undercurrents in the story."

Jason regarded her in the half-light. "I'm ahead of you in my reading. There are more twists."

Outside, a siren's wail seeped into their kitchen, a distant requiem for what remained unspoken.

Bedtime arrived. Following their nightly routine, they lay in bed and held hands. Debra started the prayer. "Dear Lord, thank You for the opportunities You've laid before us, and for the way You've opened doors we didn't expect." Her gentle voice blended with the sound of traffic filtering through the window. "I pray the meeting goes without a hitch so we can start this partnership soon."

She squeezed his fingers, signaling it was his turn.

He shut his eyes. His heart thumped in a restless rhythm. "Lord, You know things we don't. If this plan isn't in Your will, let something happen to prevent it. If we're meant to sign this deal, help us trust You. Give us wisdom. In Jesus' name, amen."

He tried to relax, uncertain which answer he feared most. Somewhere in the city beyond, a car horn blared. While Debra's light snore comforted him, he tossed and turned, dread flooding him until his consciousness faded into the hum of the room.

Windshield wipers clicked hard. Jason, tall even at ten, traced raindrops with his finger as they chased each other down the pane. His parents' voices murmured from the front seats. The jasmine scent of his mother's hair mingled with the spice of his father's aftershave.

The scene changed.

A shriek, grinding metal, splintering glass… His mother's desperate gasp filled the small space. The car lurched, spinning, the seat belt cutting into his chest. The scream in his throat never made it out.

The street faded into the background. Adults spoke in low, sorrowful tones. His world narrowed to the harsh reality that he'd lost his parents. Then Grandpa, a busy attorney, approached and hugged him.

Jason jerked awake in the darkness, his nightwear soaked with cold sweat. He had never sat in that wrecked Volvo on a rain-choked day, but the nightmares always placed him inside.

He tried to slow his breath, counting backward from ten like his previous therapist taught.

Debra stirred and placed a hand on his cheek. "Another bad one?"

He nodded and remained rigid in silence.

She didn't press and folded herself around him, holding him until he fell into a shallow doze.

The alarm clock blared at eight. Jason awoke exhausted. Debra had already left for the lab. On the kitchen countertop lay a thermos of tea and a sticky note scrawled with *Love you*. He poured a cup of tea and choked down a piece of toast.

His phone buzzed. A text message arrived from Vivian. "I'm reminding everyone. 10 a.m., Pacific Place. We'll bring the paperwork."

His stomach tightened into a knot as he packed his briefcase. The vivid dream had loosened more dread.

After a short ride on the MTR subway, he got off at Jordan and met with Debra and Professor Li in the lounge of Pacific Place, a marble world of luxury. Sunlight bared every flaw on the high-polished floor. Debra's nervous energy radiated out in the click of nails on her phone and a muscle twitch on her jaw.

Vivian swept in, a blue silk scarf knotted at her neck, her scent assertive. Esther Fok arrived moments later.

"Glad we could all meet so quickly." Vivian's voice dripped with honey.

They settled at a table tucked away from the crowd. Jason halfway listened as Esther outlined the terms again, the legalese like a net tightening around his throat. Each page they reviewed added weight on his chest.

Vivian fixed on Debra. "The university's research office already sent us an email from its compliance team. We'll need your tech-transfer timeline."

Jason breathed, but the cup in his hand trembled. The clatter of cutlery, the hiss of espresso machines, and the soft lilt of shoppers all screamed into an incoherent roar.

Debra shot him a worried glance. "Are you okay?"

Jason blinked, struggling to focus. "Yeah. Just tired. Didn't sleep well."

Vivian's eyes narrowed a fraction. "We can slow down if you want. But this is a competitive space. Any delays could impact the funding window."

Debra opened her laptop and brought up a slide. "Here is the timeline…"

Esther queried, and Debra answered. Jason tried to follow their discussions. The walls closed in. He gasped but couldn't get enough air.

"Excuse me." He stumbled into the corridor and gripped a cold steel railing.

Debra's footsteps sounded behind him. She touched his back. "Jason? What's wrong?"

He shook his head. "I—" The words cut off, replaced with wild gasps.

His knees buckled. The shriek, the grinding metal, the splintering glass from his nightmare… all flashed through his mind.

Debra crouched beside him, voice low and intense. "Breathe with me. In, out. In, out."

Sweat trickled down his spine. His stomach twisted, every muscle drawn taut. He grabbed his chest. "It hurts—"

"Are you having a heart attack?" She hugged his shoulders. "We need to get help."

His vision pinwheeled. The world shrank to Debra and to the thud of his heart. Strange. He saw everything as if in a dream.

Debra tapped her phone. "Ambulance." She spoke fast— English first, then Cantonese—chest pain, dizziness, shortness of breath. Queen Elizabeth Hospital.

Professor Li hovered, then helped ease him into a chair by the lobby doors.

The siren rose out of the street noise. Two paramedics swept in with a red bag and a monitor. "Sir, we're going to check your heart."

Before Jason could answer, they opened his shirt and pressed electrodes to his bare chest. A cuff tightened around his arm. A pulse clip pinched his finger.

"Chew these." One man tipped four baby aspirins into his palm while the other watched the EKG.

Jason ground the chalky tablets between his teeth. Numbers were called out in Cantonese. A gloved hand steadied his shoulder.

They lifted him onto the stretcher. Debra climbed into the ambulance beside him and stroked his hair. "Hang tight. We're almost there."

At the ER, fluorescent lights buzzed overhead. Debra spoke to the triage nurse in English, then in Cantonese.

His rapid breathing rattled in his lungs. A nurse took his pulse and wrapped a cold blood-pressure cuff around his arm. Another swapped the field leads for hospital ones, pressing more electrodes to his chest. Debra squeezed his shoulder. "You're safe. I'm here."

The nurse spoke Cantonese with an accent. "Any tingling sensation?"

He strained to answer. "Chest tight. Can't breathe."

The room smelled of disinfectant. Debra sat beside him, worry lines engraving her face.

At last, the nurse removed the EKG patches. "You are *not* having a heart attack."

After what felt like an eternity, his heart stopped drumming against his sternum. He blinked, tears stinging his eyes. The nightmare had released its grip, but left him empty.

The curtain lifted. In walked a young doctor with a clipboard. "You experienced an acute anxiety attack. Do you have a therapist or counselor?"

Jason's cheeks flushed hot. "I haven't for several years."

The doctor offered a clinical smile. "We'll give you something very mild, just to help you relax." She added with a wry little tilt of her chin. "This is common. Happens every day to hundreds. With life's pressures, lots of smart people experience stress."

Jason said nothing. Debra answered for him. "Thank you, Doctor."

They left the hospital as dusk bled into night, the city shining indifferently.

His body ached, his bones as hollow as bamboo.

At his side, Debra threaded her fingers through his. "Let's get a taxi home."

During the ride, she rested her head on his shoulder. He stared out. Exhaustion swamped gratitude, embarrassment, and a strange measure of hope.

He remained mute as they crossed back into their block, the taximeter clicking off. At the elevator, she hooked her arm through his, her frown still etched deep.

Inside their flat, with the door locked behind them, the world slowed. While she poured water into glasses, he slumped on the sofa and unbuttoned his shirt.

Debra set the glass next to him. "I've informed Professor Li, Vivian, and Esther that we'll need a couple days." She leaned into him. "Vivian said to postpone until Friday."

He rubbed his temples. "Thanks."

The faraway traffic hummed. Debra rubbed his arm and narrowed her gaze. "Jason, you've never had an anxiety attack before. Is this about the deal? Or something else?"

His mind jumped to Vivian, her husky tone, her lips brushing his ear, and the feverish, unwelcome urge that haunted him.

He heard himself speak in a thin voice. "Deb, I don't know if this deal is a good idea. Remember our prayers last night? Maybe God answered my plea and let this happen to stop us."

"That's fair. But we've involved the university and jumped through all the hoops. If we decide not to move forward, we have to give them a legit reason other than that God closed the door for us." She patted his hand. "Is that the real reason?"

His fingers fisted. "There's more."

She stared into his eyes, her gaze so open it hurt.

He swallowed hard. "Vivian tried to…" His throat tightened. "She tried to seduce me."

The words lingered between them, fragile and sharp. His cheeks burned. He looked down at the floor and confessed.

Debra said nothing. Then her knees rustled against his as she edged closer. "Did you…?" She started, then stopped. "Did anything happen?"

"Nothing happened." He snapped his head up and met her gaze. "During the first encounter, Pastor Wong called, and I seized the opportunity to escape. It happened again at the gallery party. By God's mercy, I also managed to get away. She's playing a game, although I have no idea what it is. After failing to seduce me, she switched her tactics and contacted Professor Li." Moisture rushed behind his eyelids. "I'm so sorry, Deb. I should've told you sooner."

Debra released a sigh. "Thank you for telling me. I wish you hadn't had to go through that alone." She pressed her forehead to his, her voice raw. "From what has happened, Vivian is conjuring up a scheme and is desperate enough to try anything." Her fingers wrapped around his. "Whatever her goal is, she's trying to pull us into it. I agree with you. We shouldn't move ahead with her."

"I kept it to myself because I didn't want to hurt you. But I can't fight her alone. Not anymore." He blinked, tears falling. "What shall we tell Professor Li and the university?"

"I'll share the details with Professor Li. He'll understand." She drew him into a tight hug. "And I plan to inform the university that we won't be able to complete this deal because of health issues."

He nodded, a weight lifting off his shoulders. They held each other. Unanswered questions about faith, business, and trust settled into a peaceful silence.

For now.

How long before Vivian made her next move?

Chapter Twenty-One

Quanzhou, Guangxi, China
May 1852

Xin pressed himself against a broken wall. "Think you the Taiping host is gone?" he whispered, his breath unsteady, palms damp upon the rough wood.

Hao shaded his eyes and listened to the hush. "A day has passed with no banner on the ridge. They must have moved on." He gave Xin's shoulder a gentle squeeze, and the severity in his features melted into warmth. "Tell me about this girl named Lan. You spoke of her in your sleep last night."

Xin's cheeks burned. "Miao Lan is compassionate, although she is a fierce kung fu master." His voice trembled. "Alas, her baba's disapproval shadows my every approach. He deems me unworthy on account of my humble circumstances. If I might secure some means to prove my merit…"

Compelled by raw emotions, he shared his discovery and unfolded the three maps on the ground. "These seem to pertain to the riddle I spoke of." He set before Hao the riddle he had inscribed on paper with his own hand.

Hao crouched low with a hunter's focus. His dark-eyed gaze darted across the cryptic lines. "So then…" He straightened up. "Treasure concealed by the infamous pirate chief Cheung Po-Tsai may lie hidden within our grasp. But tell me, given all you have shared, is it not possible others before us have unraveled the riddle and, in doing so, spirited away the gold and jewels?"

Xin took a step back and pressed his palm to his chest. "Oh, Hao, you speak truly. 'Tis possible others have labored before us. I confess, the thought chills me. Yet perhaps Cheung's cunning was such that none have claimed his trove. Pray, let us try. If even a glimmer of promise remains, it would be folly to shrink from the attempt."

"Fortune may choose us." Hao then read aloud from the slip of paper. "'Beware the curse, its silent stare, For shadows weave death's snare.' What a warning!" His lips twisted into a wry smile. "Men have killed for far less than this."

The casual words on Hao's tongue turned to iron in Xin's heart. "Brother." A shiver crept up his spine. Hao's merciless attack on his comrades sprang to mind. To banish the images of the three dead soldiers, Xin expelled a weighty breath. "Permit me to address one matter if you will bear with me. The call to find Miao Lan weighs upon me more than the treasure."

Hao's brow wrinkled. "More than silver buried under cursed stones? 'Tis a brazen caller indeed."

Xin inhaled and schooled his trembling into decorum. "I would first find Miao Lan." At her name, an ache rose within him. "I have dreamed of her death. Where have the Heavenly banners marched? I must find her and be assured of her welfare."

Hao scowled. "You plan to leave maps to a pirate's vault, all for a woman? Do you know what you ask?"

"I seek the treasure only for Miao Lan." Xin gentled his reply with an open hand. "Her absence has become a burden I cannot carry much farther." He drew a long breath while shadows shifted on the wall. "Gold may wait beneath the soil a hundred years and not complain. A life cannot."

A breeze blew over them. Hao jerked his head up. "The road leads us through butchered fields. The Heavenly Kingdom brooks no rivals. And you, Brother, you are a deserter. If they capture you, your doom is sealed."

"I have to try." Xin could scarcely hear his own voice for the pounding in his chest.

Hao grunted, half assent, half dismissal. "Very well. We will go to the Dragon Gate. An oarsman there owes me a favor. He has ferried the emperor's army." He lifted his chin toward the town. "I suppose a delay of a few hours shan't signify. We are in want of provisions. Let us proceed into Quanzhou, and, if fortune favors us, we shall secure them."

Xin swallowed, his throat tight. Hao laid a hand on his shoulder. Together they trudged forward.

A wind crept down Quanzhou's ruined streets, stirring char and ash upon the cobblestones. Xin's heart beat a muffled tattoo as he and Hao skirted a shattered shrine. The houses ahead carried the stench of suffering. Doors stood open, cast aside akin to forgotten prayers, while roofs gaped to heaven.

At least the bodies were gone. Who had removed them and given them burial? Perchance brethren from Wang Jun's faith community?

Hao surveyed the surroundings. "I trust the Taiping rebels have not carried off everything."

They crossed a hut's threshold. The dim interior bore witness to a life sundered. A comb, still tangled with hair, lay amid fractured fans and broken clay pots near a mat. Each fragment whispered of hands that once cherished them.

"I had dreamed, once, of becoming a teacher like Baba." Hao stooped to sift through a battered chest. "Not a ghoul searching for scraps among the ruins."

Xin stole a glimpse of his brother. A figure so familiar from the days of boyhood now bore the marks violence wrought. "But even teachers must eat." He bent to retrieve a small sack of dried beans from beneath a broken wooden table.

They spent the morning in silent labor, moving from house to shattered house. Xin scavenged through splintered wardrobes and overturned baskets until his satchel sagged with spoils. The clear sky watched as if daring the living to recall what had been lost.

Inside a hut by a ruined archway, Hao stripped off his stained blue-gray uniform and changed into civilian clothes. He gestured for Xin to sit before him on a cracked wooden stool. Unwrapping his dagger, Hao pressed the flat blade to Xin's scalp and shaved the crown, leaving a single wisp of pigtail. "Do you recall the vegetable patch behind our house?"

At Hao's memory-thick tone, the scent of fresh earth and green tendrils flickered across Xin's mind. He shifted on the stool. The image of their childhood floated between them. Mama plucked snow peas from tangled vines while he and Hao darted through sunlit rows, their laughter careless as any spring.

They were small again, running through the sunlit field. Hao, four years the elder, kept himself between Xin and harm. When Xin's knee met the gravel, Hao kneeled to wipe the blood with a wetted thumb and make light of it. He would count their steps from the mulberry to the well stone, set his bamboo hat upon Xin's head when the noon grew hot, and press into Xin's palm the sweetest pea, as though every treasure must be tasted by the younger first.

"I remember…" The answer caught in Xin's throat. The world they knew had vanished, its pleasures lost in the abyss.

After Hao swept away the fallen hair, he returned the dagger to its sheath. "If there is hope left, perchance 'tis only this. We must live for Baba and Mama and for ourselves."

A wry smile came to his mouth. "Let us proceed to find your girl. Understand me, Xin. If Cheung's ghost beckons me whilst we seek your lady, I will heed his call."

Xin nodded. A strange buoyancy lifted within him. "Let the treasure wait its turn."

The afternoon smog laid a sooty veil over the water as they hurried down to the Dragon Gate. They did not find the oarsman. Beneath a large willow, the migrants surrounded them. Dozens gathered, their bundles meager, children sallow-eyed and silent.

An old woman with a scar on her cheek caught Xin's sleeve. "I have not eaten—" Her words frayed, her language a mixture of Cantonese and a southern dialect.

Xin slipped her a bag of rice from his pack. "Where do you come from, Auntie?"

"Guilin," she muttered. "My only son left me and joined the Hongmen triad. He is turning into a criminal."

A rangy youth with a splinted arm approached. "Hong Xiuquan's army has turned into a tide. Fifty thousand brothers of the Hongmen have joined and said they are led by God Himself. The province is aflame."

Zhang Hao released a thin laugh. "The Hongmen, is it? Aye. Those oath-bound men, with sleeve-knives along the wharves, have plotted against the Qing since the first hour, swearing the old Ming shall rise again. Now they cast their lot with the Taiping."

Xin moistened his lips. His heartbeat quickened, even as his stomach lay like lead. If those brethren indeed bestirred themselves, deliverance might be won, but at the cost of more blood. The faces of the fallen rose before him, and he gritted his teeth. "Pray, do you know where the Taiping may be found?"

The woman blinked. "They are bound for Hunan. Rumor is abroad that they mean to seize Jiangning—Nanking, as the elders called it. Everywhere, the world is emptied for these new kings."

Xin glanced at the cloth wrapping the youth's arm. Was it not Miao Lan's scarf? He stepped closer and examined the binding. The silk showed a faded peony near the hem, and one errant thread had been drawn out. "Friend, whence came you by this strip?"

The youth attempted a faltering smile. "From a maiden. She pressed the bones true and said I must not move much. When the bandages were spent, she tore this from her own scarf."

"Was she alone? Do you know her name?" Xin's heart thudded in his ears.

The youth peered at him. "She was with a middle-aged woman and a boy. They called her Miao, I think—Miao Lan. The child carried a basket of bitter leaves and powders. They worked quickly among the injured."

Miao Lan is alive and well.

The words rang in him, bright and reckless. The iron band he'd been carrying around his chest loosened.

"I saw them too." The scarred woman put the sack of rice into a straw bag. "They went from one hurt soul to the next."

Zhang Hao leaned close and lowered his voice. "It seems your fair lady has also parted with the Taiping. I judge she fell in with Liang Fa's family."

Xin half smiled despite himself. So, Miao Lan had deserted her baba and the Heavenly Army after the Quanzhou massacre. Did she come searching for him?

He swallowed hard, palms damp, forcing his hands to still at his sides. "When did you see her last?"

"Several hours since." The youth shifted and drew a breath through his teeth. "The three spoke of quitting the district for Guangdong."

"Guangdong is too broad a term." Xin pressed his lips together. The dispatch crackled in his grasp, his patience brittle. "Did they name the port?"

The youth nodded. "They spoke of an island under the queen's flag, where the foreign steamers burn coal."

The old woman clicked her tongue. "Hong Kong, the Fragrant Harbor. All who fear the fire on the land creep thither, hoping it will not follow across the water."

Zhang Hao's gaze met Xin's. "If they seek the foreign island, they mean to put themselves under strange protection."

The youth shook his head. "They talked about going there to prevent a potential tragedy. Yet no details would they give."

Hao took a step away, then gestured for Xin to move. They left the refugees behind. The lane held the dull warmth of day. The murmur of the migrants faded.

"'To prevent a tragedy'?" Xin rubbed his thumb along the seam of his sleeve. "That is a grave phrase to spend on the road to Hong Kong."

"The island is all engines and ledgers. If harm is to befall, a small spark could grow large there." Hao adjusted his satchel. "Did you not mention that the chief pirate died in Macau? 'Tis not far from Hong Kong. While we hunt for Cheung Po-Tsai's gold in that direction, we may meet your Miao Lan."

"That settles it," Xin murmured.

As they journeyed forward, roadside villages, scorched in the Qing–Taiping seesaw of battles, yielded only bitter sanctuary.

At the foot of a broken pagoda, they camped. Indifferent stars huddled above like watchers who cared nothing for the fates of men.

Once more in the firelight, Xin unfolded the rice paper containing the riddle and the three maps. "Mark this, Hao. If we lay the charts one upon another, they agree. These lines suggest a cavern beneath a solitary peak."

Hao spat into the dirt. "All these riddles. I prefer the clarity of a sword. Yet the treasure calls, and a man must heed such music. Once we travel to Macau, we show these to the fishermen. Some of them will recognize the shore."

Xin's gaze fell on the riddle's last line. "Does this warning give you pause? Are we walking into death's snare?"

"If there is a snare, let it take you first. I shall step over your body and count the coin."

Did Hao mean it? Xin's mouth went dry. Bile rose sharp as metal.

Chapter Twenty-Two

Kowloon, Hong Kong, China
Winter 2022

The bowl in front of Jason sent up a curl of star-anise-scented steam. Somewhere below their apartment, a minibus honked twice. Then the sound slipped beneath the noise of the busy streets.

"I'm glad our life is back to its normal routine." Debra carried a teapot to the table. "You haven't had any nightmares during the past two weeks."

Jason's chopsticks paused midair. The slice of barbecued pork cooled before he slid it into his mouth. Sweet, smoky, and familiar. Yet his jaw worked too hard, as if he had to chew through the last echo of a scream. He swallowed and pressed his tongue to the roof of his mouth to steady himself. "Yeah. I'm thankful."

Debra set the teapot down. "You've read the part in Dad's manuscript about Xin's reunion with his brother, right? First, Xin met Liang Fa, and now he ran into his long-lost brother. Don't you think two such serendipitous encounters are statistically unlikely?"

Part of her job was using statistics to study the outliers that made the model wobble. Coincidence? Fate? Or God's design? He dropped his gaze to dodge the question's math. "Deb, although it's fiction and an author can do whatever he wants, Dad didn't resort to serendipity out of laziness." His father-in-law, a world-famous writer, hinted at his conversion to Christianity in his last manuscript. "As a storyteller making a point, he wrote Xin and Hao into each other's paths not because statistics demanded it, but because he intended to show that probability is a backdrop, not a destiny. What we call fate is under God's guidance."

"How about the swordplay?" Debra took the seat opposite him. "It's hard to believe a ten-year-old boy would beat Xin."

He let out a light chuckle. "You're taking it too seriously. In kung fu novels, a slight girl is able to topple a giant. Training under a master for years matters more than size. Xin trained with Miao Lan's father for about a year, while Wang Hui had probably studied under two masters since he was a toddler."

His phone vibrated. The screen lit up. He wiped soy sauce from his hand, touched the green button, and squinted at the characters before the English preview slid into place. A WeChat message from Vivian. "Can you and Debra meet with me tomorrow at my penthouse? I want to discuss the next steps. Very important."

While he read it again, Debra topped off their cups with hot jasmine tea. The steam fogged her oval face for a moment. "You look troubled. What's wrong?"

He angled the phone. The message lay between them, reflected in the gloss of the table. "Vivian. She requests we talk about the next steps." He let the last two words hang in the air.

Debra picked up her teacup. A sesame seed clung to the pad of her thumb. "That's unexpected."

"Didn't you and Professor Li tell her we decided not to move forward with the project?" He kept his voice low, as if the walls might pass the conversation along to the stairwell.

"We did." Debra blew on her tea. "We were clear."

The screen reflected his image. His hair a little wild from the humidity, he looked tired, even though he hadn't done much in the morning. Vivian's penthouse, the floor-to-ceiling glass with its harbor view, the wine, her breath on his ear… How long ago had that happened? Why did she continue to bug them? "She says it's important. Maybe she refused to accept our decision or doesn't want to."

"Vivian is a drama queen. Everything is important." A crease formed on Debra's forehead. The sesame seed on her thumb fell to the table. "We're visiting Grandpa tomorrow. Let's ignore her for now and finish our lunch."

He put the phone down and reached for his bowl. His appetite had thinned, but he lifted the noodles anyway. Outside, a patch of cloud moved in. Inside, the shadows on the wall shifted, turning the tea a deeper amber. The tightness in his chest loosened a notch. Yeah. He'd see Grandpa tomorrow. Something solid to hold on to.

By the next afternoon, the sky had lowered to a dull pewter lid, pressing the city's noise into a muted hum. Jason and Debra crossed the lobby tiles of Grandpa's building. The security guards at the desk smiled at them in recognition. One of them, the older with the cleft in his chin, offered a wave that had the warmth of routine.

Jason waved back. He'd grown up on these hellos, the nods of men who'd watched him race in and out of winter afternoons. The elevator moved them to the twelfth floor.

Mrs. Liu, Grandpa's caretaker, answered the door. "Come, come." She stepped aside for them to enter. "Mr. Guan is waiting for you."

Sunlight pooled across the living room. A clock ticked near a framed calligraphy scroll, and somewhere deeper in the flat, the kettle rumbled toward a boil.

Grandpa rose, slower than he used to, but still with a stubborn sturdiness. Jason closed the distance between them, dropped his backpack, and reached for him. The embrace brought moisture to his eyelids. Grandpa's back seemed narrower than he remembered, but the steady grip hadn't changed. The aftershave rose like a time capsule. "Grandpa, nice to see you."

"Good to see you too, my boy." Grandpa patted Jason's shoulder before he turned to Debra. "And you, Deb." He gestured for them to sit together.

Debra slipped onto the sofa on Grandpa's other side, tucking a loose strand of hair behind her ear. "Grandpa, you look in good spirits today."

"Yeah, I'm tough." He grinned, the skin at the corners of his eyes folding into familiar maps. "How's your research? Any new development?"

Debra's gaze flicked to Jason. "It went well. We almost signed a deal with a Chinese company, but it didn't go through."

"Oh?" Grandpa arched an eyebrow.

Debra's fingers danced a soft rhythm on the sofa's armrest. The tinny sound brought heat to Jason's cheeks.

He fidgeted.

Her mouth pressed into a thoughtful line. Then she laid out all the details. "We've decided not to work with Vivian. Still, I'm puzzled why she came across so desperate and manipulative."

The kettle whistled in the kitchen. Mrs. Liu's silhouette moved at the edge of Jason's vision.

"Grandpa, I almost messed up with Vivian. I try to honor God in everything I do, but when I'm tempted, my strength deserts me." He swallowed. Shame slid hot under his collar, a flush that made his shirt feel too tight. His thumb traced the cushion's seam.

Mrs. Liu returned with a tray, set the teapot and three cups on the table, and excused herself. From afar, a siren threaded the city's low hum and then faded. Grandpa closed his hand over Jason's. "My boy, I'm glad you shared everything with Deb. That takes guts. You don't have to act stronger than you are. And be wise to avoid similar situations in the future."

Jason nodded. He squeezed Grandpa's fingers back. The sunlight settled around them with the same old peace.

Debra's mouth formed a hard line. "If Vivian hadn't tried to seduce Jason and had instead approached Professor Li and me first, we might already have signed the agreement with her."

The word *seduce* hung in the air. Jason shifted in his seat again. "It's beyond odd." His voice came out flatter than he'd intended. "Why did Vivian try so hard to involve us? Why couldn't she use her own name to set up her company?"

Grandpa poured the tea. The steam rose and slipped away toward the ceiling. "Hmm." He offered them the cups. "She wanted you to lend her your names?"

Late afternoon humidity pressed against the windows. The syrupy heat seeped through even the best seals.

Debra gathered her hair into a low knot. A loose strand clung to her damp temple. "She mentioned restrictions on the mainland are strict, particularly around state-owned enterprise assets. If she does it through us in Hong Kong, she could bypass the rules. She kept emphasizing it'd be good for us too. The profit share would be generous."

"Generous," Grandpa echoed. "That word is dangerous."

Jason took a sip. The hot oolong bit his tongue, and its welcome sting gave his jaw something else to clench.

"Professor Li and I believed her at first." Debra's breath hitched. "We liked the SOE angle. Then Jason experienced a severe anxiety attack and—"

He avoided her gaze. The room tilted, and memories slammed back. Vivian's laugh, her hand slipping onto his thigh, the shock he hadn't pulled away…

"Rules are like a river. People learn to swim around them." Grandpa picked up his cup. "But when the flood comes, they drown." His gaze shifted from Debra to Jason and back. No judgment there, only the weathered calm of a retired attorney who'd watched storms roll in and out. "This Vivian woman asked you to be her local partner? I bet she promised connections, funding, and fast access."

"Exactly." Debra blinked. "How do you know?"

Grandpa shrugged. The faint scent of medicated oil floated off his shirt. "She's state-owned? That means politics all the way. And the financial arrangements are murky." He kneaded his knuckles. "She asked you to form a company on her behalf?"

The crease between Debra's brows deepened. She used a napkin to blot the ring of condensation the cup had left, as if wiping the table could clear the air.

"That's textbook 'White Glove.'" A tram bell clanged faintly in the distance. Grandpa looked out the window. "Have you heard of the term?"

Jason shook his head.

"A common practice for Chinese government officials nowadays." Grandpa lowered his voice. "They use a 'clean' local or foreign face to hold assets on behalf of the true beneficiary. That way, the real person can deny ownership or responsibility if the authorities come knocking." His gaze held Jason's for a beat longer. "High risk, especially when sizeable sums are involved."

"Do you mean Vivian tried to use us as her White Glove?" Debra's shoulders sagged. "Vivian phrased it as a standard declaration of trust."

Grandpa sipped his tea, sunlight glancing off the glaze of the cup. "If you sign a declaration of trust, you're agreeing to act as her trustee. On paper, you own the asset. But in reality, it's hers." He sipped. "She'll move money from the SOE to the new company and then, after a series of maneuvers, transfer it to her personal account in Switzerland." He hesitated as if weighing the words. "If she comes under investigation, you're implicated, even though you're innocent."

Jason's jaw flexed. His name had almost served as the handle on someone else's machine.

"Grandpa, could you explain further?" Debra twisted the napkin in her hand. "I'm still confused."

"I'll give you an example to help you understand." Grandpa set his cup down, the neat, precise clink an underscore to his statement. "Are you familiar with the case involving Bo Xilai?"

Debra glanced at Jason, as if expecting a positive response. The burn in his neck climbed a notch. "I saw it on the news but have no clue about the details."

"The tycoon Xu Ming of Dalian Shide." Grandpa inclined his head. "People called him Bo's White Glove. He handled things for the Bo family without revealing who was in charge. Flights. Hotels. School expenses. Renovations. The sort of 'help' that, on paper, passes as hospitality or a company perk. They're assets parked off the books, often through layers of companies."

"I remember a news report mentioning Xu Ming." Jason sat up straighter. "I didn't know he became rich by serving as Bo's White Glove."

Grandpa lifted a finger. "You might've read about the French villa, the one on the Riviera held through shell companies. A British fixer floated in that orbit as Bo's White Glove too. When the relationship soured and the politics turned, it all unraveled." He paused. The silence stood, punctured only by the honks of the minibuses. "The British fellow died of poisoning. Bo's wife was convicted of murder. Bo was tried and sentenced for bribery, embezzlement, and abuse of power. In the hearings, the white-glove money trails showed up line by line."

Jason stared at the coffee table. "What happened to Xu Ming?"

"He testified at Bo's trial and later died of a heart attack while in custody, at least according to the official records. He was forty-four." Grandpa tapped his cup with a fingertip. "White gloves burn fast."

Debra dropped her napkin onto her lap. "Vivian said it was just housekeeping."

"Of course she did." Grandpa folded his hands. "Housekeeping is what you call it before the knock on the door." He looked between them. "You might think you did a deal with a trusted friend. A declaration of trust here, a power of attorney there. When the tide turned, it didn't matter that you 'weren't the real owners.' The individuals on the documents, the trustees, the directors, the pretty shells in Hong Kong, were the first ones questioned."

Debra's hand stopped midair. "Vivian made it sound so common—"

"So is rain." Grandpa patted her arm. "You still close the windows."

Jason's knees had been bouncing under the chair. He stilled them with both palms. "All I can think of is that empty line beside my and Debra's names in the contract. All the promises, the shortcuts, and the ways to make the deal look clean..."

Debra's hand eased back to the table. "Jason and I pray together every night. God answered our prayers and delivered us from evil."

He slid his fingers over hers and gave a small squeeze. Heat returned to his neck. How close they'd have become ensnared in Vivian's scheme. By God's mercy, they'd been spared.

Thank You, Lord. For Your protection, for Your intervention.

Grandpa leaned forward. "Keep praying for God's grace. Let's hope your friend remains safe. Otherwise, it could open Pandora's box."

Chapter Twenty-Three

Content warning: I follow the "less is more" principle. Still, this chapter contains descriptions that some readers may find offensive.

Xing'an, Guangxi, China
Late Spring 1852

The water rippled with activity. Sampans rocked against the shore. A child coughed. A woman with a red kerchief crouched on a plank and scrubbed a pot. Boatmen at their moorings watched Xin and Hao, measuring profit against trouble. The river people were a tribe unto themselves, sun-darkened, with trousers rolled high.

"Which of you will take us to the Pearl?" Hao's voice cut through the morning air. "We pay in silver."

A fellow with a tuft of beard looked up from his junk, knife paused over a coil of net. He squinted at the dust on their hems and at Xin's bag. "Where are you from?"

"From places that burn." Hao nudged the narrow plank with his boot. The junk lifted, groaned, and settled against its ropes. He motioned for Xin to move, and they stepped forward together. The deck smelled of tar and old smoke. Water tapped at the hull. A brown sail lay furled.

Hao drew out a small ingot. "Our story would tire you."

The captain cast his gaze over his men. A lad with a smudge on his ear bent to sniff the silver. Two other youngsters came forward.

One tipped back his bamboo hat. "'Tis a long journey. Three days down the Li in fair water, another five upon the Gui, then four more through Sanshui, where the three rivers meet."

"Indeed, a long journey." The captain gazed at the ingot. "How many taels are in the piece?"

No mirth edged Hao's smile. "Five."

The man inclined his head. "May we take other passengers? For a private hire, we must have ten taels."

Hao nodded. They shook hands in a manner more binding than ink. The crew began to shift bundles of rice, a jar of oil, and a rooster in a wicker cage. Xin put his bundle on the port side, and Hao dropped his satchel on the bow.

A thin man in a tattered tunic drifted along the bank. Dust filmed his calves. His hair lay in clumps. "Master," he called, "might I come aboard? Only to the next bend."

The captain glanced at Hao. After Hao gave a nod, the crewman nearest the bow pushed the plank out, and the thin man stepped onto it. The junk rolled. He reached the deck and stumbled. His knees struck the boards with a hollow knock.

"Ah!" The newcomer hissed as if the deck had bitten him. One of his hands found the gunwale, and the other slid toward Hao's satchel.

The rooster flared its wings in a nervous clatter.

Hao caught the thief's wrist with the swiftness of a snake strike. "You have curious fingers. Do you use them to fill your bowl?"

The thief's eyes widened. He squealed when Hao tightened his grip. "I—sir, I slipped. Be merciful."

His pleas fell apart into a jumble of words. The boatmen gawked, then looked away.

"Search him," Hao commanded. "If there is a red thread twice wound about the left ankle, he is of the Hongmen and bent upon mischief."

Xin searched and found a scrap of paper with a forked mark in the sleeve and a red thread around the ankle.

"Masters, mercy," the fellow pleaded again. "I have a sick mother. There is no food. I take a penny wherever I may serve. Surely you know a man must win his rice with what talent he has."

Xin's mouth went dry. Sick mother. No rice. He had said similar phrases before Roberts put bread in his palm and said God had done it. Had that boy and this man anything in common? Hunger, fear, the bare art of survival. The faces of Quanzhou crowded him at once, a thousand mouths gaping like fish cast up on dry land.

"Cut him loose." The captain took a step away. "We make for the river. He may run to whatever master he serves—"

"Nay." A muscle twitched in Hao's chin.

Xin's chest tightened. For a heartbeat, the brother who had once laid the sweetest snow pea in his palm rose before his mind. Then the image vanished. "Hao, let him be. We had better push off now."

The man's lips trembled. A thread of spit hung at a corner. "Master—"

Hao's hands slackened, as though to release the fellow.

The tightness in Xin's chest relaxed, and his knees wobbled.

Yet in the next swift motion, Hao drew his dagger and drove it into the thief's belly. "Wrong me not."

Xin flinched. The iron smell rushed up, and the snow-pea memory turned to ash.

The crew dispersed to their stations and pushed the junk off the shore. Xin bit the inside of his cheek until he tasted blood. The captain threw the body overboard and wiped the deck clean.

While the current carried them with indifference, the thin man's pleading clung to Xin. Sick mother. No rice. Death. When Quanzhou burned, he told himself some deaths were necessary, like bitter medicine. One swallowed it and tried not to think about it. Yet the bitterness would not leave his mouth.

The river widened and narrowed, widened again, as if it were breathing. A white bird flew beyond the bend and vanished. Xin stooped on the deck, listening to the water.

"These men will not be loyal save as fear compels it." Hao stepped near and loomed over him. "You take exception to my slaying the man? We must survive before we find the pirate's cave to creep into. The crew will strip us bare and cast our bodies aside. I did it to keep them in check."

Xin lifted his gaze to Hao's. "Brother, I pursue this treasure only to show Master Miao that I am worthy to ask for Lan's hand. No more killing. No more cruelty."

"Ah." Hao sniggered. "So the girl still keeps you tethered to a post."

It stung. Yet Xin mastered himself. "If I am bound, then let it be to something gentler than iron. I am tired of being consumed by fury."

"Did you not kill a defenseless peddler and steal the maps from your hosts?" Hao rubbed his hands as if they were cold, though the day had grown warm. "Mercy is for cowards, Xin. It pacifies your conscience while someone else digs graves."

He peered at his palms and trudged away.

"Hao—" The rest snagged in Xin's throat.

The river muffled his voice, the afternoon thinning to heat.

At dusk, they tied up beside a boat heaped with long beans. Supper was porridge, pickled leaf, and fried fish. Afterward, Xin lay against the rolled half sail. The defenseless peddler's plea tapped his skull like fingers on lacquer. He reached for replacements—Roberts on love as God's command, Liang Fa on Job's patience beyond rage, and Miao Lan's lovely oval face. At last, he drifted into slumber.

They reached Guangzhou on the thirteenth day of good wind. The Pearl River lay swollen from the rains, the city rising above it. Temples looked down on them. Flagpoles with foreign colors flapped near the factories where the foreigners traded.

After they left the junk, Hao pointed at the busy streets. "Before we go to Macau, let us see what the years have done to our alley."

They passed a courtyard gate painted with images of gods. The old camphor tree smelled of mothballs. Next to it, the bean-curd man's stall displayed a new roof. A meat vendor had taken over from a cobbler, and the cobbler now occupied the other side.

The lintel of their previous house had been altered. A child sat on the step and looked at them with blank interest. A woman opened the door. "Can I help you, sirs?"

Xin swallowed. His throat refused to give him words.

Hao bowed. "We used to live here and have come to see what has become of it."

The child laughed. "Lots of people lived here."

The woman did not smile. "Sir," she addressed Xin with the glimmer of a smile, as if she knew he had a kinder spirit. "Houses changed hands in the bad years. This one cost my husband more than it should have. If you seek the old, you will only cause your heart to hurt. Would you like water?"

Xin wanted to say no and leave. Yet he nodded and peeped into what had been their kitchen. The stove had been moved. Lime now filled the crack where rain had crawled.

Hao shook his head. "Nay. We face a long journey ahead."

They walked away. Xin wished to hold his brother by the elbow, to lend strength, but Hao would not be lent to.

At the corner, Hao stopped and snickered, a flat, bitter sound. "Come. Let us find life among the living."

He led Xin through a skein of narrow alleys toward the quay. Lanterns swung on the flower boats. Laughing women, painted white and red, leaned against rails.

Hao boarded a boat as though returning to barracks where he knew the rules. Xin followed in his shadow, a chill pricking his nape.

A middle-aged woman, clad in a black satin gown with gold thread, greeted them. "Gentlemen," she cooed. "Have not seen you here before, have I? Newcomers bring fortune. Please bring yours in."

The madam's smile shone like lacquer. She turned and parted the curtain. Inside, low lamps glowed in the parlor. A boy plucked a guqin in a corner. Women leaned their elbows upon cushions and watched them with a practiced lift of the chin.

Hao bowed. "A pot of hawthorn wine and Peony, if she is free."

"Ah, so you have visited us before. She is always free for a fine young man." The madam's eyes slid to Xin. "And this gentleman?"

Xin's heart thudded. The jasmine sweetness clung to him. Shame followed. He wanted to step back into the night, onto the solid ground. Yet his feet remained rooted. Heat tickled his skin. He opened his mouth but found no words.

"He is of age, madam." Hao placed copper on a nearby table. "New to Guangdong's entertainments, but not to the world."

The madam weighed Xin with an indulgent glance. "Then the world owes him a soft introduction."

She clapped twice. A woman in a pale green robe lifted her head. Her face appeared a calm map drawn with care.

"Suyin." The madam nodded. "Show this gentleman the gentle light of our house."

Suyin set aside her fan and stood. "Sir, you look as if the boat still rocks beneath your feet, though we are moored."

"It does." Xin managed a bow. "Forgive me. I am—"

"New," she finished for him. "There is no harm in it. Will you take a thimble of wine just to warm the courage?"

Before he replied, she led him down a short corridor. The chamber at the end held a carved bed hung with pale mosquito netting, a table set with a bottle of rice wine and two cups, and other small articles. The river's slow clapping seeped through the lattice.

Suyin poured wine into the cups. "Sip. Let your breath find its pace."

He did as told. The wine slid down like fire.

She watched him over the rim of her cup. "What shall I call you?"

"Zhang Xin." He swallowed.

"Good name." She set down her cup. From the bamboo stand with the bowl, she drew a folded cloth and dipped it in water fragrant with orange peel. "Give me your hands."

He held them out. She took one first. The cloth began its slow devotion, a patient chase along each line and knuckle. She grasped his other hand and laughed under her breath.

A shiver ran through him.

"Why do you tremble?" Her nails skimmed, then soothed. "'Tis no sin." She wrung the cloth, let a droplet slide to the pulse at his wrist, and followed it with the pad of her thumb. "'Tis only a door," she murmured and caressed his fingers, "and every man ought to open it."

"I—" The words caught in his throat.

She drew the netting down. Within, she unfastened his garments in a practiced gentleness. Closing his eyes, he imagined the courtesan to be his beloved Miao Lan and surrendered his boyhood.

In the hush that followed, he opened his eyes. The lamp painted the wall with shadows. A Bible verse once read in a small tract rose unbidden. "What? Know ye not that he who is joined to a harlot is one body? For two, saith he, shall be one flesh."

Why was his flesh so weak? Never had the weakness of his flesh shown more plainly than now. He sat up and grabbed his garments. Bitterness coated his tongue. A faint drip from the eaves echoed his remorse. Was it raining? *Oh, Miao Lan, what have I done?*

He had long considered Lan his lamp, yet he had brought soot onto her light. Could he, with any honor, pretend to a spotless love, as though the stain would wash out with morning?

A warm palm rested on his thigh. Suyin's purr brushed his ear. "Your brother has purchased the whole of this night for you."

Her fingertips drew slow, widening circles. His breath grew short. Unbidden heat rose anew. He sank his head back on the pillows and yielded to the merciless tyranny of her touch.

Chapter Twenty-Four

Guangzhou, Guangdong, China
Late Spring 1852

Xin followed Hao across the narrow plank into the morning light. The world moved on, as though nothing remarkable had occurred.

"Well, little brother, did you enjoy yourself?" Hao winked.

Xin shook his head. Heat crept over him anew. At last, he spoke. "I am thirsty." Thirsty for water to wash the night from his skin.

"Good." Hao laughed, clapping him on the back. "Come. I'll take you to a place where tea is free."

They passed baskets of fish at the market. Smoke joined the steam of rice. Children ran with reeds. The ordinary day declared itself without remorse. The two strolled beneath a weatherworn signboard. Within, a modest tearoom awaited. "Two cups," Hao said to a youth. Then he dropped his voice. "And tell your master my fingers itch."

The youth slid a panel aside behind the brazier and guided them down narrow steps into a place with low tables. The oil lamps flickered. Six men bent over dice and cards.

"Ah, my friend," greeted a man with a black pin in his hair. "Your luck went to the hills last time. Has it descended again to the plain?"

"It lives in my sleeve." Hao chuckled. "This is my younger, Xin. Fill him a cup before the dust kills him dead."

The youth put down the teacups and withdrew. Xin raised one and sipped. The thin brew slid into him like forgiveness without new strength in it.

Hao drew coins from his packet. "Did you come to look?" he spoke over his shoulder. "Pray, rattle your bones."

"I have no taste for it." Xin pressed his lips thin. "I would rather depart and call upon Roberts."

"The missionary?" Hao's mouth slanted. "Did you not part with him in ill humor? If you will not throw, at least keep me company."

He slipped into a seat at the nearest table. The dice danced. A sea of coins gleamed in the middle.

Xin stood behind his brother for the first toss. His focus soon shifted to the bulge in Hao's neck when chance favored him. A similar scene had delighted Xin when they were boys and Hao discovered a thrush's nest or coaxed tricks from pebbles. Now it disquieted him.

Laughter mingled with curses. Hao lost the first two, won the third, and lost again. Then he tapped Xin's elbow. "Let me borrow to reverse the tide."

"I have none to spare." Xin knitted his eyebrows. His hand moved to the packet on his belt. "This is for our journey to Macau."

Hao rose. "Nay?" he said, as if tasting a foreign sound. "Do you set the law upon me?"

Xin's heart knocked against his ribs. "Brother, we came for tea. Enough."

The man with the hairpin narrowed his eyes. "The boy may count his coppers. If he desires virtue, let virtue be his hearth."

Hao yanked Xin forward by the sash and plucked at the belt. The knot slipped. A string of copper cash snapped loose and skittered across the table. Conversation hitched. Dice stopped clacking. Even the lantern's hiss seemed too loud beneath the low, smoke-blackened beams.

Heat flared through Xin. He grabbed Hao's wrist and twisted. "You shan't take mine."

"Ours, little brother." Hao reached again.

Xin tightened his grip until Hao flinched. "Not this time."

"Ah." Hao exhaled. "Hear him. When did you grow taller than I?"

"When you led me where I did not want to go." Xin bit his lip.

Hao's grin showed teeth stained with tea. "You were led nowhere your feet did not follow."

Xin trembled. He loosened his hold and tugged at his brother's sleeve. While Hao jerked free, Xin seized Hao's collar and slapped him hard.

Hao's head tilted to the side. He raised a fist. A blow landed on Xin's chin.

Men dispersed. The lamps swung. The cups rattled.

They grappled at the table. The coins leaped. The dice scattered.

Xin looped an arm around Hao's ribs. Hao targeted Xin's ear with his teeth. Xin cried out.

The housemaster appeared. "Take them up and throw them out."

A knot of men thrust between them and drove them up the steps into the late afternoon light.

A dog barked. Children stared and scattered.

Hao's lip bled. Xin's ear burned.

Each looked anywhere but at the other. Then the old pull drew their gazes together.

"You would clutch a handful of coins," Hao growled, "as though they were your soul."

"You sold mine," Xin spat into the ground, "last night."

Hao sniggered. "You stayed. Do not put all the blame on me."

"I did stay." Heat flooded Xin anew. His breath fluttered. "The blame is mine. Yet you—" He inhaled hard. "You would cast me after your dice, if I let you."

Hao wiped his mouth with the back of his hand and stared at the smear of red as though it were nothing. "Keep your remaining coins, if there are any. Return to the Taiping and sip your water. Their virtue shall rinse your tongue. I shan't trouble you again."

He turned to leave.

Xin grasped his sleeve and released it. "Brother, I do not wish to lose you." The words scraped his throat. Emotion pulled at him until his knees weakened.

Hao's shoulders jerked. "Then learn not to hold." He walked away.

"Do you still desire Macau?" Xin cried after him and hurried his steps. "We cannot go there without money."

"We will make money." Hao halted, a sinister light in his eyes.

"How?" Xin's courage wore thin, near to snapping.

"By calling on Roberts." An easy smile spread over Hao's face. "The foreigner owns a tender heart. You speak of your thirst for the right way. He may open his purse."

A knot tightened in Xin's stomach. "I shan't deceive him."

"Deceive? Nay." Hao wagged a finger. "He is forever buying virtue with silver. Give him the pleasure. If it troubles your stomach, deem it a loan and pledge him with clear thanks."

"That is crooked," Xin murmured.

"Crooked?" Hao's brow twitched. "Do we want to sail straight to Macau? A straight journey may begin at a crooked door. Come."

He set off without looking at Xin. They passed along the walls toward the Pearl River. The city's din faded, leaving only the whisper of the camphor trees. Beyond the great gate loomed a square white house, its casements flung wide to the breeze.

Xin's breath snagged as he took in the well-remembered vegetable garden. The air smelled of damp soil. The scent opened an unguarded tenderness he kept buried. He smiled and winced in the same heartbeat, unsure whether to step forward or turn away before the past pinned him where he stood.

At the gate, a boy with a shaved crown looked them over. "Whom do you seek?"

"The teacher." Xin bowed. "Tell him Zhang Xin has called."

The boy's gaze paused on Xin's bruised ear, slid to Hao's split lip, and moved away again. He went within, returned, and drew the door wider. "Enter. He will see you."

Years had flown by. Yet the room appeared much the same as on the day of their first acquaintance. On the walls hung the same great cloths, embroidered with foreign characters, mountains, and sheep. In the corner, the old wooden chest continued to yield a harvest of books and ragged papers.

Roberts stood before him, still tall, spare, and somewhat bent. "Xin." He greeted in Cantonese, bearing a foreign tilt. "How many years has it been since you left with Hong Xiuquan? Why do you not remain with him? Of late, words spread that the Taiping have captured Daozhou and Chenzhou in Hunan and are marching toward Nanjing."

Xin bowed low. Shame burned on his tongue and into his cheeks. His fingers worked within his sleeves to hide their tremor. "Teacher, you were right when you warned me of the peril of following Hong. I could bear it no longer." A breath shuddered out of him. "I crave your pardon."

"Pardon is given where repentance stands true." Roberts inclined his head toward Hao. "And who is this fellow?"

"Let me present my elder brother." Xin drew a step aside. "His name is Hao."

"Welcome, Hao." Roberts, with a small motion of his hand, guided them to the sitting area. Outside, a bell tolled. "The Taiping have not reached us. Yet, the provincial authorities have tightened the defenses of the Pearl River. Fighting in neighboring Guangxi has sent refugees our way. We have been much occupied." He let out a heavy sigh. "Fear drives men into sin. But the Lord abides the same. Xin, why are you here?"

Xin swallowed. Should he tell the lie his brother fashioned on the road?

Hao's nostrils flared. His breath rushed out and carried words. "Teacher, we are in peril. The Qing have put out word for us, and Hong's people would also seize us. We are between two nets. If you can lend us a little silver for boat hire and passage, we will seek to reach Hong Kong under British protection."

Roberts's gaze fell on the stain at Hao's lip, the bruise at Xin's ear, and then returned to their eyes, as though he had resolved where truth must reside. "Xin, is it true you are being pursued for having deserted the Taiping?"

Xin frowned at the feet he could not keep from shifting. "Indeed."

Silence ensued. When at last Roberts spoke, his voice carried the same unshaken gentleness. "I cannot turn away someone who confesses and seeks to do right. If you are hunted for righteousness' sake, you are blessed. Do you promise before God to walk henceforward in truth?"

"I do," Xin whispered. His heart ached over the lie.

"Then you shall eat rice here and sleep safe under my roof." Roberts gestured for them to sit. "The river in the dark is no place for tired men. In the morning, I intend to find out what means I have."

The same boy brought them simple bowls of rice topped with pork and vegetables, then set up two mats at the far end of the room. Roberts prayed with them in his halting Cantonese. Xin tasted a sweetness like before as he thought of the night he had first bowed his head in this house. When the candles were pinched out, he lay long awake listening to the frogs by the ditch, while Hao's steady breath filled the narrow space.

At dawn, Roberts roused them. "Follow me." He led Xin into his study. From a drawer, he retrieved a boat-shaped piece of silver and wrapped it in paper. "This is sufficient to pay your ride downriver and leave somewhat for food and the ferry to Hong Kong. A boatman at the ferry, Old Li, knows me. Show him this note, and he will not cheat you." He looked into Xin's eyes. "Remember. Do justice, love mercy, walk humbly with your God."

Xin took the parcel. Moisture pooled behind his eyelids. "Teacher…" His throat tightened. "I will not forget."

After a simple breakfast of congee and pickled vegetables, Roberts walked them to the lane, his slight figure straightened for the effort. They slipped into the bustle of porters, laborers, and vendors already up with the sun. When Xin turned once, the missionary waved as if in blessing. Then the crowd swallowed him.

They kept to the narrow ways and reached a quiet stretch behind a line of junk hulls. Hao released a low whistle, tapping his sleeve. "Our fortune mends, little brother."

Xin frowned, uncomprehending. Hao opened the fold and showed a coil of foreign watch chain and two gold coins, their milled edges bright. "The foreigner keeps his chest poorly. While he took you to his study, I kept watch with profit."

The world tilted. The paper-wrapped ingot burned in Xin's hand. "Hao, you have done a wicked thing. We must return them."

Hao's mouth twitched. "Return and hang a bell around our necks? Do you suppose he will thank you?" He lifted his chin. "Did you not steal the treasure maps from the very family who hosted you? Why are you so upright now?"

Heat pricked Xin's skin. He opened his mouth, but his throat closed up. *Upright.* The word scraped. He shut his eyes. The cries of the boatmen and the wet slap of oars sounded from very far away. Roberts's figure, somewhat bent yet steadfast, rose with the light upon his worn face.

"God forgive me," Xin whispered.

Hao patted his arm. "Come. You desire the pirate's treasure, do you not?"

They trudged down to the water. A boatman with a patched sail squinted at them and at the scrawl on Roberts's note, then spat into the river before nodding them aboard. As the boat pushed out into the brown current, the city's watch gongs sounded. The small ingot lay heavily against Xin's heart. It burned there, an accusing fire.

Chapter Twenty-Five

Kowloon, Hong Kong, China
Winter 2022

Across the shadowy skyline, neon traces lingered in the morning mist. Jason stood at the kitchen counter, clutching his phone. The alert pulsed with a sick insistence. "Sandy Yang, socialite and mainland Chinese businesswoman, died after falling from a luxurious yacht. Joe Niu, a business associate, is in custody on suspicion of murder." The article spiraled into conjectures about affairs, debts, and the pressure-cooker lives of the elite.

Debra, still in her pajamas, hovered by the table. "Did you see this?" She held up her tablet. The screen light cast her face half in blue. "News about Sandy Yang and Joe Niu, Vivian's friends who almost bought properties through you."

Jason's chin moved before he nodded. The clock struck seven times. Sunlight seeped through the window, striping the countertop between them.

His body turned wooden—the same dead weight he'd carried into funerals and morgues since his parents' death in a car accident. Lilies and wool. Air too cold for breath. The old grief came down on him with a new sensation. Guilt? Remorse? In therapy, they'd said there was a difference. In him, they felt the same, a pressure that wouldn't let him fill his lungs.

Debra's fingers found his. He flinched, then let her anchor him.

"You met both of them not that long ago, and they gossiped about Vivian."

"Yeah." He stared at the sunlight bands on the counter, not sure why he whispered the word. "Yeah." He spoke louder this time as if doubling the word might make it truer or undo whatever had happened.

His phone buzzed. He picked it up and put it on speaker. "Jason Guan."

Vivian's low voice flowed through. "Have you seen the news? Sandy is dead."

He hesitated. Did she want comfort or corroboration? "I have. The news said Joe is the suspect."

"Not that simple." Vivian switched from Mandarin to Cantonese, each syllable edged with steel. "Sandy had too many powerful boyfriends. Joe was last in the queue."

Jason remained quiet, a sinking realization in his gut.

"She chose risky men." Vivian released an audible sigh. "Joe divorced his wife because of her. He thought it would win her. But Sandy never followed the rules." She switched back to Mandarin, softer now, yet no less intense. "She played the dudes like a game. When the game ended, someone always lost. Sometimes it's not the one you'd expect."

He fixed his gaze on the thin crack trailing along the edge of the table. "She must have known it would catch up with her."

"Sandy thought she was clever. That's why she laughed at the rules. But even clever ones run out of luck." Vivian sighed again. "The people above us don't forgive."

A pause. Raindrops pattered on the window. When did it start raining? Was today one of those days when the sun and rain shared the earth?

Jason's mouth turned dry. He licked his lips. "Vivian, why are you telling me this?"

She released a brittle laugh. "Although you're a bit naïve, you and Debra managed to avoid harm. You are either super lucky or your God is the real thing. In my circle, few would escape unscathed."

The line clattered. She hung up.

Rain beaded on the glass, each drop catching another. Naïve. The word stuck under his skin. Sandy's face flashed in—eyes blown wide, a tremor in her mouth. He put his phone down and exhaled hard.

Debra's arms slid around him from behind. "Vivian sounded scared."

He pulled her to the front. "She did." He folded her closer, trying to make his body a wall. "She said we're lucky we didn't get sucked in." He attempted to make it sound lighter, but the words fell flat.

She leaned into him. "There's so much darkness out there. I can't imagine a life without God's presence."

"Yeah." He rested his chin on her head. The clock ticked too loudly. His heart thudded, a hammer in a quiet house. "So much evil. Everything could change in an instant, and you'd never see it coming."

Her palm flattened against his chest. "We asked God to keep us safe, and He protected us."

"God is in control." He glanced out at the rain. "For a while, we were walking across a bridge in the fog, and the only thing between us and a fall was something we couldn't see or touch."

She nodded. "God's mercy is beyond our comprehension. Even if we make a wrong choice, He guides us back to the correct path."

The rain drummed on. The sick chill within him faded, replaced by warmth. "It's a blessing we share the same faith and pray together about almost everything."

A faint smile broke out on Debra's face. "That wasn't the case for Zhang Xin in Dad's manuscript. The poor guy lost his virginity to a prostitute. I wonder how that will affect his relationship with Miao Lan when they meet again."

Jason's chuckle snagged in his throat. His arm tightened around her, and he brushed a thumb along her cheek, as though reassuring himself she was real. "Few men could withstand a seduction of such directness." His gaze drifted past her shoulder. "If God hadn't intervened…" He released a slow breath, his thumb stalling against her skin. "I'd have yielded to Vivian's scheme and become her White Glove." His muscles tensed, even as his shoulders curved under the pressure. "The truth is, I was a step away."

Debra's lips found his. When she drew back, she rested her forehead on his. "I love you. Not the idea of you. But you, the man who fought to honor God and didn't fall. And if you had fallen?"

Her fingers threaded along his nape. "I would have loved you too. There's grace for what we did or almost did. With God. With me."

He flinched again, the word *grace* cutting a groove through the shame. "I don't deserve—"

"Neither do I. We're all sinners." She kissed the corner of his mouth, a promise pressing into his skin. "Mistakes don't own you. You're mine, and I'm yours."

His breath shuddered. He clutched her tighter. "I never want to hurt you."

"We're under the same yoke," she whispered. "When you can't stand, I'll stand by you. When I falter, you'll carry me. Those are the vows we made to each other on our wedding day."

He searched her face, the iron in his jaw giving way to tenderness. "No matter what?"

"No matter what." She kissed him again, slower this time.

The kitchen felt safe, a fragile sanctuary held together by faith and love.

After breakfast, he left home and trudged to the second-floor office he shared with Uncle Brian at DreamAchieve Realty. The building seemed quieter than usual, the hush deepened by gloomy headlines and the patter of steady rain against the windows. Across the room, two assistants hunched over their desks, gazes fixed on glowing screens. In the group chats, links about Sandy's death mingled with memes and daily chatter, as if the tragedy were another blip in the stream of passing stories.

The door swung open, and Uncle Brian walked in, eyebrows knit. "Jason, did you hear the news about Sandy and Joe? Also, Grandpa mentioned the conversation you and Debra had with him about the project you two almost partnered with Vivian. Come on. Let's grab a coffee. I want to talk to you."

Jason swallowed again, but his mouth stayed sand dry. He grabbed an umbrella and trailed half a step behind Uncle Brian on the walk to Le Jardin. The slap of their shoes against wet pavement synced with the thud in his chest.

After their orders came, he hid behind a ginger ale. The fizz needled his tongue, burned his throat, and made his stomach feel hollow.

Uncle Brian sipped his coffee. "The news about Sandy and Joe is everywhere. Unbelievable. And to think we just met them several weeks back at the yacht party. Did Vivian contact you?"

Jason nodded before his voice would work. "She called. Said—" He steadied the glass with both hands. "Said Sandy's death is worse than it looks."

"Hong Kong isn't what it was." Uncle Brian let out a slow exhale. "Mainland money, politics. None of it clean anymore. When a person falls, it's often not an accident. You can't trust those people, even when they smile at you."

A server set down a plate of apple strudel. Uncle Brian waited until she turned away. "I've seen men disappear over deals like the one Vivian wanted from you. Paper companies, shell games, funny money. Someone gets burned. If they don't use you, they erase you."

The cinnamony scent rose like a memory of safer places. Jason gaped at the pale soda. A sudden, feverish relief left him lightheaded. "I'm glad Debra and I told her no."

Classical music washed over them. Uncle Brian reached across and squeezed Jason's shoulder. "Maggie and I have been praying for you. God answered our prayers. We must stay clean, or we'll get drawn into dangerous schemes."

Jason drained the last of his drink. It lit a cool trail all the way down and did nothing to steady the tremor in his body. Ice rattled against glass as he set it down too hard. "If the police learn about my interactions with Sandy and Joe—"

Uncle Brian turned his mug a quarter inch, lining the handle with the seam in the wood. "Tell the truth, but nothing more."

Tell the truth. The words landed heavily. The image of Vivian's fingers on his thigh flashed behind his eyes. Shame crawled up his neck. "How about Vivian? She sounded desperate."

"Pray for her." Uncle Brian squinted. "She needs God."

Jason smeared the water ring on the table and swallowed a bitter taste. A world of money, power, and beautiful corpses beckoned, and he'd glimpsed its price.

On his lunch break, he declined Uncle Brian's invitation to dine together and walked rain-slicked streets by himself toward a noodle shop. Each headline on newsstands along the street whispered, "Femme fatale." Glossy magazines splashed with the same grainy photo—Sandy, legs crossed, champagne tilted, wore a red gown. "Mistress at the top. Murder in the heights."

Inside the restaurant, Jason wrapped his hands around a bowl of steaming beef brisket to warm the chill in his body. A recent message from Joe Niu sprang to mind. "Jason, wanna grab a drink? I need to talk. Trouble with S..."

He pulled out his phone and reread the small talk—the back-and-forth about expensive flats, plans that never materialized. His jaw clenched. What could he have done to prevent this tragedy? If he hadn't been so focused on closing a deal...

He nudged aside the chopsticks next to the bowl, his appetite gone.

"These circles eat people alive," Vivian had said. What did she mean? Was that melodrama or a warning among survivors?

Maybe he'd take the afternoon off.

By the time he reached home, the rain had stopped. Debra was reading the *South China Morning Post* in the living room. "It's like a plot from a superficial soap opera." She shook her head. "So young, so beautiful. And look at Joe. His whole life gone for a woman who didn't even care about him."

Jason squeezed onto the sofa with her. "They lived in another world. Different rules, different morals."

She flipped to a page. "The newspapers are packed with details. Joe's fingerprint on the railing, surveillance footage of a heated argument, and a minute-by-minute timeline of events. Sandy's designer bag, scattered with lipstick and receipts, is cataloged too. Lawmakers demand answers about 'corrupt influences' from the mainland. Everyone loves a scandal."

His phone pinged, Vivian calling again. He braced himself. "Vivian, I—"

"I'm being watched. They froze my business account. Don't mention me to anyone. Understand?"

His stomach crawled. "What's happening?"

"I have no clue." Her voice cracked, a hairline fracture. "Remember, you know nothing. Please, Jason. For old times' sake."

The line went dead. In the silence, his mind rewound to his high school years. Vivian hid behind her glasses, cornered in the hallways by other girls. He had smiled at her once, and she remembered that to this day.

A watery shimmer of city light flickered over the window. He glanced at his lovely wife. For a second, everything—the scandal, the fingerprints, the frozen account—appeared tangled with his quiet life, as if the line between spectator and suspect was dissolving.

If the authorities learned of his connection with Vivian through the property transaction records, would they come for him?

Chapter Twenty-Six

Pearl River, Guangdong, China
Late Spring 1852

The tranquil reed beds along the banks lapped the Pearl with tired water. The junk's deck stank of dried fish. Xin looked toward the stern. Their hired skipper, Old Li, sat with his toes hooked on the tiller and his focus upon the currents. "Ah Fai, is dinner ready?"

"Ready as it will be," came the answer from the little stove-box forward.

Ah Fai set out four bowls while Old Li eased the tiller and let the boat ride the fair tide. They ate in silence—plain rice, mustard greens, and salted fish—with jasmine tea cutting the briny air.

As the last light slid off the reeds, the Pearl took them on, and the sail flapped in the dusk wind. Xin leaned against the mast. Had they stayed in Guangzhou for only three days? So much had come to pass. He could not banish Roberts's image from his mind. When the missionary should discover that they had stolen his watch chain and gold pieces, what would he think?

"Xin," called Hao. "Never have I seen a river so thronged. Is every soul bound for Macau?"

Dark hulks shouldered past. A fisherman's lamp bobbed up, glimmered, and was swallowed again. A sharp prow sheared by within an arm's reach.

"Macau?" The skipper lifted his head. "Reverend Roberts wrote you were for Hong Kong."

Heat rose in Xin's cheeks. He and Hao exchanged a glance.

In the dimness, the whites of Hao's eyes showed like shells. He chuckled. "Old Li, you have crossed every channel in this south country and know the headlands as a farmer knows his field. We've a wish to show you something—only you must keep a closed mouth about it."

Old Li did not turn. "A man learns to shut his mouth. Else he swallows mud." His foot tapped the tiller. The junk's nose slipped a point, skirting a slow black barge. "Bring your things here."

Xin crouched, tugged open his satchel, and drew out the small parcel. His chest now tight, he crept aft, where the oil lamp was caged in a paper hood.

The hood of the oil lamp breathed with the ship's sway, washing a honeyed circle over the boards.

Hao helped spread the maps on the deck. "See this?" He pointed. "A tract of jagged rocks lifting from the sea."

Old Li's breath smelled of dried squid. He dragged his fingers over the coarse sheet where the red lines crawled. "Ah, warning of treacherous tides and the invisible teeth of undercurrents." He slid his nail to the second chart. "Boulders arch to cup a cove, and water lies under their lee." His thumb hovered over the neat script, and he read it out, "'Avoid the undertow and trust instead in the guidance of the stars above.'" He looked up. "Who gave you this?"

"A friend left them in a chest." The misleading statement splintered like cedar under Xin's tongue. He toed the floorboards, drawing his sandal along the grain to avoid meeting Old Li's gaze. "Do you recognize—"

"Hush." Old Li cocked his head, as though listening to the river. Dogs barked. The lights of a village rose and sank upon a low shore. He spat over the side. "I have seen rocks shaped like ox horns before." He squinted at the fine chart. "A cove with a pull beneath it. The writer warned you to keep clear of the suck and take your bearings from the sky. Good counsel."

"Where?" Hao inhaled.

Old Li grunted. He moved on to the oldest sheet with the faded figures and the solitary man's outline on the shore. "Behind this tongue of sand is a pool good for junks to ride when a northeast comes hard. There is a mark where the man's arms flung wide." He glanced at them. "Some call that rock a standing man. Pirates in my father's time drew him to give their men the sign to run in." He returned to the margin of the first map, where faint red lines stitched the edge. "If the painter painted true, a cave lies nearby as well. The sea marauders kept jars in such holes." His shoulders jerked. "'Tis Cheung Chau Island, near Hong Kong."

Hao exhaled. "Cheung Chau? Are you certain?"

"As sure as sunrise. The pair of pointed outcrops nicknamed the Ox Horns confirm it."

Xin gathered the maps. The world formed into lines—downriver, past the forts, into the island-studded sea.

"Can you bring us there?" Hao's voice trembled.

Old Li's lips curled up. "If the tide serves, I shall be able to nose a junk into a teacup." A muscle twitched in his chin. "A man does not pour tea for strangers without asking what thirst they carry. Why there, and why now?"

Xin pinched the cord around the rolled papers.

Hao's attention shifted to the smoke from the lamp.

Old Li chuckled. "You wear it plain as wet cloth. Cheung Po-Tsai's largesse, eh? A chest put away in a sea hole, the old pirate's gold will make every poor man a prince. So the story runs."

"We only—"

"Hear me out." Old Li held up a hand, stopping Xin. "Some fifteen years ago, when my hair had less white, a fresh-painted government vessel arrived in Cheung Chau. A neat craft, with a small gun forward, and a strip of green on the men's sleeves. The soldiers, a dozen or more, ran toward the ox-horn rocks." He settled back. "We waited near the shore, thinking to sell them fish when they returned. One tide turned, then the next. No men came back."

Creases formed on Hao's forehead. "They were taken?"

"By whom?" Old Li arched an eyebrow. "Their vessel stayed in the lee with nobody aboard. The villagers removed the mast and took her in. They maintained the cave had swallowed them."

Night deepened. The smell of lamp oil crowded out further words.

Within the berth, Hao lay curled like a child, his breath steady and untroubled. Beside him, Xin reclined, his eyes turned upward to the pitch-black vault of the deck above. Ever since Old Li recounted the vanished Qing soldiers, the warning from the second riddle would not be stilled. "Beware the curse, its silent stare, For shadows weave death's snare."

He shifted his body. The planks creaked.

Curse, silent stare, death's snare.

Sleep eluded him. Xin rose and climbed onto the deck. The Great Dipper hung low. The pale road of the Milky Way lay across the sky.

Water slapped the hull. Then the junk swayed. The stern swung, and the rope on the bow cleat squealed.

Quick footsteps sounded. Old Li appeared. "If the current flows straight under the boat, we will drown."

"What?" Cold tightened Xin's chest. He leaned over the rail and saw only darkness.

Old Li slid the tiller bar across. "Undercurrent."

The old man's calm steadied Xin. The stern yawed again, the mast trembled, and the furled sail rattled.

"Indeed!" Xin planted his feet wider on the planks.

"You know the sky?" Old Li's chin flicked upward.

Xin swallowed the taste of salt and iron. "Reverend Roberts once showed me how the Little Ladle points to the north." Aye. Under a sky crowded with stars, a lantern swung on the mission roof, and the parson's finger mapped the constellations.

"Find the North Star. Keep her head on it. If she falls off, shout. I will carry out the kedge in the skiff. When I bid you, walk her up. I'll haul."

Xin swallowed again. In a breath, Old Li cast off the skiff with the kedge aboard. The junk trembled as the kedge warp came taut, humming. Xin worked the stern sweep to keep her nose straight.

"Hold her steady. Do not mind the water. Look at the sky!"

Xin fixed his attention on the pale light.

Old Li let the kedge go with a grunt. A soft plop, then the line in the skiff ran out. "Now, walk her up!"

The bow wavered after Xin shoved the sweep. "She falls off!"

Old Li's line took the strain. The kedge bit, and the junk inched ahead. The stern wavered again, but the star held.

Then, all at once, the grip loosened. Water lost its teeth. The hum softened to a purr.

"She lets go."

Old Li hauled twice more, came alongside, and tossed the kedge inboard. He grinned at Xin.

They made fast the sweep and the lines.

The old man flicked his fingers like a fisherman shaking out a net. "The river pulls to its own. If you have no mark to hold by, you will sideslip with the current. Then 'tis too late."

Was Old Li speaking of the river or something else?

"The pull is not always water." He pointed toward the sky. "It can be anything. Only a sure light shall draw you clear."

Xin ducked his chin. With treacherous ease, the maps had slid into his satchel, whilst the Wangs trusted him and left their house in his keeping. His heart throbbed.

"Reverend Roberts has been my friend these many years." Old Li retrieved from his tunic a folded paper. "You yourself brought me this note of his. In it, he writes he found you, a lad of fifteen, astray in the street. For three years, he cherished you as his own son. Yet you turned from his entreaties and left with Hong Xiuquan. When he saw you recently, he perceived a shadow on your soul. Since he had no chance to speak with you, he begged me to do so in his stead." He clamped a hand on Xin's shoulder. "Roberts loves you dearly."

Old Li said nothing more.

Tears rolled down Xin's cheeks. "I stole the maps." The silence drew the words out of him. "They are Liang Fa's. I told myself he had no use for them."

The old man remained motionless.

Xin's head dropped against his chest. "And that was not all. I have been with the Taipings. We stormed a town by the bend. A man fell. I had a sword. A shout commanded me to be quick. I—" The sound in his throat stopped. He forced it out. "I thrust. He had no weapons."

His hands trembled, as though the warmth of that blood was still on them. "And Guangzhou—" He wrung his fingers. "Hao and I visited a flower boat. I assured myself there was no mischief so long as 'twas confined to two adults."

The deck tipped. He leaned against the railing to steady himself. Moisture wetted his cheeks.

Old Li released a sigh. "You can strain until you give out, but the river will still take you if you rely only on yourself. A light exists beyond us that doesn't fail when we fail. I once laughed at His name, yet age has taught me that Christ is the surer guide."

Guilt pressed like stone. Xin closed his eyes, sick of the noise in his skull. "I'm too dirty."

Old Li tugged at his sleeve. "Repentance is not the same as drowning in sorrow. You have been searching inward. Turn your eyes upon Him. He was nailed to the cross and took our curse upon Himself. Yet He says, 'Come.'"

"I am…" Xin faltered.

"A sinner." Old Li nodded. "As I am. We have all added to the world's hurt. You have. So have I. So has anyone who ever tells a lie or lusts after a woman who is not his wife. No one could boast before Him."

An image of a cross flashed through Xin's mind. Christ crucified, and himself nailed there with Him. "I had often asked how a loving God could permit the world's suffering, not discerning that my uncleanness had swelled its measure."

Liang Fa's words—"When I consider the cross, I perceive myself crucified there instead of Jesus Christ"—had once perplexed him. Now they fell with weight.

"What do I do?" he whispered.

Old Li patted his arm. "Ask Him to forgive you. Trust that He grants it. Then walk in His light. That is all."

They stood, dim figures beneath the mast. Old Li lifted a brief prayer into the gloom, akin to greeting a friend. Xin followed and bared the worst of himself. When at last he fell silent, the fog in his soul lifted.

Chapter Twenty-Seven

Kowloon, Hong Kong, China
Winter 2022

Jason stood by the living room windows. Night had descended. A siren wailed in the distance. Inside, soft jazz crooned. The street noise, disconnected from the comfort of their apartment, seemed like part of another universe.

Debra walked out of the kitchen and plopped down onto the sofa. "I finished reading the chapter about the brothers' trip down the Pearl River." She sat and tucked her legs beneath her. "Xin finally acknowledged the fact that he was a sinner. Like so many of us, he's added to the world's hurt. He accepted that Christ died on the cross on his behalf."

The lamp made a soft island of light over her lovely face. Jason lowered himself beside her. "Faith is a journey with twists and turns. Dad allowed Zhang Xin the room to be complicated, just as we all are."

Debra picked up the tablet from the coffee table and tapped it awake. "I wonder what will happen next. Dad loved happy endings. Yet with Hao by Xin's side, the situation became precarious. I fear for them."

Her brow creased, seemingly tender with concern for fictional men as if they were neighbors. The sight warmed him. He chuckled and grasped her hand. Her fingers were cool in his, a streak of ink smudged on the side of her index finger. He had a sudden, ridiculous urge to kiss the smear away, to keep her clean of every worry. "Hao was a soul traumatized by the war. Want me to tell you the ending? He—"

"Don't spoil it." She leaned into his arms.

His chest loosened under her weight. Everything—the hush, her hair against his jaw, their shared faith, and their love—aligned. He drifted in it, grateful.

The intercom buzzed. The sound needled the quiet.

Debra straightened up. "Who's visiting at this hour?"

He stood. "I'll check." After speaking with the security guards, he mouthed, "It's Vivian."

A moment later, she walked in, clad in a T-shirt and blue jeans, a sapphire pendant in the hollow of her throat. Jason studied her face, trying to read the urgency there. The room's warmth faded, and he squared his shoulders on instinct.

Vivian settled into the armchair. Her gaze shifted from its usual confidence to searching uncertainty.

He prepared tea. The movement steadied his nerves. Still, a tremor skated along the rim of a saucer when he set it down. Debra helped place a cup in front of their guest. The air carried the soy-slick tang of the dinner they'd shared just an hour ago.

Vivian broke the silence. "Do you remember how I used to sit at the back of the classroom? I always tried to keep out of sight."

Of course he did. The last row, her head bowed over a frayed notebook, the invisible gravity she'd carried. Heat prickled along his neck. He nodded, but said nothing.

"People change." Debra's voice sounded gentler than usual. "Vivian, you're not that girl anymore."

Vivian flashed a wintry smile. "No, I'm not." She exhaled. A muscle in her chin twitched. "After high school, my parents were disappointed I didn't get into the University of Hong Kong. I left for a Shanghai college, intending to escape from them and my boring life. Unknown to me, school in China is a different battlefield."

Jason stood, then sat back down. Not knowing what to say or do, he fixed his gaze on his teacup.

"In freshman year, I met a man from Hong Kong, Liam Sima. He was older, slick, handsome, and generous." Her voice thickened. Was it longing or regret? "He took care of me and introduced me to another world. Nightclubs, business meetings, vacations… I passed through life as someone important. For a while, I believed I was."

Jason traced the rim of his cup, searching Vivian's face for the vulnerable girl who used to wear her anxiety in every hunched posture.

"Liam ran a company, Shi Bong Holdings, that specialized in 'services' for powerful men." Her lips twisted. "I trusted him and didn't ask what the business was. Soon, I became one of those services."

She paused. A dense stillness descended.

"I was bait. We'd socialize at lavish hotels and parties. Men would come. A hidden camera filmed us in action. Liam then used it for leverage."

Her admission landed, ugly and heavy. A slick of cold sweat crawled down Jason's spine. If he had succumbed to her seduction, he'd be a file on her drive, a thumbnail labeled with a date and a price.

Debra's fingers entwined, knuckles turning white. "How—"

"I loved Liam," Vivian whispered. "After a while, I became good at it. He taught me how to read men's appetites and weaknesses. I helped plan the setup. Eventually, we had videos in our system about high government officials and executives in SOEs. Our business wasn't selling sex. It was selling secrets."

She looked away as if ashamed. The neon outside blinked, the strobing lights like silent judgment. "Sandy and others joined later. For some, it was just money. For me, it was blind love at first, then survival. When I realized Liam never loved me, I managed to get into Sinogene Pharmatech." She raked her hair back from her forehead. "That's how I became 'successful,' and why Du Jin-Dong, my so-called boyfriend, keeps me close. I know too much."

A knot tightened in Jason's stomach. No wonder Vivian had tried to seduce him. That approach with men had never failed her before. Yet he escaped, and she switched tactics.

"And Sandy?" Debra's question sounded barely above a whisper.

Vivian blinked, fingertips worrying the hem of her sleeve. "She was talking about using what she knew to bargain for her freedom. Joe Niu loved her, but she never returned it. Men like Joe don't understand the game."

Jason pressed a palm to his stomach to pin the churn in place. "Vivian, why are you telling us this?"

"I'm next." The corners of her mouth quivered. The words scraped out. "I thought I could move money out and start again. It fell apart."

Debra reached for her arm, tears shimmering on her lashes. "You can start again."

Vivian flinched away. "No. They'll never let me go."

His throat turned dry. He gulped some of his tea, then wrapped both hands around his cup. "Vivian. What do you want from us now?"

"I want—" Her lips parted in a voiceless struggle. Her eyes drilled into his. "Maybe I just wanted someone from the old days to know who I really am before I disappear."

He fought to gain understanding. "Disappear?"

She released a broken chuckle. "People who hold too many secrets have to run or hide or worse."

A stillness fell, heavy with memories and regret. After Vivian left, Jason drew the curtains open and peered down. On the street, she slipped into the night, her head held high, her steps measured.

During their nightly routine before bed, Debra whispered prayers. Jason heard his name and Vivian's, hope bleeding into fear.

Afterward, he stared at the ceiling, light slanting through the blinds. Gratitude flooded him once more. "Vivian said we're super lucky or our God is the real thing."

"Yeah." Debra fluffed the pillow. "God answers prayers. Some people call it coincidence, though. But a friend texted me a quote today from William Temple, some archbishop guy in England. He said, 'When I pray, coincidences happen. When I don't, they don't.' Isn't that great?"

Jason smiled and leaned into her arms. Slumber soon overtook him.

✳ ✧ ✳

In the days that followed, the news flooded every corner. Sinogene Pharmatech Holdings came under investigation by the Chinese authorities. Vivian's boss, Du Jin-Dong, was the first to be named, followed by a dozen others. Embezzlement, bribery, misappropriation of state assets, sex scandals… The waterfall of exposure tumbled downward.

Each headline assailed Jason with the sick conviction of what the next act would bring. Two weeks later, while he was accompanying his clients, an expat couple, through a final walk-through of an apartment in Repulse Bay, his phone vibrated. He glanced at the display and answered.

Debra sounded flat. "Vivian is in custody, accused of financial crimes, conspiracy, and corruption."

For a breath, the sea beyond the glass tilted. A metallic taste coated his tongue. "Got it." He gave a brief response and slid the phone into his pocket.

Don't think. Not here. Not now.

Autopilot took over. He pointed out the storage space, the lighting, and the new carpet, his heart thudding. His clients thanked him, and he closed the deal with a pasted-on smile.

Once he reached the subway station, he clicked open the phone. Photos showed Vivian in handcuffs, face shielded by police. Reports speculated on her role as "the glamorous accomplice," "the queen bee of corruption," and "the Hong Kong connection." Images recycled from magazine launches and yacht parties painted her as a femme fatale.

Back at home, Debra sat on the couch beside Uncle Brian. They spoke in hushed, anxious voices. The mug on the table had grown a skin.

Jason's pulse ticked at his throat. He collapsed into the armchair. "What's the matter?"

Debra wrung her hands, turning her wedding band so fast it flashed. "DreamAchieve Realty is becoming famous." Her sarcasm carried an edge. "The name showed up in various places."

He forced a chuckle. "That's a surprise."

"We may be in trouble," Uncle Brian muttered, gaze skittering. "Hong Kong real estate intermediaries have anti–money laundering reporting obligations. I checked our file, and you didn't file a report with the authorities after you helped Vivian purchase the penthouse."

The word *didn't* slammed into his chest. The room closed in, air thinning to a whistle in his ears. His fingers dug into the armrests. "I didn't file because there was nothing to file."

His uncle flinched and cleared his throat. "At that time, did you know the source of Vivian's funds?"

Jason smoothed a wrinkle on his shirt that wasn't there. "Vivian paid by cashier's check, not by bank transfer, for privacy reasons."

Uncle Brian rapped his thigh with a fingernail. "You wrote 'client known to me' on the due-diligence checklist and ticked the not-applicable box on the enhanced-due-diligence line."

Right. Jason remembered the form. Heat crept up his neck. He swallowed, jaw tense, and met Uncle Brian's gaze. "Vivian had stamped tax returns and a letter from her Macau bank." He shut his eyes. In his mind's vision, the scalpel-thin line of light under the penthouse door when they did the second viewing appeared brighter than the sun.

"DreamAchieve is mentioned in the papers they seized from Vivian's office."

Debra patted his hand. He opened his eyes.

Uncle Brian rose, then sat again. "I called a solicitor. Yip & Yip. They do regulatory work. Ms. Yip can see us at four. She said we shouldn't delete anything or talk to anyone."

On the street below, a bus coughed, a horn popped. The one question Jason didn't want to voice found its way out. "What will the penalty be for me?"

"Fine. License suspension. Jail for egregious." Uncle Brian reached for the mug, then lowered his arm. "ICAC may get involved if they decide DreamAchieve made it easier for her."

The ICAC, the Independent Commission Against Corruption. Bile burned Jason's throat. He forced it down. "Do they have evidence against Vivian?"

"They raided her office." Debra glanced at him. "People talk. Names leak."

He leaned forward. The armchair creaked. "Okay." He rose. His legs felt like he'd stayed too long at the cinema. "We go to Ms. Yip this afternoon."

He winced at a flash of Vivian's image. Her perfect nails tapping the counter, her whisper in his ear, her caressing his thigh… "Why me?" he once asked. To which, she had smiled. "Because you're my old classmate and don't ask the wrong questions."

The intercom buzzed. Debra and Uncle Brian froze. Jason answered.

"Security here. You have visitors. Shall we send them up?"

He exhaled. "Yes, please."

A minute later, the lift chimed, and footsteps approached.

He opened the door the width of the chain.

A woman showed him a name card. Hong Kong Police. Commercial Crime Bureau. Another person, a man in a navy suit holding a canvas bag, stood behind her.

"Mr. Guan?" Her Cantonese came across crisp. "Inspector Kwok and my colleague Inspector Situ here. We need to ask you some questions."

He undid the chain. "Come in." His voice sounded lower than usual.

They stepped out of their shoes and onto the flat. The man set the canvas bag on the floor with care. Inspector Kwok glanced at the mug on the table, then at Jason's face. "We understand you assisted Ms. Vivian Jiang with the purchase of a property at Mid-Levels. Our source indicated that her money originated from a BVI holding company, Larkspur Ventures, and was then routed through a Macau bank. If you don't mind, we want to look at your records pertaining to that transaction."

"Do you have a warrant?" Uncle Brian stood.

Inspector Kwok met it with a professional smile. "At this stage, we are making inquiries. You may decline. You may also invite us to sit and speak. We will obtain the appropriate paperwork if necessary."

Don't move. Don't talk.

The attorney's advice rang true. Jason squinted. "We've engaged counsel and will schedule an interview at your convenience with our lawyer present."

Kwok's gaze held his a second longer than polite. "Of course." She reached into her jacket and slid a card onto the table. "Please don't destroy any documents related to Ms. Jiang. It would be a criminal offense to do so."

The inspectors left. Brian sank onto the couch. The flat squeezed in. Jason picked up the card. The ridged edges bit into his fingers.

Debra's hand found his. Her touch steadied him, her presence a balm. "We visit Yip at four o'clock."

Chapter Twenty-Eight

Pearl River, Guangdong, China
Late Spring 1852

The river had worn itself into a hush. Mist hung low over the water.

Xin wrung water from his sleeves and descended into the berth. Hao stirred, hair slicked to his brow.

"Brother"—Xin sat beside him—"whilst you slept, we were caught by a hidden current. It nearly swallowed us whole. With death so near, my sins rose before me. Then Old Li told me how much Roberts loves me, and straightway the matter was plain. When Christ suffered, I was there. My hand swung the hammer. I was the thief beside Him. Yet He forgave. If He forgives me, He will forgive you. Turn not your back upon Him."

Hao yawned. "You sound like those foreign liars in Guangzhou." He sneered. "Always whining about their god nailed to a stick." His mouth twisted. "Did you not seek heavenly peace? Where is it? You clutch at dreams, Xin. Do you think a dead man on a cross can wipe away what we have done?"

The words cut deep. Xin's fingers trembled. He spread his palms against the rough planks to steady the drumbeat in his chest. "When I shut my eyes, I saw myself on the cross. He had taken my place on that cursed tree. But it didn't end there. He rose. His resurrection gives us hope."

"Fool." Hao ground his teeth. "Pray to your ghost if it comforts you. Get away from me."

A tightness closed Xin's throat. He swallowed against it. Heat prickled behind his eyelids. He inhaled hard until the ache eased. "Lord, help him," he whispered and, with a heavy tread, returned to the deck.

Old Li stood at the stern, palm resting on the sweep. The ferryman's profile seemed carved by the current.

The river's chill lived in the tender place beneath Xin's ribs. He bowed his head, jaw tight. "Old Li, is peace nothing more than what a strong man holds by force?"

"The strong man's force fails." Old Li traced a circle on the sweep with one finger.

Xin's shoulders twitched. In his mind rose the dull thunder of fists, the flare of banners, the hiss of arrows, and the clatter of spearheads rattling in a hundred grips.

Old Li's finger kept its calm orbit. "I have known a peace that endures when my strength is spent."

The words landed warm, weighty. Xin gaped at Old Li.

Old Li let the sweep catch the water, then eased his pull. "Years back, when a flood stranded me in the city, I stayed with Roberts. He spoke of Nicholas Ridley, an Englishman who was burned for his Christian convictions." He shifted his weight. "On the night before his execution, his brother offered to remain with him in the prison to provide comfort. He declined and replied that he would go to bed and sleep as usual. Ridley knew the peace of God, did he not?"

Xin opened his mouth to answer, and nothing came out. He shut it. The current licked the hull.

Old Li's lips curled up. "Roberts also told of Jesus' own words. 'Peace I leave with you; my peace I give you. Not as the world gives.' A gift unbought. I have not found that kind of peace anywhere except in Christ."

The breath Xin drew shuddered on the way in. The eastern sky had turned pale. He directed his gaze toward the thin blade of light. Alas, peace did not come after the Taiping seized a city. It climbed into the boat last night, when the river's perilous current surged against them. He cleared his throat. "I heard peace speak through you when the water struck. And for a moment, I was not afraid."

The mist thinned, birds piping tentative notes. Old Li pressed the sweep, and the boat answered.

Hao's harsh shout rose beneath the deck. "Lies, useless lies."

Xin flinched. Heat burned his cheeks, yet a thin thread of hope held fast. "I am a man in debt. Yet Christ has forgiven me. I plead with God for His forgiveness to reach Hao like the dawn."

As if summoned, the horizon unbarred its light. One ray, then another, broke from the dark. The junk nosed down the Pearl River's broad mouth. The brown river chop lengthened into a long ocean swell, and the tide carried them eastward past Macau into the South China Sea. A scatter of islets stitched the water.

Hao emerged from the berth and leaned on the bulkhead, his eyes narrowed in a half-scornful gaze. "Pray, cast aside your useless talk. Cheung Po-Tsai has long gone to his grave. Yet whispers remain that broken bands of sea marauders still haunt these seas."

"Indeed. Wolves roam this coast." Old Li scratched his chin. "But their packs are scattered. No longer do they rule the waters with fleets of a hundred sails. These days, they creep in a single junk or in twos and target the smaller craft."

Hao patted his belt. "A petty trade. They dare not attack the merchant armadas, nor the foreign brigs with cannon. Instead, they prey on fishermen and small traders, boats with little more than a few sacks of rice aboard."

"Aye." Old Li nodded toward the misty horizon. "And in these areas, even a single junk flying false colors may be more than enough to bleed an unwary crew."

"Why do we worry?" Xin sat on the planks. The current muttered, a comforting sound. "God's grace is sufficient. Brother, you slept through the worst of the river's wrath. Christ delivers all who call upon Him."

Hao let out a cackle. "Will this god of yours strike down pirates when their hooks bite into our deck?" He spat over the side. "Better to trust the steel in your fist than some spirit's whisper."

Xin's lips tightened. "His mercy is greater than our strength. Even you, Hao, could find rest in Him."

Hao stepped close until his shadow swallowed Xin. "Rest? Rest is for corpses. Remember Quanzhou? Who shielded you from the Qing soldiers who wanted you dead? Not your Christ, but me."

His brother's mockery pierced Xin's soul anew. An image from his boyhood rose before him. The river ran high. The rope-bridge strained and sang. Hao stepped out, laughing, feigning a fall. Xin clung to the willow trunk, the color gone from his fingers.

Afterward, in the cool shade of the pines, Hao vowed, "When I grow up, I will set a bridge that shan't sway. Mothers and children shall pass over it as on the floor of a house."

Years passed. While others drifted, Hao tried to make good on his word. He patched nets at night for coin, carried sand in winter, and learned the weights of plank and stone. Before the undertaking was concluded, the Qing soldiers arrived and snatched him away.

Where had that kindhearted boy gone? Why did he become a man whose gaze ran ahead of him, measuring exits and distances? He struck first and never inquired. A plea was wind. Mercy, once his habit, slipped from him like a shadow.

Oh Lord, let Your grace shine upon Hao.

Perhaps Hao might soon find light on a gentler path.

A breeze swept over Xin. Two low-built junks with patched sails emerged from behind an island. Soon, the dull beat of drums carried across the water.

Old Li's hand paused on the tiller. "'Tis as I feared. Make ready."

He stood and lifted a lantern high, swinging thrice in a practiced arc.

Hao sprang up, eyes alight with a fierce delight. "At last! We shall see if your God delivers you!"

Cold knifed down Xin's spine. Across their bow, a junk loomed, its shadow blotting out the dawn. Gunfire cracked. The ball thudded into the mast above his head. Splinters peppered his sleeve.

"Down! Down!" Old Li's voice cut through the smoke.

Out of the smoke came a hiss and a clatter. Iron claws of grappling hooks rang against the rail. The ropes thrummed as the pirates hauled in rhythm. More hooks arced across. Water gurgled between the hulls until the two boats kissed with a grinding thud.

"Cut those lines!" Xin lunged to kick a hook free. The hemp burned his palm, and he stumbled back.

Hao heeded not. With a shout, he snatched an oar from the rail and swung it at the first man to leap onto the deck. The fellow's jaw fractured beneath the blow.

Xin moved into a corner. His heart pounded as more raiders poured across.

Old Li planted his feet and lashed out with a pole, knocking down one assailant. "Ah Fai, bring up the weapons."

The deckhand flung open a bag and smacked a sword into Xin's palm.

A pirate lunged. Xin slid aside. His sword found the man's ribs. The raider crumpled. Xin gasped at what he had done.

In Xin's peripheral vision, Hao's oar crashed against one attacker's leg, spun in the air, and cracked another across the temple. Yet each strike left him open, and a knife nicked his arm. Scarlet seeped from his sleeve. He bared his teeth. "You think me weak?"

Old Li parried a cut from a pirate's saber, countering with a sharp jab of his pole. "Xin! The left!"

Xin pivoted and whipped his sword in a tight arc. The cross guard snagged the pirate's collar and yanked him off-balance. The man thudded onto the deck.

More bodies crashed in, the reek of tar and brine thickening. Xin and Hao were driven into a corner patched with splinters. Hao's oar felled two assailants, yet a third slipped in close and smote him beneath the chin with a short cudgel. He staggered, blood spilling from his mouth.

"Xin…" he rasped. "Falter not."

"Brother!" The word tore out of Xin before he could breathe. Heat rushed to his face. Then a cold hollowness opened inside him.

A rogue surged in. Xin's vision tunneled, the world shrinking to the swing of an arm and the pound of his heart. He stepped into the attack and rammed his sword into the foe's side. "I won't falter," he hissed, dragging the blade free. "I swear it."

Hao clutched his wound, fingers slick with blood. His eyes found Xin's—pain, defiance, and the bewildering tenderness of their boyhood flickering at once.

Xin's throat cinched shut. *Nay. Not him. Not now.*

He grabbed Hao's shoulder. "Hold fast, brother—stay with me." His voice cracked.

"Help is coming!" Old Li yelled.

A glimmer of sails broke from behind a nearby isle. A faint chorus of hymns wafted over the water.

"Our brethren have heeded my earlier signal." Old Li straightened, color returning to his face. "Fight them off a moment longer!"

Ah Fai leaped up, his blade cutting into a pirate's elbow.

As the Christian boats drew near, the attackers faltered. They dragged their wounded away, leaving a dark smear that thinned in their wake. Two dead remained where they fell. Then the marauders fled back to their junks, and the deck returned to peace, save for the soft slap of water against the hull.

Ah Fai helped Old Li dump the corpses into the water.

Hao's face twitched, blood at the corner of his mouth. "It… was always the river… that I feared."

The words cut into Xin's soul. Memories rushed back. Bare feet on slick stones, he fell, and Hao pulled him up. Xin gathered Hao tighter, as if love were a weight heavy enough to keep a body from drifting. The sun hid behind a cloud, indifferent.

"You see… your prayers… did not save me." Scorn curled Hao's lips. "The world is… rotten. Trust nothing but… your…"

"Hao, do not forsake me. We will bind the wound." Xin choked up. *Oh Lord, save Hao.*

So many memories… Summers and swollen rivers, nights shared on a mat with their knees touching, boyhood oaths uttered in a world both vast and simple.

Hao's eyes fixed upon the sky, bitterness fading into vacancy.

Xin laid Hao's head on his lap, his heart a storm of grief. *You know us by name. Then why did You not answer my prayer and spare Hao?*

Old Li laid a hand on Xin's shoulder. "He is gone. The Lord has taken him, as He takes all men in their hour."

Xin stared at his brother's still face, tears falling down his cheeks.

Chapter Twenty-Nine

In the battle's wake, the waves lapped as though mocking the carnage on the deck. Xin wrapped Hao's body in a sailcloth. His lips trembled, but no sound escaped.

Silence. No more of his brother's scornful remarks or his laughter that Xin remembered from childhood.

Old Li placed a hand on his shoulder. "The sea gives and takes. That is her bargain since before our fathers had names."

The sailcloth turned stiff where the blood had dried in the sun. Xin bowed over the shrouded form. The deck smelled of powder and iron. He tried to respond and found his throat a locked door.

"Do not fight the silence. Sometimes 'tis the only wise sound a man hears." Old Li's shadow fell over Hao's covered head. "He was a sharp one. Quick with his tongue."

Xin swallowed. "He said God was for fools and hell did not exist."

Old Li shifted his weight, the boards creaking. "Aye. He mocked. Perhaps 'twas his way of holding fear." He patted Xin's shoulder again. "Do not let his last words cut you twice."

Footsteps sounded. A group of Christians approached and stood at a respectful distance. A girl wearing a cross on a cord stepped closer. She glanced from the sailcloth to Xin. "Only God knows who are His."

Xin's fingers tightened into fists. Would Hao fall into hell? "If he goes down, does he go down to the bottom? If the Judge looks upon him and remembers his scorn—"

Another man came forward. "The Lord alone knows who are saved and who are not. We shall commit the matter unto Him."

Old Li turned to the speaker. "Brother, will you lead us in a hymn and in prayer?"

The wind hissed. Somewhere below, the bilge sloshed. The girl with the cross hummed a line from a hymn. The rest joined her, and they began to sing.

Afterward, the catechist prayed for resurrection and reunion, with the humility a man bore before the Almighty. After the loud amen, Xin's body ceased shivering. Not yet unto peace, but unto the possibility thereof.

With needle and twine, he pressed the point through stiff sailcloth, each stitch a small surrender. At Hao's face, he paused. "Will he be warm?"

Old Li patted his back. "The dead don't feel cold."

Xin nodded and tied a round stone to the feet. "Lord, look kindly on my brother. If he mocked You, remember also his little courage."

Toward the rail, they moved. The waves whispered, indifferent. They slid the body into the water with a soft splash. Xin stared at the place where the ripples widened and thinned.

"Only God knows." He drew a breath and tasted salt and smoke.

"Come, child." Old Li tugged at his sleeve. "The voyage remains."

"Aye," Xin whispered. "The voyage continues, but never the same."

✳ ✧ ✳

The Christian boats sailed alongside their junk. The fleet turned toward a hidden cove. A cluster of huts on stilts stood, braced against the tide. After they disembarked, Xin, accompanied by Old Li, walked toward a larger dwelling in the center of the settlement.

Liang Fa sat within. His white beard fell on his chest. Yet his eyes shone with a tranquil fire. Beside him sat Wang Jun and his wife, Ying Si-Fen. The aged preacher rose and greeted Xin. "Old Li told us what happened. You have passed through the furnace and not been consumed. Blessed is the man whom the Lord delivers."

On his knees before he knew it, Xin bowed his head, and he could not lift his gaze from the mat. At length, he found his voice. "Teacher Liang, I have a matter on my conscience. Please forgive me. I took the treasure maps from your trunk."

"Rise, my son. I have already forgiven you in the name of our Redeemer."

Heat and cold swept through Xin at once, and the ache gave way. He stood and wiped his eyes.

While Wang Jun kept his hands within his sleeves, Ying Si-Fen placed a small cup of tea before Xin. "Please sit." She gave her husband another cup. "Upon our return, we discovered the maps gone. Since the treasure is a fatal snare, we sought you in every quarter to avert calamity."

"Indeed." Wang Jun sipped his tea. "We have been seeking you. Many scour the islands for Cheung Po-Tsai's buried treasure, not knowing the hoard is tainted with deadly poison. Men have fallen dead for only a touch."

Chill crept up Xin's spine. He sat down. His fingers lost their steadiness. The room drew close about him. "Is it so? How did you gain such knowledge?"

Ying Si-Fen leaned forward. "He was compelled to witness it. Years ago, a band of Qing soldiers forced him and an aging brother, Bai Dian, to lead them to a cave."

Wang Jun's face twitched. The tremor spoke of old torment. Remorse pricked Xin for pressing him, and he held his tongue.

She returned her focus to Xin. "Finding the buried treasure, the soldiers laughed and cried out for a blessing. Then they clawed at their throats and fell."

Xin's mouth turned dry. He gaped at Wang Jun. "How did you escape?"

"They tied me and Bai Dian to a stone pillar." Wang Jun inhaled. "The men used hammers and chisels to break an aperture in the wall. They crawled in. Bai Dian and I strained against our bonds to peer into the breach and beheld the entire scene. After the soldiers collapsed, we tried to loosen our bonds to no avail. By God's mercy, Si-Fen, following close upon the soldiers, loosed us. Our dear brother Bai Dian has since gone to the Lord at a ripe old age."

Xin looked from one to the other. The night pressed close. Beyond the rocks, the surf muttered like an old man in troubled sleep. "Is there a remedy to remove the poison?"

"Perchance." Ying Si-Fen inclined her head. "Cheung Po-Tsai warded his wealth with a sailor's cunning, not a sorcerer's spell." A weary sigh escaped her. "Greed slays more than storms. As Christians, we are taught to lay up treasure in heaven, not clutch at the glitter of this passing world."

Xin lurched to his feet, then sank back, his heart knocking against his ribs. The room swam as if the air were water. "I have heard Miao Lan is with you." His voice wavered between hope and fear. "Where is she? Will you lead us to the pirate's gold? She and I must secure it so her baba may approve of our suit."

"Take heart. Some treasures are not buried in caves." She turned toward the doorway and flicked two fingers, a quiet summons. "Please ask Miao Lan to come."

Light footsteps sounded. A slender figure burst into his sight. Miao Lan entered and walked up to him. "You are safe, Xin. Praise the Lord."

His tongue failed him. The chamber held its breath. Somewhere, a gull cried. The wind fretted the lattice. Her touch burned upon his sleeve like a coal, and he dared not stir for fear the moment should be shattered. His gaze fixed on the loosened thread on her cuff. The faint jasmine scent in her hair leaped into his nostrils.

She hesitated, her lips quavering. "My baba is no more. He fell at Quanzhou. I am released from his disapproval, and Uncle Liang Fa has become my guardian."

Released.

The word struck Xin. Sorrow for her loss ran through him, keen as a blade. Old Miao's intense gaze, the line of his mouth that could be stern or kind, the war cries, the last glance backward that a father might give for his beloved daughter…

Yet under the mourning surged a joy that shamed him for its boldness. He yearned to hug her. Instead, he pressed fist to fist, as if he would chain desire with his bones. "Then naught stands between us save our own hearts. If I have any worth, 'tis yours. The treasure can remain buried with its poison."

Tears welled in her eyes but did not dim their brightness. A tender smile touched her lips. "My heart has long since been yours."

He lowered his head lest she detect the moisture behind his eyelids. When he looked up, her hand still lay on his sleeve. "Lan, let me carry a part of your grief. I am not strong. But for you, I would be stronger than I have ever been."

"You're strong even when no one sees." She dabbed her face with a handkerchief. "Remember the rainy night at the ford? You gave me your cloak and shivered. You trembled for my sake."

The gull cried again, nearer now. He thought of Quanzhou, the rumors and the fear, the night Hao brought him to the flower boat… Still more confessions to make. Perhaps later.

✳ ◇ ✳

Days passed in mourning for Lan's father and Hao. Xin walked as one still under a shadow, yet Lan's presence seemed a lamp in the darkness.

He sighted the aged preacher beneath the camphor tree.

"Come." Liang Fa motioned to the bench. "Sit with me a little, my son."

In silence, Xin bowed and obeyed, breath caught somewhere high in his throat.

Liang Fa regarded Xin. "Your steps are heavy. How stands your heart?"

Clenching his knee until his knuckles blanched, he forced the sentences out. "A matter gnaws at my conscience. In my folly, I visited a prostitute with Hao. Ought I to tell Lan? I fear to cloud her heart and stain our bond."

Heat climbed his neck. A pulse hammered at his temple. He dared not lift his gaze.

"Truth is the safer ground." Liang Fa thumbed through his white beard. "Miao Lan has already acknowledged her own sins before the Lord. She will forgive you, as one forgiven."

The tautness ebbed from his muscles. His fingers unhooked from their grip on his knee. The breath he had hoarded for days slipped out of him. His voice dipped lower. "Duty tells me to keep the memories alive so the dead won't grow cold. But when Lan speaks, it's as if a shutter lifts and spring air rushes in. I'm ashamed to find comfort so soon."

The elder nodded. "Do not feel guilty for setting your grief down. What matters is whether you are true. Will you protect Lan with your life?"

Xin's breath caught anew. "I am resolved. Only—" The word snagged in his throat. "Only the custom is against us. To wed in mourning is to draw scrutiny. They will say we have forgotten the deceased's names. I would not have our joy tread on their memory."

"The Bible teaches us to greet the morning even when the night is not over." Liang Fa stroked his beard. "Join your life to Lan's. In such a time, let your house be a sign of hope."

Xin stood and bowed again. "Indeed. Would you preside over this matter for us?"

Liang Fa rose to his feet. "I shall send word to Reverend Roberts that he may officiate at your nuptials." He winked at Xin. "You may likewise restore the watch chain and the gold coins to him."

A hush gathered around them, akin to the curtain lifting at dawn.

✳ ✧ ✳

The day turned. Weeks slipped by.

Outside, the wind shifted, sending a dry rustle along the dusty road. The peril beyond the gate had not vanished. Rumors spread that the Taiping had seized Nanjing and were pressing north toward Peking, seat of the Qing.

Inside the community's chapel, Ying Si-Fen adjusted the red veil over Lan's face. Xin wore a magua in sapphire blue paired with a long robe, while the bride was adorned in a red silk gown embroidered with a golden phoenix.

Bamboo benches lined the walls. A single candle flickered on the table that served as an altar. Roberts lifted both arms, and the murmur stilled. "Beloved, in a season of tears, the Lord appoints gladness. These two would be bound, not to forget their grief, but to bear it together and thereby to live."

He beckoned. Xin and Lan moved to stand before him. The candle flame leaned, then straightened.

"Zhang Xin"—the missionary fixed his gaze on Xin—"do you take Miao Lan to be your wife, promising to keep her in sickness and health, in want and in plenty, to honor her as your own life, and to walk with her in the fear of God and the peace of neighbors, as He shall give you strength?"

"I do," Xin responded in a firm voice.

"And you, Miao Lan," Roberts continued, "do you take Zhang Xin to be your husband, promising to stand with him at all times, to comfort and to counsel, to labor and to pray, as God shall grant you days?"

"I do," she affirmed, and the answer kindled warmth in Xin's heart.

Roberts laid his hand on their joined fingers. "Then, in the sight of God and of this community, I bind you in holy matrimony. What He has joined, let no one divide." He stepped back and waved. "Go in peace and shine."

Night deepened. The people feasted on rice, fish, and farm-grown vegetables. Stars spread their quiet light above, as though heaven itself smiled upon the humble company. Wang Hui brandished a stick by the fire. Ying Si-Fen laughed and drew him away, while Liang Fa and Wang Jun looked on with affection. Old Li lifted a hymn of thanksgiving, and all voices joined.

Xin sat with Miao Lan at his side, her hand in his.

Lord, set us on a course guided, not by men's wrath, but by Your peace.

Chapter Thirty

Hong Kong, China
Winter 2022

A tide of noises crested against the courthouse's stone façade. Reporters clustered at the entrance, cameras flashing, microphones thrust forward. Jason bowed his head and moved among them, his suit collar damp where nervous sweat seeped through.

"DreamAchieve Realty!" one man shouted in Cantonese.

"Did you help launder mainland money?" came a sharper question in English.

His shadow bounced on the pale gray ground beyond his shoes. The shouts blurred together into a metallic roar.

Next to him, Debra tightened her grip on his sleeve. Clad in a simple navy dress, she was a shield, unyielding in presence.

"Keep walking," murmured Ms. Yip, their counsel. Her heels clicked on the steps. "Don't answer. Not a word."

Jason obeyed. His voice wouldn't work even if he tried.

The courthouse doors swung open. Inside, the clamor subsided to an austere hush. The Hong Kong regional emblem hung above, a spot once occupied by the queen's portrait.

Pausing by the defense table, Jason stole a glance at the gallery. Grandpa sank into his seat, his jaw locked. Uncle Brian flanked him on one side, and Debra's mom—Maggie—on the other, her hair swept into a neat bun.

Mom had called Debra and said that Grandpa's caretaker, Mrs. Liu, planned to stay home with Mateo. The child was spared this spectacle, tucked away from the storm.

Jason settled down, back rigid, palms flat on his thighs. When the robed magistrate entered, everyone rose. Jason's knees turned to damp sand as he obliged.

The prosecutor, a balding man with rimless glasses, launched into the case. "DreamAchieve Realty facilitated the sale of a luxury Mid-Levels penthouse to Vivian Jiang, an executive from the mainland biotech sector. The funds traced through Macau and shell entities. Under Hong Kong's anti–money laundering regime, every licensed agent must file a Suspicious Transaction Report. Mr. Guan failed to do so."

Failed obligation. Willful negligence.

Jason's chest tightened. Once more, he scanned the benches, catching Debra's steady gaze. Her lips pressed together as though in silent contemplation.

Ms. Yip rose. "My client does not dispute that the transaction occurred under his facilitation. He does not dispute that he failed to file the required report. But let the court consider this. There is no evidence of collusion, no proof of enrichment beyond a standard commission. Mr. Guan was misled by a former classmate he trusted." She waved a hand, her cadence deliberate. "A woman who concealed her dealings until she herself was exposed. My client's error is naïveté, not corruption. He has cooperated fully since, and he poses no ongoing risk."

The prosecutor countered. "Naïveté does not absolve duty. Our system depends on vigilance. If every agent claimed ignorance, the gates would stand open to illicit capital. Mr. Guan's lapse undermines the integrity of Hong Kong's financial defense."

As the prosecutor and Ms. Yip traded voices, Jason sat rigid, nails biting his palm to stop the tremor. The prosecutor's syllables thudded against his chest, while Ms. Yip's steadied him. Each word, either indictment or defense, peeled him bare before the room.

At the end, murmurs rippled among the spectators. The magistrate raised a hand. Silence fell. "This court will recess before sentencing."

The gavel cracked like thunder.

Once inside the holding lounge, Jason stared at the dull linoleum floor. The hum of fluorescent lights gnawed at him.

The guard at the door allowed Debra in. She crossed the small space and sat next to him on the hard bench. For a moment, she said nothing and only reached for his fingers.

"Breathe," she whispered. "God hasn't abandoned us."

Jason swallowed. "One form," he croaked, remorse scraping his throat. "One report. Ten minutes. That's all it would have taken. And I didn't."

The admission weighed down his shoulders.

"You didn't." She nodded. "And now you admit your negligence. That's the difference. Repentance means God can work with you."

He pressed a palm to his eyes. "Maybe I didn't file it because I was blinded by greed and overconfidence. I—"

Greed. Overconfidence.

The words scorched his tongue, cinched his ribs, and heat climbed his neck.

She leaned into him. "Don't let the enemy drown you in regret. There's already grace."

His mind flitted back to the manuscript about Zhang Xin. The man's wrongdoings had piled high as mountains, yet when he confessed everything and surrendered to Christ, he received salvation.

A man guilty of far more than I am found forgiveness. Why can't I believe it for myself?

He swallowed again and shook his head hard, trying to jar loose Vivian's perfume, the glassy laughter, the city glittering beyond the penthouse windows…

Debra's grip anchored him as the images surged and broke, and he exhaled. "Lord," he mouthed, voice raw, "I'm sorry."

A deputy cracked the door and gestured for Jason to move. He stood and followed the officer to the courtroom. Murmurs faded. He shrank into the chair next to Ms. Yip, a vain attempt to make himself smaller.

The magistrate's tone sounded flat. Still, every word cut.

"This court finds Mr. Guan breached his obligations under the Anti–Money Laundering and Counter–Terrorist Financing Ordinance. While there is insufficient evidence of collusion or personal profit beyond commission, the failure to file a Suspicious Transaction Report is a grave negligence. The court imposes a fine of three hundred thousand Hong Kong dollars. His real estate license is suspended for six months. Imprisonment is not warranted. Let this stand as a warning."

Jason's breath escaped in a rush. His knees nearly buckled. The fine stung, the suspension hurt, but there was no prison.

He glanced back at his loved ones. Debra sat straighter. Uncle Brian smiled. His mother-in-law covered her mouth, her eyes glistening. Grandpa grabbed his cane and gave him the faintest nod of approval—an acknowledgment of endurance.

Outside the building, reporters swarmed. Microphones jabbed.

"Did DreamAchieve know?"

"Were you protecting Vivian Jiang?"

"No comment," Ms. Yip snapped and steered him toward the waiting taxi.

Debra clung to his arm, chin high as flashbulbs burst around them.

* ✦ *

The taxi shifted away from the frenzy of cameras and shouts. Inside the cab, Jason slumped against the vinyl seat, his breaths uneven. Debra held his hand, her thumb circling his knuckles as though to steady his pulse.

Before them, the taxi carrying Grandpa, Uncle Brian, and Debra's mom sped ahead. The city blurred past. At last, the cab pulled up to the apartment tower where Uncle Brian and Mom lived. They entered through the side entrance and rode the elevator in silence.

The apartment door opened onto the scent of jasmine tea. Grandpa walked toward the armchair by the window and propped his cane against the side. Mrs. Liu emerged from the hallway, Mateo perched on her hip. The boy squealed at the sight of his parents and kicked his little legs.

"Ah, Mateo." Mom rushed forward to gather her son into her arms. She kissed his cheeks as if to draw courage from his laughter.

"Thank you, Mrs. Liu." Brian slipped her an envelope before guiding her out. She waved at Jason and left.

The apartment settled into a hush. Jason sank deep into the sofa, elbows on his knees, palms pressed to his face.

Uncle Brian poured tea, then set a cup before Jason. "So, a fine and suspension. I consider it a fair outcome."

The word *fair* snagged in Jason's chest. His knee wouldn't stop bouncing. He jerked up his head. "I—Uncle Brian, DreamAchieve Realty—"

Heat flooded his ears. He pushed for the rest of the sentence, but his jaw clamped until it ached. All he could manage was a shaky breath and the sick weight of what he couldn't say.

Uncle Brian wagged a finger. "Not now. We'll talk about the company later. For tonight, try to relax if you can."

Grandpa cleared his throat. "The law has spoken." His Cantonese carried the cadence of old courtrooms. "Justice is not always mercy. Today, you were given both."

Jason stilled. His aging grandfather's gaze, sharp as ever, fixed him in place.

Uncle Brian leaned forward. "Do you remember the manuscript we've been reading together?"

Jason nodded. Had his loved ones also reflected on Xin's journey while waiting at the courthouse?

Uncle Brian pushed his cup aside. "Xin did things far worse than mere negligence. When spiritual conviction struck him, he confessed his sins, repented, and clung to Christ. He was made new."

The words pierced Jason's chest. He stared down at his feet again. "Xin didn't drag his family into a scandal with him."

Grandpa touched his cane. "Don't mistake consequences for condemnation. You'll bear the fine and the suspension. That is just. But you aren't defined by this failure—unless you choose to be."

The city hummed outside the windows. Mom patted Mateo's back. "Jason, Deb told me what happened between you and Vivian. It could have been much worse. The Lord's protection is upon all of us."

Debra shifted closer and slipped her arm through his. "Hong Kong has turned Vivian over to the Chinese authorities. She is still waiting to be sentenced. Rumors say it'll be severe. Considering her and Sandy, we're truly blessed."

For the first time since the verdict, a breath moved through Jason without choking him.

Grandpa closed his eyes as if in prayer, then opened them. "Let's remember today. Not for shame but for God's grace on us."

Silence ensued. Mateo babbled and clapped, oblivious to the weight of grown-up sorrow, his laughter rising like a bell.

Jason reached out to touch the child's hair. A life untouched by deceit, by fines, by the judgment of courts. What would he grow up to be?

A thought settled within him. If God's mercy saved Xin in 1850, perhaps it could cover Jason too.

❋ ◇ ❋

After the family dinner, Jason and Debra returned to their flat a few blocks away. The lights of Kowloon shimmered beyond the windows, yet he kept his focus on the floor, unable to take them in.

Debra drew him to the sofa, then left for the kitchen. Porcelain clinking drifted back. When she returned, she set a cup of tea before him.

"I disgraced you today," he murmured, his voice rough.

"You think my dignity depends on you being spotless?" She sat beside him and rested a hand on his wrist. "Jason, look at me."

He forced himself to lift his head.

Her gaze locked with his. "You didn't lie to the court or to me. That's courage."

His gut knotted. He swallowed. "I feel filthy. Like there's tar under my skin that won't wash away."

She leaned on his shoulder. The jasmine scent of her hair softened the heaviness in his chest. "Very few men could have escaped the traps Vivian set for you. But you did. Don't forget that." Her voice quieted. "I believe God shielded you then, and He isn't leaving you now."

Jason's throat tightened. Tears blurred his vision. He sank into her warmth, and the dam broke. Tears flooded down his cheeks. His shoulders shook.

Debra held him close, stroking his back. "You haven't been sleeping well since the two inspectors from the Commercial Crime Bureau visited us. I pray you won't have nightmares tonight."

His sobs slowed, and exhaustion drew him into slumber.

Epilogue

Cheung Chau Island, Hong Kong, China
Winter 2022

The ferry bucked over the whitecaps. Jason stood at the rail with a cake box balanced in the crook of his arm. His stomach rode the same jagged rise and drop. Debra pressed into his side when the ferry yawed, and his body adjusted automatically. Ahead, Cheung Chau Island rose out of the blue. The tiny harbor curved like a hooked arm around the sea.

"Are you sure it's okay to put the buttercream in the sun?" Debra hugged the bag of toys for Mateo, voice pitched to ride over the engines.

"Hey, it's winter." Jason's lips crinkled up. "And we'll store it in the fridge soon."

Her eyes caught the pale sun and sparkled. The light in them comforted him, a knot in his stomach easing.

A horn blasted as the ferry slid into the crowded harbor. A boy sprinted along the rail and was caught by an older woman, perhaps his grandmother. The sight hit a nerve. How easy it was to go too far without meaning to, how much depended on someone catching him in time.

"Careful," he said, though he wasn't talking to the boy.

After disembarking, they stepped in with the crowd. The island's narrow lanes swallowed them, bright with food stands. The smell of fish balls and caramelized sugar drifted from a stall.

"Did you see the WhatsApp message from Uncle Brian? He ordered a few dishes from the nearby restaurant, and Mom prepared a basketful of red-dyed eggs for good luck." Debra hitched the toy bag higher on her shoulder. "Mateo is turning one. How did that happen?"

"Everything happens fast."

His gaze flicked toward her face again. Was she thinking of the courthouse, of the judge's stern voice? She was too kind to mention it. Yet how could they forget?

Grandpa's beach house loomed ahead. Salt touched Jason's tongue. He'd spent numerous summers here with Grandpa and Uncle Brian, scraping his knee on the same rock every year and eating buns from the ferry pier with sugar stuck to his lips.

As they stepped onto the porch, Mom opened the sliding door. The laces of her apron billowed. "You're late." She pressed her cheek to his, then swept Debra into a hug.

"Traffic on the high seas." Jason chuckled, lifting the cake high.

"Don't joke," she scolded with a grin, took the box from him, and checked under the lid. "Ah, not melted. Great."

They entered the living room. Uncle Brian staggered in with Mateo on his shoulders, hands clamped around the infant's ankles to prevent a tumble. "Birthday boy coming through."

Mateo wore a bib that declared, "I am 1" in crooked stitches. A white smear on one cheek made him look like a tiny wrestler. He had Uncle Brian's hair clutched in one fist as if steering a very confused horse. Spotting Jason and Debra, he dropped both chubby arms and nearly fell backward in his excitement. "Ba! Ba!"

"Not Ba." Mom clucked. "Say Jie-Jie and handsome Ge-Ge."

"Guh—" Mateo scrunched his nose. "Ge-Ge." It came out on a triumphant breath.

He reached out. Jason offered his thumb, and the little fingers closed around it. They were damp and impossibly strong. "Hey, birthday tiger."

Grandpa shuffled in from the backyard, wiping his palms on a towel. "Even though it's winter, the ocean is not too rough today."

Jason stepped forward and took his elbow, feeling the old man's wiry strength. With the relief came the same fear that had been in his chest since Grandpa's hospital stay last year because of COVID. "You look well. Where is your cane? You don't need it anymore?"

"I saw a crab as big as your palm." Grandpa ignored the subject of his health and set down the towel. "Too quick for me." He surveyed the cake. "From that fancy shop with the gold box?"

"Man Wah Road." Mom giggled. "Very fancy, right?"

She'd turned a heap of cushions into a corner throne for Mateo's first-birthday photo. Strings of paper lanterns hung across the wall, each lantern bearing Mateo's face.

Someone—Grandpa?—had arranged a children's Bible, a toy stethoscope, and a calculator in a loose crescent on the floor. According to the custom, the baby's future would be set by the first thing he reached for. Jason had laughed the first time he saw it. Now, watching his tiny brother-in-law, he wanted him to reach for something that signified kindness and blessing from the Lord.

"Wait, do we have enough utensils?" Debra called. "And napkins."

"Stop fussing," Mom scolded once more with a smile. "You fuss when you're happy and when you're sad, so you confuse me."

Jason caught Debra's gaze across the room and watched the way her eyes shone. How she enjoyed her mother's teasing! "May I say a few words before dinner?"

Uncle Brian flopped down on the rug beside the cushion throne. "No more bad news, please."

Mateo crawled onto his dad's lap to sit like a lord surveying his court.

"Tea first," Grandpa put in.

Jason headed to the kitchen to oblige, grateful to have his hands occupied. He carried a tray with a clay pot and five small cups out to his loved ones. They settled around the coffee table, the sea audible beyond the porch screens.

"Good news and bad news." He cleared his throat, his thumb worrying the edge of his teacup. "Dr. Baker told me the immigration paperwork is done. The bad news is that, because of my recent court case, I have to provide the Canadian authorities with a Hong Kong police certificate."

Mom turned to Jason. "I hope your court case won't pose a problem. No one should be punished for telling the truth and following their conscience."

"They moved faster than we thought," Debra added, as if she needed to fill the space of what-ifs with more words. "If everything goes well, Jason will start his job with Dr. Baker in early spring."

"I'll pray for you." Grandpa looked at Jason without his usual grin. "Since you were a child, you've shown an interest in wetland conservation. I know how much it means to you."

The words slammed into Jason's chest. He swallowed, trying to smile as heat stung his eyes. All at once, he was working in the Mai Po Marshes again, mud on his boots and a migratory bird calling nearby. He pulled Grandpa into a tight hug, cheek brushing the familiar scratch of stubble. "Thanks," he managed, voice rough. "I was never good at real estate, anyway."

"Speaking of real estate." Mom glanced at Mateo, who had discovered the calculator and was busy pressing its buttons. "Did you see last night's news? Your friends, Joe Niu, Esther Fok, and Vivian Jiang, have all been transferred to the mainland, and they'll await trial there."

"And Vivian's boss, Du Jin-Dong, is still being held in a prison in Guangzhou. The court that handles serious economic crimes hasn't set a trial date." Uncle Brian bounced Mateo on his knee. "The only exception is Liam Sima, Vivian's first boyfriend. Somehow, he managed to flee to the US."

Jason's heart thudded. Too recently, Vivian sat in their apartment without makeup, telling them she'd been a baitfish in a net, and through it, she'd looked at Debra, as if pleading for support.

Mom glanced at him. "You and Deb did the right thing to stay away from her."

The machine of memory had gears that clicked even when idle. Jason sucked in a breath. "Vivian once commented that either we're super lucky or our God is the real thing." He shifted his gaze toward the water. The sun had moved farther west. "Zhang Xin, in Dad's manuscript, wasn't so fortunate. He got sucked into his brother's world and soiled himself."

"Even so, when Xin confessed his sin, he received forgiveness from the Lord." Uncle Brian put Mateo on the rug. The baby grabbed the children's Bible and gnawed on the corner. Uncle Brian plucked it out of Mateo's mouth and turned it upright so the cartoon animals looked up.

Jason's eyes stung without warning. He thought of Vivian in high school, a girl who had not yet learned how to paint a face as armor. "I wish I'd shared the gospel with Vivian."

Would it have made any difference?

Mom herded them to the dining room like a cheerful drill sergeant. Debra helped her heat the food—barbecued pork, drunken shrimp, spicy tofu, stir-fried mixed vegetables, and red eggs. Jason's stomach grumbled. This was home.

In the cool pause after dinner, with plates stacked and chopsticks corralled, Uncle Brian clapped. "Before Mateo falls asleep, let's have the cake."

One large candle was anchored in the buttercream sea and lit. Jason lifted his phone, the family's unofficial documentarian. Debra sang, Uncle Brian bellowed, Mom trilled, and Grandpa hummed in a key of his own, somewhere between haunted kettle and distant bagpipe. Jason's shoulders shook as he tried not to laugh. The camera wobbled.

Mateo squinted at the cake, then introduced it to his fist. The frosting came up in a majestic, gloppy paw. He licked it with serious concentration.

Jason's laugh burst out. For a heartbeat, the rest of the world receded until there was only this room and these people, the warmth of them knocking around inside his ribs. Love swelled so fast it stung his eyelids.

He set his phone aside and dipped his hand into the cake. It was ridiculous and perfect. The gesture said what words couldn't. *We love one another no matter what.*

Debra gawked. Then she grinned and dug in with a theatrical flourish. All her earlier fuss about the utensils had been for naught.

The End

Did you enjoy this book? Have you read Book 1, *Echoes over Stormy Sea*, and Book 2, *Thunders over Idle Land*, in the series? Dive in now.

Free on KU
Hero's Journey
Loyalty
Redemption
Transformation
ECHOES
OVER
STORMY SEA
DUAL-TIME ODYSSEY
1
R. F. Whong

Hero's Journey
Forgiveness
Redemption
Transformation
THUNDERS
OVER
IDLE LAND
DUAL-TIME ODYSSEY
2
R. F. Whong

A Note from the Author

Hello and thank you for sharing this journey with me. Writing this book was a special and emotional experience, and I cannot say how honored I am that you joined me through these pages. If you like the book and have a moment to spare, I would appreciate a short review. Thank you for your help.

About the author

Although I grew up in Hong Kong and Taiwan, my family members live in different parts of the world, a common phenomenon for most Chinese my age because of political conflicts.

I work for a small biotech company and have published 120+ scientific books and papers (under my legal name).

While I am relatively new to the realm of creative writing, I'm thrilled that I was chosen as a featured author by the Minnesota Anoka County Library in 2025 and by the Suffolk Virginia Authors Festival in 2026.

One of my books, *Echoes over Stormy Sea*, has won several awards, including being recently chosen by readers as a winner in the HOLT Medallion Contest.

Amazon Best Sellers

Our most popular products based on sales. Updated frequently.

I currently live in the Midwest with my husband, a retired pastor. We served together at three churches from 1987 to 2020. Our grown son works in a nearby city.

Check out my other books.

The Way We Forgive (Women's fiction): https://www.amazon.com/dp/B0BQ5LNLNB

Blazing China (family saga): https://www.amazon.com/dp/B0CD9P49HW

Detour to Agape (sequel to *Blazing China*; contemporary romance): https://www.amazon.com/dp/B0CD9P29GJ

Prestige of Hearts (contemporary romance): https://www.amazon.com/dp/B0CV4FL3CH

Center of Enigma (Paradise PA Mystery Book 1; mystery/suspense/thriller): https://www.amazon.com/dp/B0D9R2M134

Essence of Illusion (Paradise PA Mystery Book 2; mystery/suspense/thriller): https://www.amazon.com/dp/B0DFVPKW3N

Allure of Elegance (Paradise PA Mystery Book 3; mystery/suspense/thriller): **https://www.amazon.com/dp/B0FCP1BV32**

Series Page: https://www.amazon.com/dp/B0DFNXPSGW

Love Under Holy Skies (contemporary romance): https://www.amazon.com/dp/B0F362Q7T8

Echoes over Stormy Sea (Action/Adventure; Dual-time Odyssey Book 1): https://www.amazon.com/dp/B0DPGQ6TZP
Thunders over Idle Land (Action/Adventure; Dual-time Odyssey Book 2): https://www.amazon.com/dp/B0F49GFHW6
Fire Between Two Skies (Action/Adventure; Dual-time Odyssey Book 3): https://www.amazon.com/dp/B0G2YZZ8LG
Series Page: https://www.amazon.com/dp/B0F4LKXS2W
Zenith of Tea (Historical romance) https://www.amazon.com/dp/B0GNNFT2XM
Eclipsed System (Sci-Fi)
https://www.amazon.com/dp/B0GX32N1MX

Nonfiction (under Ruth Wuwong):

Are your health and finances linked? A Christian Entrepreneur's Quest:
https://www.amazon.com/dp/B0BQ5JXFYY
Wander Or Not: https://www.amazon.com/dp/B0CXJ79MWF

To connect with me, please go to www.ruthforchrist.com.

Follow me on social media:

Amazon: https://www.amazon.com/author/love.respect.grace
Goodreads: https://www.goodreads.com/author/show/42632055.R_F_Whong
Bookbub: https://www.bookbub.com/authors/r-f-whong
Twitter/X: https://twitter.com/RWuwong
Instagram: https://www.instagram.com/ruthwuwong
Facebook: https://m.facebook.com/ruth.wuwong

www.ingramcontent.com/pod-product-compliance
Lightning Source LLC
Chambersburg PA
CBHW011322310726
48973CB00011B/3028